ENGLAND'S
MESSIAH

ENGLAND'S MESSIAH

Martin Saunders

Copyright © 2004 Martin Saunders

10 09 08 07 06 05 04   7 6 5 4 3 2 1

First published 2004 by Authentic Media
9 Holdom Avenue, Bletchley, Milton Keynes, Bucks,
MK1 1QR, UK
and PO Box 1047, Waynesboro, GA 30830-2047, USA

The right of Martin Saunders to be identified as the author of this work has been asserted by him in accordance with the Copyright, Designs and Patents Act 1988.

All rights reserved.
No part of this publication may be reproduced or transmitted in any form or by any means, electronic or mechanical, including photocopy, recording or any information storage and retrieval system, without permission in writing from the publisher.

British Library Cataloguing in Publication Data

A catalogue record for this book is available from the British Library

1-86024-474-2

Cover artwork by Al Gray
Cover design by David Lund
Print Management by Adare Carwin
Printed and Bound in Denmark by Nørhaven Paperback

For Joanna

Acknowledgements

With thanks to John Buckeridge, James Davies, Malcolm Down, Matt and Steph King, Andy Peck, Keith Saunders, Trevor Smith, Liz Williams and David Woodford.

With extra special thanks to Jefferson Buckeridge for lending me his football comic, and starting the whole ball rolling.

Some people believe football is a matter of life and death. I'm very disappointed with that attitude. I can assure you it is much, much more important than that.
Bill Shankly, Liverpool Manager 1959–1974

Harry stared fearfully at the soggy, microwaved pie in his hand. The pastry was sagging badly, and there was an indeterminable, and not wholly pleasant, smell arising from it. 'Meat pie', said the sweaty plastic wrapper – although it claimed nothing more specific than that. The first bite would therefore be an educational one, but Harry was hungry, and, after bracing himself slightly, he sank his teeth hard into the crust. The ensuing screams as boiling 'meat' gravy scalded his lips, his tongue and the bald patch of the man in front of him, were drowned out somewhat by a sudden swell of excitement around him.

A half-hearted shot sailed hopelessly wide of the left-hand post, and everyone slumped back into their seats. It was the first time that the crowd had been remotely roused in nearly an hour and a quarter of a dire football match. Two tired teams at the end of a tiring season; twenty-two players earning the kind of money that could bring an end to third world debt, each one dreaming of his summer holiday in the Caribbean. It all added up to a lifeless, turgid, thrill-free evening's entertainment. And it was raining. Harry wasn't sure who he pitied more – the 40,000 drenched mugs around him who'd paid thirty quid each to watch this rubbish, or himself, for having to go back to the press office afterwards and write 500 words about it.

Harry pushed the pie back into its wrapper, and placed it carefully under his seat. The man in the row in front of him had removed the last traces of gravy from his head, and Harry didn't want to risk a repeat offence. The stinging in his mouth had dulled the hunger anyway. Instead, he sat back and concentrated hard on the last twenty minutes of the match, scanning the field desperately for something worthy of a mention in a newspaper report. Besides seeing the two club mascots having a fight before kick-off – an amusing sight since one was dressed as a chicken and the other as a goat – Harry hadn't yet found much material.

On one of the substitutes benches, Harry noticed a sudden flurry of activity. The supporters had picked up on it, too, and soon a huge incessant roar was building on all four sides of the ground. A track suit was unfastened, and Harry made out the bleached-blonde locks of Mark Lewis, Merseyside's new 16-year-old wonder-kid.

Just five minutes later, Lewis made his impact. Picking the ball up just inside the opposition half, he showed good skill to beat the first defender and advanced towards the penalty area. Then the centre half, clearly caught off-guard by this sudden change of gear, instinctively retreated, giving Lewis the time he needed to set himself for a shot. Twenty yards out, he let fly with that marvellous right foot that the media had spent the last week raving about. And as he did so, before the ball had even come close to the line, every man in the stadium knew where it was heading. Half a moment later, the net was bulging, Lewis was celebrating, and the crowd was on its feet.

'Lewis, Lewis,' they chanted, crowning their new messiah – the golden boy with the potential to lead Merseyside to glory and England to a European Championship.

Mark Lewis played six more games for Merseyside, scoring no goals. He never played Premier Division football again.

One

Harry Foster's life had been dominated by a clutch of things that seemed important at the time. At a few years short of 60 he was in a position now to look back, as if looking out at dawn across an empty beach. And the beach was empty, even though once it had seen a Manhattan skyline of finely-crafted sandcastles. Over the years they'd been washed back into the sea, kicked down by passers-by, or toppled by the wind. That's what happens to sandcastles.

To blame: a sad imbalance of priorities; an obsession with rising from the squalor into which he was born; a love affair which had begun before he was even old enough to understand it. The object of his affections, the medium for his rise, the alpha of his priorities, one thing alone: football.

Football. That beautiful, despicable, elating, agonising game. That most simple, that most complicated of all sports in the world. Where eleven men are charged with the power to divide a city or unite a nation. Where they chase around after a little ball, through which dreams can be realised and hearts can be broken. Football: which some see as a microcosm of life itself, and which others see as irrelevant and ridiculous. Which some love, truly, like a wife; which others hate, with the venomous passion usually reserved for one's sworn enemy. Harry Foster chose the former – perhaps the former chose him. Either way, his ravenous mistress swallowed his life.

Harry switched his gaze from the long empty beach in his mind to the short full glass in his hand. He rolled the melting ice cubes around and watched them water down his Scotch. Then he swigged at the bitter liquid, letting it burn on his tongue for a moment to remind him he was alive, and put it back down on the desk in front of him.

The phone rang. Harry had given up leaping out of seats long ago, back when the last of his genuine friendships dried up. He knew who this would be. Slowly, he dragged himself out of his study, trudged into the hall and looked lovelessly at the buzzing appliance. There had been twenty rings or more before an answer came – the person making the call clearly knew to wait.

'Foster,' said Harry, his dried-out voice made drier by the alcohol.

'Harry,' came the reply, full of forced enthusiastic niceness. 'I'm afraid there's a problem with your copy.'

Harry paused, then slowly growled: 'I'm sorry?'

'A problem,' repeated the voice confidently, 'with your copy.'

'There's no problem with my copy, son. It's good copy.'

'I'm sure it's excellent copy Harry, but the editor doesn't like it. He's not happy with the comments you make about Alan Burton. . . .'

'Burton's a silly little boy who needs bringing down to earth before he really hurts someone.'

'That might be true Harry, but he's also the new face of *Active For Men*. And the editor is a minority shareholder in the company that makes the stuff. Sorry Harry – we're going to need something else for the main body of your column. Maybe you could . . . .'

Harry slammed the receiver back down into place, and stormed into his study, muttering like a petulant child. A few years back, this sort of setback might have thrown him into a rage, but not now. Now he was too used to it, too familiar with the ways and workings of a modern media company; in essence, too cynical. In truth, he'd known all along, even as he was writing about this vile little footballer-turned-fashion-model-turned-thug, that the article would almost certainly be pulled. He'd even known about his editor's personal interest in seeing the player's profile remain positive. And yet, partly out of some perverse desire to see his cynicism proved right, and partly to see if he could get it into print before anyone noticed, he'd submitted it anyway. So now he didn't feel angry, nor aggrieved, just a little frustrated that he'd have to write another 500 words for *Foster's Eye* the next morning instead of sleeping in until twelve, and a little smug at having known his unscrupulous editor so very well.

Slumping back into the creaking leather of his easy chair, Harry returned to his now well-diluted poison. He took a sip, but the taste no longer pleased him, and so the rest of the glass was swiftly poured into the nearest suitable receptacle: a large, withering pot plant that looked as if it was watered more often with whisky than water. Dispensing then with a favourite evening pursuit, he subsequently moved on to another: and one that usually followed a particularly heavy session of the former. Reaching behind him, and again without ever coming close to leaving his chair, Harry took hold of a thick flaking volume, the low-budget appearance of which was at odds with every other item in his lushly-furnished home. It was a photograph album, old and worn and musty-smelling.

Crossing his short legs and pushing himself further back into the chair, Harry opened the book at the first page, revealing a dull and entirely monochrome collection of grubby-faced children in a range of concrete locations. He didn't spend long there, nor did he grace the next few pages – full as they were of long-dead family members and forced expressions that tried to make the best out of poverty – with more than a passing glance. But then, something caught his eye. A boy, no more than 6 years old, clad in a torn pullover and mud-wrecked shoes. A boy with a 7-inch grin cleaving across his face, and a haircut straight out of his mother's best pudding bowl. A boy whose expected yet arresting appearance in this photograph album was now causing Harry to stare intently. A boy with a football under his arm.

'Harry, son, look at the state of your shoes! Your mother'll have my neck if I bring you back looking like this. Get yourself down to the stream and wash them off – quick!'

Little Harry scampered down to the water with his grin still intact, and clinging on hard to his new favourite possession. Before attending to his own mud, he first cleaned the ball, removing the last traces of 'Happy Birthday Son', which had been inked onto one side, in the process. And after lovingly rendering it spotless, he devoted a few brief seconds to his hole-ridden shoes, dipping them into the stream and receiving a sock-full of water as thanks. He squelched back up the bank, ball still in hand, and kept on grinning.

It'd been a great hour. Harry didn't have hours like this too often, even on his birthday, and he was savouring every last moment. Time alone with Dad, for one thing, was a rarity for a boy with seven siblings, but the chance to play football with a perfect sphere – instead of a crushed tin or an out-of-date vegetable – was something else altogether. And this was *his* ball. No one could take it away from him now – his parents had promised him that.

As they walked back hand-in-hand to the family flat, Harry and his dad took turns to dribble the ball across uneven pavements, through groups of gossiping girls and around the creeping concrete of their estate. Not once, in the ten-minute journey between the park and home, did either of them lose control of it. Harry was a good footballer, just like his father before him, and they both knew it. He had a natural aptitude for the game – even when playing it with a mouldy potato. That was why Harry had been given a new ball for his birthday that year, when the rest of his brothers and sisters had received home-made cards and kisses for theirs. That was why his dad had been working extra shifts at the car plant. That was why his mum had cut her smoking from forty-a-day to twenty. Where football was concerned, Harry's dad was convinced that his boy was a bit special. When they reached home, they stopped outside. Knowing what he had to do, Harry picked up the ball and offered it to his father, who obligingly placed it in an outdoor cupboard and locked it out of sight. Then they knocked at the door, and Harry's mother appeared, with babe in arms and two toddlers in tow. Inside, all the children were cramped into the front room, as were three grandparents and a favourite aunt. Sitting on the rickety table in the middle of them all was a home-made birthday card and an orange.

'Happy birthday Harry!' cried the chorus in unison.

Harry smiled up at his dad, and his dad winked back.

Finally, the page turned, and the earnest flicking began again. Now he skimmed through team shots, images of the same boy – a little older each time – holding medals and trophies and more muddy shoes. Then everything leapt into garish, cheap and unfocused colour, and there were family holidays at assorted campsites; teenage girls with fat smiles and tiny shorts; long-haired young men with bloated self-rolled cigarettes and John Lennon shades.

Harry looked up at the clock, and realised that time had run away with him – that evening, as in life. He closed the book and swung to return it to its shelf. But as he did so, a crumpled something sneaked out of the bottom of the album, and fluttered down toward the floor like a falling leaf. Harry reached forward to catch it, but somehow it evaded his grasp and found its way underneath his chair. Annoyed, he slunk to his hands and knees, and poked his head down under the seat, banging it on the wooden frame in the process. An arm flailed out towards the crumpled something, but it was too stubby to reach. Then an umbrella was procured from its resting place behind the door to assist in the effort. Eventually, after much bad language and further head-banging, the crumpled something was retrieved.

The photograph in Harry's hand was of a girl, perhaps 19 years old: tall and pretty with sun-kissed hair and a ring on her finger. But he spent barely a second looking at it. Instead, instinctively, he flipped it over and revealed a scribbled inscription on the back. It said: 'Blackpool, 1969'.

The girl had candy floss in her left hand. The boy had a newspaper in his right. Their other hands were joined together tightly, and although they said little as they wandered up and down the beach, that couple had an aura of inseparability and contentment about them. She ignored the admiring glances aimed so barefacedly at her by the men seated along the front, simply pressing herself tighter toward the only one that mattered. He responded with proud silence as the same men fired jealous, green rays at him, affording himself a little smug grin now and then. The couple were happy, they were quiet; they were clearly in love. If Blackpool council had wanted to award prizes for the King and Queen of the promenade, they'd have needed to look no further.

She stopped and turned to him. She was a little taller than he was, and so looked down slightly when she spoke. 'I'm having a wonderful time,' she said softly.

The young man smiled and looked towards, though not directly at, her.

'Me too. It's lovely up here this year.'

'And it's great,' she continued, trying to work her way into his direct line of sight, 'to get away, just the two of us. I mean, it's great to get away from everything back home.' She paused. 'Harry? Isn't it?'

Harry gave a non-committal nod of the head, and looked out to sea.

'Yeah. I suppose.'

The girl was deflated, and started walking again. Harry joined her, still holding her hand, and once more there was silence and jealous glances for the King and Queen. But then Harry spoke:

'I was thinking though, maybe we could drive back on Thursday night.'

The girl stopped again, and this time looked hurt. She knew what the answer would be, but still she felt compelled to ask:

'Why's that then?'

'Well, because we will have had four good days up here, and then I can still get to the training session on Friday.'

'But we were already leaving early so that you get back for Saturday. I thought they'd let you off of training this week?'

'They did, but I'm not feeling all that sharp. I could do with a run around before the game.'

'So you want to cut our holiday short because you're not feeling *all that sharp*? Did I blunt you then Harry? Would you rather have not come away this week? Would you rather have kept yourself sharp at home?' Her voice was becoming increasingly tense.

'No sweetheart,' he implored, 'that's not what I meant. . . .'

'It's the same thing with you all year long,' she barked, ignoring the pointing, jeering bystanders. 'You never take your mind off it. All the time, you're just thinking about the next match.' Her voice began to crack – she was not accustomed to raising it. 'You don't care about me – not really. Not like you care about football.'

He stretched out his arms and she meekly fell into them, waiting and hoping for reassurance. It came, complete with forced sentiment and dramatised feeling:

'Jessica. Jess. You know I'm crazy about you. You're more important to me than any stupid game.'

'Really?'

'Of course. It's just that, well, I have to work hard at it, don't I? So that I can earn a contract. You want me to get a contract, don't you?'

'Yes – you know I do, more than anything. . . .'

'That's why I seem so obsessed with it. Because I want to earn a living through it. Because I want to earn a living so that we can get our own place, and pay for a nice wedding, and all that.'

'I know. I love you, Harry.'

'I love you, too, Jess.'

Evening had quickly become night, and there was a chill in the air. Shaken out of his recollections by a growing draught and a realisation that the boiler had failed again, Harry returned the crumpled photograph to its proper place in the album and shuffled out of the study. Adhering to a long-ago-concreted routine, he wandered into the kitchen, poured a mug's worth of milk into a pan, and set about heating it on the stove. While he waited for it to bubble, he began to run through possible subjects for his column rewrite. What could replace his ill-judged rant about the conceited young thug? An attack on the underachieving national team perhaps? That was always a popular subject. Or a rapturous eulogy on the brilliance of Gary Wilson, the Stanford United centre-back recently turned pop singer? (An option guaranteed to win points with the celebrity-obsessed editor.) He wasn't sure. And then somewhere in the thought process, both Wilson's wailings and England's failings dropped out of his head and were replaced by a beautiful blonde 19-year-old on a Blackpool beach.

'Harry. . . . ' Jessica began, a little nervously. 'You remember Carnaby Street?'

'Remember it? I spend every Saturday night there.'

'You know what I mean. *That* time in Carnaby Street?'

'Yeah, I know what you mean.' Harry was pretty sure, although not definite that he knew what she meant. He had been to some pretty wild parties.

'Did you mean what you said?'

'I always mean what I say.'

'About wanting to marry me, soon?'

'I always mean what I say,' he repeated, suddenly flushed and trying to hide it. 'I do want to marry you.'

'Soon?'

'Sure.'

'When?'

The milk boiled over and fizzed and splashed on the hob. The sound shook Harry from his daydream, but it was too late to make good cocoa from this pan. Being well past midnight though, it was also too late to start over again, and so for once, Harry ventured upstairs without a warm mug in his hand.

Stumbling around in the bathroom, as usual, because he couldn't be bothered to turn the light on, as usual, he managed to fill his mouth with a brush and something minty. Then he stared at the bulky shadow in the mirror, granted his teeth a half-hearted half-minute, and headed for the comfort of his self-deprecatingly large bed. He worked his way into the middle, as usual, and propped himself up on three tiers of pillow, as usual. His left arm reached out instinctively for a television remote control, and found it instantly. Still enshrined in lazy darkness, he pressed knowingly at the same buttons as ever and relaxed in front of a giant screen that flooded the room with grass-green light. But tonight, as the Brazilian World Cup team of 1970 danced for his pleasure on a 42-inch canvas, Harry's mind wasn't on the game. It was still on Blackpool beach, one year before those players set his world on fire, with the wife he never had.

Two

The chill December wind bit at Harry like an angry Rottweiler as he trudged across London's Ariel Fields. The coffee flask tucked under his arm offered little warmth, and the boggy ground beneath his feet helped even less. Head down, he persisted, as he did every Saturday morning, past rows of men with dogs, beyond joggers in unfashionable track suits and around the edges of poor quality football matches played by fat men with hangovers. Eventually he reached his destination, a small wooden bench watermarked with half-removed graffiti. A cold, half-eaten kebab had got there before him this week, but a well-aimed karate kick was enough to remove it. Suddenly very content, Harry perched himself in the centre of the bench, crossed his legs and unfolded his copy of the *Daily Reporter*. A cluster of well-placed evergreens kept the wind from him – that was precisely why this was his favourite bench; in the summer they shielded the sun – and allowed him space to sit back, relax, and scour his fellow columnists for spelling mistakes.

He was heartened to discover three typos on the hated celebrity gossip page, including one, amusingly, in one of the headlines. The appearance of the title 'Carter's Licky Escape' would surely mean the end of at least one sub-editor's career, unless of course the country's premier TV chef had somehow cheated death via the use of his tongue. That idea, of course, was almost as unlikely as the possibility that Harry's column might for once have been printed un-butchered. He didn't hold out a shred of hope that this might be the case. Flicking, as he always did at this time on a Saturday morning, to his regular spot, six pages from the back, any doubts were placed immediately at ease as he took in the headline:

'Why England can still win the World Cup'. He read it out loud to make sure he wasn't dreaming. Even to a man who had become well-accustomed to creative editing, this was still something of a shock. Harry's hand shot instinctively into his jacket, retrieved a mobile phone, and hit the speed-dial.

'*Reporter* Sport,' answered a young, naïve, efficient-sounding man.

'Alex Knight, now!' bellowed an old, cynical, irate columnist.

A short time passed as the frightened lackey plucked up the courage to fetch his superior. Harry clenched his fists tightly, so that his nails left little depressions in the skin. Out of the corner of his eye, he noticed a couple of tramps kicking a ball around.

'Hi Harry,' said a voice eventually.

'Burke?' Harry replied, unsurprised but trying to sound surprised, 'I asked to speak to Alex.'

'Yes, Alex is a bit busy right now. Can I help you at all?'

'You know what this is about Burke. Alex knows what this is about. That's why he's pretending to be busy.'

'I'm sorry,' replied the voice, a little too innocently, 'but I don't know what you're talking about. Is there a problem with the paper?'

'Apart from the fact that it's generally very poorly written, and edited by a team of under-evolved monkeys you mean? Yes, there's a problem with the paper. I wrote an article for it, and then someone in that office replaced it with a different one.'

'I don't think that would have happened Harry. Are you sure you're not still half-asleep?'

Harry was getting really aggravated now. A vein on his temple was beginning to gently pulse.

'Now listen Burke. Someone has made some very significant changes to my piece which completely alters the tone. The version that you've printed makes out that I think there's some kind of hope for this England team, when clearly I do not. They haven't got a chance of winning the next World Cup – they've barely got a prayer in qualifying for it.'

Burke paused for a moment. Then he tried:

'Are you sure you didn't write something a bit more hopeful than that?'

'Burke, I wrote the words, "This England team is very, very bad indeed." You've printed the words, "This England team has shown only flashes of its true quality."'

'But isn't that pretty much what you were saying?'

'WHAT?' Harry's unexpected scream unsettled one of the tramps, who fell over and head-butted a tree. 'Burke, that is exactly what I was *not* saying. I'm trying to point out to the nation that we need to get real about this England team and stop kidding ourselves that they're any good. The press has spent the last year making excuses and perpetrating the myth that they're one of the best teams in the world. In fact, they're a bunch of spoilt pop stars, with too much money and far too little passion, and they need a good wake-up call. I try to give it to them, and you turn the whole thing into yet another exercise in excuse-making and myth perpetration.'

'But that's what people want to read, Harry.'

'That's it Burke – get me Alex Knight. I know he's cowering behind you somewhere.'

'He's not available right . . . .'

'JUST GET HIM.'

'I'll go and see . . . .'

Harry huffed and gurgled, his face darkening like a burning sausage. He cursed and ranted under his breath as he brought himself right to the boil in preparation for his confrontation with the sports editor.

And then suddenly, in a single moment, none of it mattered anymore. Because before the eyes of Harry Foster, reporting veteran of countless World Cups, European Championships and EFF Cup ties, one of the greatest pieces of individual footballing skill ever to grace British soil took place.

Three of the four men kicking a ball around in front of Harry's bench were shabbily dressed, clearly drunk and in all probability, residents of this very park. The other, a leaner, more conservatively-attired figure, looked positively conspicuous by his normality. He – tall, young and handsome – appeared to make up one team on his own; the others, handicapped by long coats and blurred vision, made up the other. From the looks of what Harry had seen so far, as he'd glanced up occasionally from his tirade against Burke, it was no contest. The sober man was already five goals up when the miracle happened, even though he'd generously handed his opponents a fistful of chances to score (drunk homeless men, it seemed, have turned missing open goals into an art form). Then, as the cynical, beetroot football pundit looked on, the young man produced a moment of flair of which the greatest Brazilian of 1970 would have been proud.

Starting on his own goal line (two trees, 10 metres apart), he approached his first opponent, a howling red-bearded Glaswegian with a can of 8 per cent lager in one hand, and beat him with a clever side-step. Then, increasing his speed a little, he left a second man trailing as he made his way toward the other goal (two trees, 1 metre apart). So, between him and a six goal lead in this most prestigious of matches, stood an enormous beast of a man in a patched-up leather coat and gardening gloves, whose bulky frame filled the goal almost entirely. Seeing barely a chink of light in his target, the sober man stopped the ball for a moment and thought. Then, in a flash, he drove the ball hard – and quite deliberately – at the left hand tree. Fooled, the 'goalkeeper' leapt, or rather, fell awkwardly, to his right, arms flailing and nowhere near the ball, which returned at speed towards the attacker. At which point, as Harry's pupils widened, the young man flicked the ball up into the air, spun on his heel and somersaulted himself upside down. Then, as gravity brought the ball back towards earth, he brought out a foot, swung gracefully, and made quite perfect contact. A second later, the ball had travelled directly into the centre of the recently vacated goal; a second after that it was still travelling. Picking himself up off the floor, the young man simply turned and retreated to his own pair of tree-posts, helped on his way by a cry of 'lucky' from the pot-bellied heap on the ground. He saw nothing out of the ordinary, and no cause to celebrate – after all, he had already been 5–0 up.

Harry, on the other hand, had seen something very out of the ordinary. His jaw had plummeted, and like the ball it still seemed to be travelling. His hands were alternately shaking and engaged in eye-rubbing, such was his surprise and disbelief. If that goal, such as it was, had been scored in a major final, it would have been deemed worthy of winning the tournament. Action replays would have filled television screens; fans would have used pint glasses and crisp packets to recreate the moment on their pub tables. And, of course, Harry would have revelled in describing it to his readers through a hundred still-inadequate superlatives. But the stage on which this drama had been played out was not a major final. It wasn't even a real football match – just a kick-around in which 75 per cent of the participants would have failed sight, let alone drugs, tests. And the only person who'd seen it was him.

'What's up Foster?' a gravely voice on Harry's mobile phone attempted to shake him from his daze. It was Alex Knight, the sports editor, whom the worm Burke had finally persuaded to talk to his heavily-cut star columnist. 'Foster?'

'Er . . . yeah . . . .' slurred Harry, his eyes still fixed on the goal-scorer's slender body.

'Burke says you wanted to speak to me. He said it was urgent.'

Harry thought for a moment, realised that he no longer cared at all, and switched off his phone. Then he kept on staring, his jaw still open, and contemplated the marvel that had just occurred in front of him.

He'd seen a lot of things. Decades of football journalism had made him an eyewitness to some of the greatest and most memorable moments in the sport's history. Impossible tackles incredibly made by fearless defenders; goals scored from halfway, from the most acute angles, from unlikely body parts; 70-yard passes of astonishing accuracy. Each stuck in the memory, glued into the magic football photo album on the inside of Harry's eyelids. Each had taken place in a moment of great importance – often turning a game on its head or even single-handedly claiming a trophy. But none of them, no matter what the context, what the prize, matched up to this: a simple, unlikely flash of brilliance, which had appeared, just for a moment, on the boggy, uneven ground of Ariel Fields. It was the finest piece of skill that Harry Foster had ever seen, because – gymnastically speaking at least – it was absolutely perfect.

The 'goalkeeper' was still lying prostrate in the muddy grass, but his eyes were no longer open. The combination of heavy drinking and light exercise had got the better of him, and he was now fast asleep. His two colleagues looked too fearful to continue without him, and regrettably, it looked as if the game would have to end prematurely. The crowd, understandably, was disappointed, and scratched its head.

The mysterious genius shook hands with the rest of his opponents, and set off on his own, back across the fields. Instinctively, Harry folded his newspaper, stood up, and began to follow. He was excited – full of questions for this man. Who was he? Which team did he play for? Why on earth was he messing about with tramps on a match-day morning?

Pacing briskly in pursuit of the track-suited superstar, Harry managed to get to within twenty feet of the player. Tiring, he decided to launch into his first question from a short distance, in the hope that the man might stop and wait for him to catch up.

'Excuse me,' he called, panting slightly.

But instead of turning, the man sped up, gradually at first, before breaking into a run. Harry, with thirty years of football stadium pies inside him, could only look on in disappointment. And then, that disappointment turned again to wonder, as he watched this enigmatic figure disappearing through the Saturday morning haze. What pace he had! Not just a tremendously skilful player then, but a lightning-quick one, too. Who did he play for? Who was he?

An hour later, the doors of the *Daily Reporter* sports office were crashing open as a round, excitable old hack burst through them. His wrinkled face was alive in a way that it hadn't been for years, and his startled colleagues could clearly discern a wide grin pasted across it. His head was bursting with words, yet as he strode past five of his football-fanatic colleagues, he said nothing.

Surprised, Alex Knight poked his head out of a glass-partitioned office.

'It's Saturday Harry,' he called. 'You're not supposed to be in today.'

Arriving at his desk, Harry switched on the computer, tapped his fingers as he waited for it to initialise, and replied with nothing.

'OK,' said Knight, slightly nervously, 'maybe I went a little bit far with the edit yesterday. Do you want to come in and talk about it?'

Again, the response was silent. Then Harry's PC finally spluttered into life, and he was away, typing with the kind of speed and intense concentration usually reserved for five-minutes-to-deadline.

This behaviour continued – to curious glances from all around the office – for another twenty minutes, until suddenly, and with a deep, satisfied sigh, he stopped. Then he stood, still beaming, and strode across to his editor's office, via a printer.

Inside, the sycophant Burke was taking detailed notes as Knight whispered and hissed. The younger man seemed to be taking a quite perverse pleasure in writing so copiously, despite the fact that his fingertips were turning blue from the pressure. But as Knight noticed the figure in his doorway, the deputy was instantly dismissed, bending and cowering as he went, like a rebuked pet.

'Harry! Come in – this is an unexpected pleasure.'

'I'm still angry about the column Alex.' Harry kept smiling, as he spoke.

'Sure. Sorry about that, I must have got the wrong end of the stick with what you were trying to say.'

'I think I was pretty clear that the stick only had one end. But that's not what I wanted to talk to you about. Have a look at this – it's Monday's column.' He handed Knight the printout that he had just produced, and leaned back into his chair.

'Monday's column?' repeated Knight, incredulously. 'But this weekend's matches haven't even been played yet. How did you write a column about the weekend's football before a ball was kicked?'

'Just have a read.'

Knight did as he was asked, and Harry set about trying to study and gauge his reactions. After three minutes, during which Knight didn't so much as blink, the bald-but-goateed sports editor lowered the paper and responded.

'This is different,' he said ambiguously.

'Good different?'

'I'm not entirely sure. It's certainly very subtle. Is it supposed to be another attack on the England team?'

'Not really Alex. I'm being positive for a change.'

'Yes, that was what worried me.' For the first time, Knight allowed a tiny droplet of emotion seep from his pores, as the first twitches of a smile began to emerge on his face.

'So do you like it?'

'On one level, I do, yes. It's certainly the best piece of prose you've knocked out for a very long time. And it's a nice story, and it's positive for a change . . . .'

'But . . . .'

'But, it's not a Monday column. Monday is always a review of the weekend – and you know that.' Knight watched his columnist slump like a punctured balloon animal. A moment later, he was re-inflated by 'I could see it in the Saturday slot though.'

'So if I come up with something else for Monday, you'll run that next weekend?' Harry suddenly realised how keen he was to see this particular string of words in print.

'Why not?'

'Great. Then consider yourself forgiven for that shocking piece of butchery in this morning's rag.'

'You're too gracious Mr Foster.'

Harry rose to his feet, engaged in a rare handshake with his editor, and left the office happy. On his way out, he noticed the little goblin Burke, crouched outside. He'd been listening to every word.

Before the goblin could re-enter his master's dwellings, however, the door had been slammed firmly in his face. A moment later the blinds closed, too. Inside, Alex Knight was engaging in a more thorough second reading of a marvellous story about three tramps, a mysterious stranger, and the greatest goal ever scored.

Three

Wednesday morning. In the foliage-heavy coffee bar of an exclusive London hotel, two well-dressed men were deep in conversation.

'I'm not doing this for less than a hundred grand,' said the taller, younger, better looking of the two – a spotless, clean-shaven man with crew-cut hair and an undeniably pleasant aroma.

'Of course not,' reassured his fat, perma-tanned and very possibly wig-bearing companion.

'Up front.'

'No problem. We'll start the bidding at 200 and let them bait us down.'

'After tax.'

'After tax? Be reasonable Billy. They're not going to give you £150,000 up front. You're only 23 – it's not like you've got all that much of a life story to sell.'

'You what?' Unaccustomed to being treated with any kind of disrespect, playful or otherwise, the good-looking man was not impressed by this.

'I mean . . . er . . . that it wouldn't be a very thick book. Because you're only young . . . .'

'And do you know what, you greasy little criminal?' the good-looking man interrupted. 'I've achieved ten times as much in that time as you have in your whole life, and you're about 50.'

'I'm 43.'

The good-looking man glared across the table, and was about to launch into a second volley of abuse when he was interrupted by the arrival of a third man, who again came immaculately presented in something expensively Italian. He introduced himself as Eddie Chung, Chief Commissioning Editor of Torpedo Books, and from the look of him – or rather, his cuff-links, wristwatch and achingly-costly diamond-stud glasses – he was in a position to furnish them with as much cash as they could possibly desire.

'Eddie,' began Perma-tan, 'it's great to finally put a face to the name.'

'Mr Sprout, yes?' asked Eddie, almost certainly with his tongue in his cheek.

'Stout,' corrected Stout (who, ironically, had changed his name from 'Sprout' twelve years previously). 'But please, call me Lenny.' (On his birth certificate, it said Lesley, spelt for a girl, which his mother had desperately wanted instead.)

'And you must be Billy Regan,' said Eddie, offering a hand to the good-looking man. 'I'm very honoured to meet a true English superstar.'

'We'd like two hundred grand after tax. . . . ' snapped Regan, before Stout pushed himself between them.

'I think I'll do the negotiating Billy, if you don't mind.'

Eddie Chung gave a wide, forced smile, and sucked a little air in through his teeth. Then he looked at his watch and said:

'Harry Foster should be here in a minute. He's the writer I had in mind for your book. I mentioned it on the phone to you I think Mr Stout.'

Stout didn't have a chance to formulate a response. From behind him, Regan was making high-pitched noises.

'Harry "Foster's Eye" Foster?' he squawked. 'The bloke in the newspaper?'

'That's right Mr Regan.'

'He can't write it. He hates me.'

'He certainly does not Mr Regan – he adores you. He's very excited about this project.'

'He said I wasn't fit to be the boot boy for the England team.'

'I'm sure that was a joke.' Eddie suddenly became a little flustered. 'In fact,' he lied, 'he told me that he thought you should be the next captain.'

The high-class decorum of the place then vanished, along with Eddie Chung's credibility, as Harry Foster appeared, in jeans and trainers, asking other patrons in a loud voice whether they'd seen 'a sneaky-looking Chinese bloke and the worst footballer in the world.' Unfortunately, he then went on to ask Stout, too.

The three Italian-suited men stared, flabbergasted at the rudeness of the dishevelled figure standing before them. Harry knew his options, and quickly chose one:

'Morning chaps. Sorry I'm a bit late.'

Around forty minutes passed, during which much coffee was consumed and many heated words were exchanged. None of the parties seemed able to agree on a single point of the deal. Billy Regan wanted pots of money for the rights to his life story, along with assurances that he'd be shown in the very best possible light. Harry seemed far more interested in protecting some degree of journalistic integrity – pointing out that Regan's well-publicised brushes with the law could not simply be glossed over – while Lenny Stout kept going on and on about the film rights. The conversation was not heading to an obvious resolution, and though this frustrated the watching publisher, he had the sense to realise that some time apart was badly needed.

'Can I suggest, gentlemen,' offered Chung, straining for a smile, 'that we break off now and reconvene at a later date? We're all London-based, so it shouldn't be too difficult to get around a table again this side of Christmas.'

Regan huffed like a spoilt child, and without saying anything, gave the table a hard shove in Harry's direction in order to release himself. He then clicked his fingers, and Stout quickly came running, following on his client's heels like an eager hound. They left noisily, and without any suggestion that they might be prepared to pay for their drinks.

Harry and his publisher looked at each other. Harry's eyes were full of self-righteousness, while Eddie Chung's were a mixture of angry disappointment and been-here-before resignation.

'Harry, what on earth was that?'

'What?'

'That performance. Is my money no good to you anymore? This is a £20,000 job for you, plus more if the thing sells anything like as well as it should.'

'And I'm very grateful that you thought of me to write it. But if I paint Billy Regan as some sort of gentleman, scholar and saint, my credibility will disappear down the toilet.'

'It's very simple Harry. You just write about the bits he wants to talk about, and you leave out the bits which he doesn't. Good news for you – less to write about.'

'What do you want me to do then Eddie? Do you want me to reform him into some sort of role model? In his career he's made more front-page headlines than back – drugs, prostitutes, tax evasion. Apart from the fact that a book about his life that omitted all those incidents would only be about four pages long, you'd also mislead people into thinking that he was a good guy, when clearly he's as corrupt as he is talentless. If he wants to admit his past and then apologise, then all power to the man. But that's not what they were suggesting. This whole thing is a stinking exercise in public relations – they're probably just trying to smooth over his image in preparation for the release of the Billy Regan action figure.'

Surprised by the force of the blast, Chung was unsure of what to say next. Morally speaking, Harry had a point; financially speaking, that really didn't matter.

So he just said: '£20,000 Harry. Twenty grand. And I know the *Reporter* doesn't pay you half as well as it should. You could really use that money.'

Harry looked down for a moment. 'What do you mean by that?' he asked, not really wanting an answer.

'I've seen your house. The mortgage must be very expensive.'

'I manage.'

'And then I understand you've got a few other outgoings that your salary won't stretch to. Expensive tastes, if you know what I mean. . . . ' Chung's tone was getting ever more sinister, and a defeated Harry chose that moment to interrupt:

'If I do this – if – then I don't want my name to be anywhere near it. Not on the cover, not inside, not even on that little bit of author-asserts-the-right small print. This will be proper ghost-writing – I'm the ghost, and that makes me invisible. Understand?'

'Excellent.' Chung reached for his mobile phone. 'I'll call Mr Sprout and tell him the good news.'

Harry's outstretched hand dissuaded him from making the call.

'I said "if" Eddie. I still want some time to think about this.'

Petty thieves incarcerated for their crimes are often found stealing again on the day of their release. In the same way Harry, stung by the revealing remarks of his publisher, headed directly from the hotel to the den of his principal vice. Although embarrassed that word had got to Chung about his problem, he bore little thought to his crumbling self-respect as he pushed open the door, strode to the counter and asked:

'What time's the first race of the day?'

Gambling is a lonely, obsessive, painful pursuit. Like the coin slot on a fruit machine it greedily sucks its victim in, casting its spell, convincing that fabulous rewards are just around the corner. And as mounting frustration leads the gambler to stake more and more in the hopeless pursuit of simply getting back to where they once were and breaking even, the addiction begins to guzzle at the individual's whole life. If they can afford it, they get burned and possibly learn a lesson. If they aren't blessed with limitless funds, no mercy is shown. But between those two extremes – the rich playboy who wastes a couple of million and the poor loser who ends up living in a second-hand car – lies someone else. They aren't rich enough to gamble without a conscience, but aren't poor enough that their home is placed on the line with every bet. They're angry that they've lost more money to the bookie than they've made; they're sure that tips and knowledge will help them to turn it around in the end. Yet somehow, despite studying the form to degree level, and befriending countless jockeys, stable managers and sheikhs, they never do manage to turn it around. They win three bets but lose six more, and so find themselves inching ever further away from the mythical realm of profit. And when they do get lucky, and finally the 20–1 shot comes in with £100 staked on the nose, somehow that money simply disappears in a subsequent flurry of rash bets on 'dead certs'. So they still leave the bookmaker with less than they entered with, and they still curse their luck, and vow not to make the same mistake again.

But that was yesterday. Here Harry was again.

For three hours and more, Harry sat in a smoke-saturated corner of a less than salubrious bookmaker's shop that he may or may not have spent a day in before. Old men, their craggy faces turned grey by the weight of their disappointments, lined the walls around him. He could see some younger men, too, perched excitedly on cracked plastic stools, their hands at their mouths from the excitement. They were still standing at the top of the helter-skelter; soon they, too, would be grey.

The 2.15 from Littledock was gearing up to start. A white ticket clenched in Harry's hand contained his last glimmer of hope for the day. His cash had reached its end again – his psychiatrist never allowed him to carry plastic – and if this horse failed, he'd have to contemplate leaving this room that had been his home for most of the day, and do battle with public transport.

Harry's horse, a hotly tipped 12–1 shot, was on the inside lane of a field of twenty. And at the very first fence, the horse ejected its jockey in a kind of slingshot motion which amused everyone except the jockey, and the thousands of poor fools who'd listened to the tip. They included a now penniless Harry. As he made for the door, he noticed the depression that his presence had made in the soft foam of the stool he'd been occupying, and realised how pathetic he was.

That feeling continued and developed as he made his way through the bustling streets of a rain-peppered West End. It was a feeling which always arrived when the money ran out – the gurgling plughole of emotion that remained when the buzz of addiction had drained away. In these moments, the abject stupidity of burning one's money on the horses came sharply into focus, as if a pair of long lost spectacles had suddenly been re-discovered and placed over his eyes. Harry was an intelligent man, and he knew that his habit was ridiculous – but that knowledge wasn't nearly enough to make him stop gambling.

Disgruntled, disappointed and disgusted with himself, he lumbered down the steps of the first tube station he came to, and slouched his way home.

That evening, he found himself again in the study of a house too large for one man; a house with beautiful big windows across which the curtains were always drawn. Sitting once more in his favourite chair, with a dangerously full glass ever-present in his hand, he tried hard to relax, but could find no comfort. In an hour, the Docklands vs Moss Side game was going to kick-off, and that meant a ninety-minute reminder of the morning's ugly meeting. Billy Regan, the Docklands striker, was a certain starter – the manager knew better than to leave out a prima donna like him – and this would provide a good opportunity for Harry to witness this changed man in action before he made his final decision about the book.

But before that, there was a whole hour to kill. Deciding against another trip down memory lane, at least until after the match, Harry shunted a nearby photo album out of his line of sight and instead grabbed a computer printout of the coming Saturday's article. The bad luck of the day so far had wiped his mind of the refreshment he'd felt in his encounter with the mysterious tramp-beater the previous weekend, but the words in front of him soon brought it all back. He smiled again as he read his own reflections.

> . . . I'd grown bored of a sport dominated by sponsorship, sidetracked by scandal and undermined by money.

And then, in the most unlikely situation I ever could have imagined, I stumbled across the reason I fell in love with football in the first place . . . .

Harry had already decided that on Saturday morning he would actively seek out the gifted stranger again, if only to show him the article. Of course, it was unlikely that he, like Harry, had a regimented routine which meant he spent every Saturday morning of his life at Ariel Fields Recreation Ground, but even a remote chance meant that Harry had to try. Although quite what he'd say if by some coincidence the player was there again, he hadn't yet worked out.

'Hi there.'
'Hello.'
'I was watching you play football with tramps last week.'
'Right.'
'And then I chased you across the park, but you managed to get away.'
'Uh-huh.'
'So I told 6 million people about it.'

No, that wouldn't work. He'd need to think more carefully about it. But he did need to say something. This man had infected his thoughts for the past five days; only the bitter medicine of the bookmaker had given him temporary respite. He needed to know something – anything – about him. Who is it that wastes an extraordinary sporting gift like that by playing with three drunk men and not so much as a real goalpost. Who was he?

Harry's ponderings led him to the bottom of his glass and to 8 o'clock, when the match was due to start. Grabbing another drink on the way, he chose the comfort of his living room above the bigger screen at the end of his bed. After all, Moss Side were a notoriously negative team, and he needed to give himself every chance of staying awake.

For forty minutes there was little incident. Moss Side's Portuguese striker Hugo Veiga – one of the two supposed 'superstars' on show; Billy Regan being the other – was having the best of the game, hitting the post and demonstrating a couple of his eye-popping tricks for the watching cameras, but ultimately delivering nothing important. And then, just before half-time, the match came alive. Regan, until that point totally upstaged by his rival, found himself completely unmarked as a Docklands corner sailed into the penalty area. Leaping like a Jack-in-the-box, he made great contact with the ball, and planted it exactly where he intended: directly into the top left-hand corner of the goal. Docklands were up 1–0, and so it stayed until half-time.

Conceding a goal just before the interval is most painful. One team has usually allowed their minds to drift for a split second towards the warm dry benches of the changing room, while the other has sensed the slight lull in their opponents and taken advantage. Thus each player blames himself, and his colleagues, while the manager, whose carefully-thought-out team talk has been thrown into chaos at the last minute, is likely to place a rocket behind each of them and light the blue touch-paper.

That meant that as the second half kicked off, Hugo Veiga was in need of no more motivation. A minute after the restart, he collected the ball just outside the Docklands area, deceived a defender with a clever pirouette, and blasted the ball in from 20 yards. Such was the ferocity of the shot that the goalkeeper had barely even decided to dive before the ball was past him. 1–1.

With the scores evened up, the game again sank into relative mediocrity. Regan was trying to find more spaces in the defence, but failing, while Veiga had dropped back into midfield to try to preserve the draw. And nothing much happened then until the ninety minutes were up.

With some sections of the crowd already heading for their trains, and the referee looking at his watch, a young Moss Side striker – a Manchester-born lad called Wayne Borrows – took advantage of a misplaced Docklands pass and dribbled, completely alone, towards goal. His entire team waited nervously in their own half, not wanting to throw men forward and then concede a sucker-punch goal themselves. But Borrows was young, and held little fear, and so advanced on regardless, frightening a Docklands centre-back into crassly bundling him to the ground. The referee blew his whistle, but not for full-time.

With ninety-two minutes on the clock, Moss Side had a free kick on the edge of their opponents' area. The plucky Borrows picked the ball up as if to take the kick himself, but a bark of Portuguese quickly led him to drop it. Up stepped Hugo Veiga – well known as one of the Premier Division's top free-kick takers – and the rest was almost to be expected. Seemingly without effort, he won the game for Moss Side with a beautiful bending shot that the Docklands 'keeper could only admire. The final score was 2–1, with no time left even to restart the game.

Harry, although not a Moss Side supporter, punched the air in excitement. He even poured himself another drink to celebrate. Then he turned back to the television screen, and was sickened by what he saw.

Billy Regan, horrified at being upstaged by this foreign invader, had been unable to control his rage and had flown into a violent tantrum, kicking the shocked Hugo Veiga and spitting in his face. There had been no provocation besides the scoring of a goal (although later Regan would claim that Veiga offered him a 'taunting smirk'), and so the referee had little doubt about issuing a red card. A general ruck ensued, between at least ten players and with the increasingly worried-looking referee at the centre, and all the while Veiga lay writhing in pain on the grass, with a stud-marked gash weeping blood across his thigh. Fascinated, the television director kept a camera on the still-raging face of Billy Regan, and followed him as he wrestled with his own coaching staff, kicked water bottles, and bawled abuse at fans. And this was England's national hero.

Harry switched off the television set and sat for a while with his head in his hands. Eddie Chung had been right – he did need money – but did he really have to earn it as some sort of glorified PR-man for this animal? In an instant he had clarity, and the decision was made. Although a little drunk, Harry decided that this would be a good time to deliver it.

An e-mail, to land on Chung's desk the next morning, would lay out his final decision in certain and unarguable terms. It was to be a firm 'no' – on the grounds of integrity, good taste and simple common sense. It didn't matter how much debt he was in – he had built a reputation as an honest, respectable journalist over the last few decades, and he was not about to set the Billy Regan bulldozer on it now for a few pieces of silver.

But as his computer booted up, Harry saw the crumpled printout on his desk and had a much better idea. In the last week, an unknown quantity had re-ignited his passion for the game, and a quantity he knew far too well had all but extinguished it again. Therefore it was only fair that if he was to tell his readers about one, he should also mention the other. And a blatant attack on Billy Regan in *Foster's Eye* now would certainly scupper any chance that he'd still be asked to write his book.

He turned off the computer again and picked up a pen. Settling into his chair, he took another swig of whisky and began to scribble on the original article:

> ... They say that Billy Regan is our next great hope. Well if he's our hope, then all hope is lost. He's violent, he's a cheat, and he's generally despicable – and this is supposed to be the heroic figure we encourage our children to imitate?

That should do it, he thought. But he didn't put the pen down. Instead, lubricated by the drink, something inside of him poured out onto the page, and he continued:

> Whatever happened to England's heroes? We want footballers to be proud of, not spoilt brats like Billy Regan. Where's our St George – fit to lead us into battle armed with honour, dignity and sportsmanship? Regan cannot be our next great hope. Let's pray that God sends us someone else.

Four

Saturday morning arrived with a surprising explosion of sunshine. Although a light frost covered the ground and coated cars and buildings, and though the air was decidedly chilly, the brightness of the day somehow overcompensated. It was impossible to feel cold, despite the temperature being barely above zero.

The absence of wind and rain had already brightened Harry's outlook when he picked up his copy of the *Reporter* (never, ever trusting paper-boys to deliver reliably) and flicked to the back. And his mood improved even further as he realised not only that Knight had published his article complete and unedited, but that he had also commissioned some whizz-kid to illustrate the piece with a computer-generated artist's impression of the Ariel Fields wonder-goal. (That it was a fairly faithful recreation of what actually happened filled Harry with not inconsiderable pride: clearly his descriptive skills were still in fine condition.) Armed then not only with a story, but also an unexpected picture, Harry set off at full pelt toward the park, hoping to find both his mystery man and the answers to a myriad of questions that had kept him awake at night for a week.

On arrival, however, he was sorely disappointed. No tramps were to be found by that favourite bench; no mythical miracle man belting balls at trees. Instead, the oak-wood goal stood untended, and birds, who last week had demonstrated the good sense to stay away from flailing men with little self-control, were settled on the branches. Once again kebab meat lined Harry's seat of choice – at least one reassurance that the world hadn't moved on completely – and the offensive graffiti was twice as rife as it had been before. But as for the sublimely gifted stranger, he was nowhere to be seen.

This week's takeaway consumer had not been as careful or considerate. As well as a mess of meat, a heavy smudge of chilli sauce had been smeared (probably by the same unsuspecting fellow's trousers) across the bench, and the crumbling wood beneath looked even less inviting than usual. Instead, then, Harry propped himself against one of the goalpost trees, and looked again at the article. Despite his other disappointments, he smiled at the thought of three readers, all somewhere else in London, who would not be so happy with his words. Harry's mobile telephone was switched off, and that was just as well, because just about now, a heavy-handed publisher, a brutish footballer and his tacky agent would all be choking over their cornflakes. Billy Regan and Harry Foster were unlikely to speak, let alone write together, ever again. That made Harry feel very satisfied indeed.

As did this rather beautiful illustration; a masterpiece that had in all probability been woven together by robots in about fifteen minutes. And although Harry didn't know how this was possible, it didn't bother him. He was far too impressed by its accuracy. Folding the paper up so that only the graphic could be seen, he walked across and stood in the very spot where the miracle had taken place seven days earlier. As he did so, and as he thought of all the millions of readers who'd be perusing this abstract departure from the usual *Foster's Eye* fare, he realised that he, and only he among all of them, knew where to find this tiny theatre of dreams. This was his place – his new footballing Bethlehem – and no one else could ever find or share it.

For a third time that morning he read the piece (he seldom read his own work, saving to check for signs of crass editing), and this time his heart suffered a sudden bout of anguish. Although all along he had known how unlikely a reappearance of the wonder-boy would be, he'd somehow never actually considered the most obvious eventuality. All week he had been formulating questions, sweating over words of introduction, as if he was certain to meet the stranger again – as if they'd arranged to meet here. And now he was feeling the force of realisation full in the face.

His reading was disrupted, albeit briefly, by a dull thud behind him. It sounded like the slap of boot on leather, and, knowing that a talent-free football game was going on nearby, Harry found it easy to ignore. He read on, congratulating himself on some witty slurs on Regan's character.

Seconds later the noise could be heard again, and this time louder. Now Harry *knew* it was the sound of a ball being kicked, and this time he didn't even stop to consider it.

A third time the silence was broken, and this time from a distance of only a few feet. So, Harry realised, either the pitch had been extended in an unlikely direction, or the sound was not what he had first assumed it to be. He spun on his heels, dropped the newspaper to his side . . . and took in a sight that sent his spirits hurtling skyward.

'It's . . . you,' he spluttered, frightening the ball-juggling figure before him into losing his concentration, and the ball.

'Um . . . yes?' the ball-juggler replied.

'You're the guy who was playing here last week,' garbled Harry excitedly.

It was. He nodded.

The two men looked at each other for a moment. One, tall and blonde with boyish good looks, was getting very uncomfortable very quickly. The other, shortish, fattish and oldish, with a gambling addiction and a drink problem that showed through the lines on his face, was rapturous with pleasure. And though he'd been through this unlikely meeting fifty times already that morning, he was now at a loss for words. He was just grinning, inanely, as if someone had just removed his brain.

In the end, a few nervous words burst out of the blonde man. 'Do I know you?' he asked, edging backwards very slowly.

A few words from the planned conversation filtered back into Harry's brain. He replied therefore with, 'I'm your biggest fan.'

'My what?' came the confused and no more reassured response.

'Your biggest fan,' Harry repeated, never doubting himself. 'I watched you last week – playing with those tramps.'

The blonde man thought for a moment, and then, struck by a moment of realisation, asked: 'Were you the man on the bench?'

'That was me!' Harry beamed, proud that he'd even been noticed.

'Oh. I assumed that you were with them.'

Harry's face fell a little, although not completely, and he chose to mostly ignore being compared to a homeless person. Instead he decided to press on – after all he had a lot of questions, and he knew from experience how fast this man could run away.

'Harry Foster,' he said quickly, extending a hand.

'John Christie,' came the reply, still a little tentatively.

'If I'd known that yesterday, John, you'd be famous by now.'

'I'm sorry?'

Harry had attempted the joke to put John at his ease. Instead it was too cryptic and had the opposite effect. This was all too obvious on his face – he looked only a few breaths from shrieking, 'What do you want? Please don't hurt me!' – and Harry realised that he needed to make sense, and fast. His best effort was to unfold the newspaper and hand it to the trembling youngster.

John read the words, and looked at the graphic, and all the while his jaw descended incrementally. Finally, and still no more relaxed, he asked, 'Is this me?'

Harry smiled, trying desperately to look not in the least bit sinister. 'Yes, it's you John. You're the mysterious goal-scorer.'

'But I was only playing in the park.'

'I know.'

'I was just kicking a ball around with a few strangers.'

'Yes,' Harry grinned, 'I know.'

John's heart was racing so fast that it nearly leapt out of his chest. His wide blue eyes were darting all over the page, searching for a sign that this was a joke or a dream, but finding none.

'But . . . .' he stuttered, 'why would you write about this?'

'Because it amazed me. It staggered me. It captured my imagination for a whole week. I've been watching football for well over forty years, John, and nothing has ever got me going quite like that goal.'

This seemed a little too much like madness to John, who nevertheless was relaxing now, if only due to the sheer ridiculousness of the situation.

'With respect, Harry, I think you should be writing about the goals they score in the real world, not people messing about in the park.'

'With respect, John, you didn't see it.'

John looked at the ground with embarrassment, not because of some swelling pride, but because this still sounded like lunacy to him. Harry, meanwhile, had a hundred questions, and proceeded to launch into them.

'So, do you play for a team around here?'

'No.'

'You don't play at all?'

'No.'

'Do you live locally?'

'Yes.'

'And you come down here every Saturday morning?'

'Yes.'

Harry sighed. This was hard work. 'You're not making this very easy,' he said, trying not to snap.

John looked at him for a moment, almost formulated the word 'no', and then thought better of it. Instead he said, 'I'm sorry sir, but I'm not *finding* this very easy.'

Harry could not recall the last occasion on which he was referred to as 'sir'. It made him smile to hear the word now. It seemed to him that this man, still no less mysterious to him save that he now had a name, was gentle, nervous, humble . . . and far too respectful for someone of his age. No wonder he didn't play for a team – this man bore no relation whatsoever to the footballers that Harry knew.

Eventually he did manage to string a few sentences together, and to look Harry in the eye. He explained that he was a local lad of 22, who lived on the local estate with his mother and sister. He was an electrician by trade, also in this little area of Ariel Hill, where he grew up, went to school and did all his grocery shopping – a micro-universe which he barely ever saw a need to leave.

As he explained this to Harry, who also revealed a few personal details, omitting his addictions and glamorising his love life a little, the old reporter noticed a strange, captivating quality about him. It started somewhere in his eyes, but once you'd caught sight of it you could trace it through all of his features, and in his movements; even in his words. In essence it was wise yet innocent, old yet young, weak yet powerful. Harry couldn't quite put his finger on what it was exactly, but it was almost unearthly, and once he had noticed it, he found it impossible to turn his face away.

Before long an hour had passed, and John explained that he now had to go.

'You haven't got time for a drink?' asked Harry, slightly desperately. 'The Locomotive on Bristol Square has illegal satellite and we can watch the Saturday football.'

John tried hard not to look appalled at this suggestion, but couldn't stop his face from falling. 'Sorry,' he said, 'I've got to go and look after my sister.' He began to back away.

'OK,' said Harry, his hundred questions now replaced by a thousand more, most of them on the unresolved topic of why on earth such a naturally gifted footballer didn't play for any sort of team. Hurriedly he added, 'Will you be here again next week?'

'I'm always here on a Saturday,' John replied. 'Why don't you come in your trainers next week and we can have a kick about?'

'I'll see you then,' said Harry, waving to a figure who had already backward-stepped his way into the distance.

John waved back, then turned, and ran even faster than he had before. Then Harry was alone and slightly pained, feeling like a poet ripped from his muse. But when he glanced again at his Bethlehem, his smile returned. He would certainly be back next week.

'But now,' he thought, 'the pub.'

The bar of The Locomotive was thick with smoke and heaving with loud customers. These were generally not members of the 'top half' of the Ariel Hill community: the rich city professionals and media types who had swamped the place over the last few years, and of which Harry was definitely one. Moreover, the kind of clientele that this place attracted was that basement-level element of the 'bottom half' that liked nothing more than to burgle the five-bedroom houses of the top. But it served alcohol cheap, and showed more football than any other pub in the universe, and those two factors alone outweighed any negatives and made it Harry's favourite watering hole.

Karen, the not-especially-pretty barmaid who liked older men and always flirted embarrassingly with Harry, saw him coming and instinctively reached for a glass. Nodding, but trying to avoid eye contact, he gladly grabbed his drink and tried to head for a quiet corner. Karen called him back:

'You alright Harry?' she squawked, in her fingernails-down-a-blackboard voice.

'I'm fine thanks Karen. Very well,' he answered, looking at the scratched wooden floor.

Harry didn't ask, but regardless of that Karen replied: 'I'm not bad Harry. Always happier for seeing you though.'

Again Harry forced a smile; again he refused to make any eye contact. He could tell that she was leaning towards him though, because the stench of very cheap perfume had heightened considerably. When he did look up briefly, he saw that she was leaning so dramatically that it was a wonder she hadn't toppled right over the bar. Swallowing hard, he resolved to walk away and break her heart once again. As he did so, she called after him:

'I hear you've got yourself a new girlfriend!'

She hadn't heard that of course. It was the thing she always said to try to find out whether he was in a relationship, and it never ever met with an answer. And even if she had heard that, nothing could have been further from the truth. Alcohol-fuelled liaisons at book launches and charity dinners aside, Harry had barely enjoyed any romance in decades. A worn photo, removed sporadically from a heavy album in Harry's study, was the only proof that he'd ever even had a girlfriend. Not that Harry was unattractive. He was a little overweight, and not especially striking, but he did have, and had always had, a certain roguish quality that had endeared him to a fair share of admirers. It was just that he only had room for so much passion in his life.

Three hours and six whiskys later, Harry's passion was roused. Along with the rest of the regulars, Harry shuffled into the 'secret' back room (another bar, the same size and shape as the real one, which everyone in Ariel Hill, including the police, was well aware of), and took his seat for the afternoon's football match. It was a far-northern derby, between Tyneside and Teesside, and it was being transmitted to The Locomotive via a small television station in Oslo, Norway. In an effort to circumnavigate the laws preventing domestic Saturday afternoon games from being shown live, the football-obsessed landlord here had bought himself a quite horrendously large satellite dish, not dissimilar to the ones used by NASA to communicate with craft in deep space, after hearing that you could pick up foreign coverage of the English game. He was right, and, having made his (illegal) discovery widely known, he now saw his pub fill every Saturday with local fans – including several members of the local constabulary – who all agreed that this was a fantastic idea and that they were only perpetrating a victimless crime.

Tyneside were Harry's second team, and his favourite in the Premier division. For most neutrals, they were an exciting and well-liked side, known for their attacking style of play and led by their enigmatic and popular manager, a former Italy goalkeeper named Roberto Spagnoli. He had boldly claimed that his side were in the mood to 'trounce' their local rivals, and with that statement in mind he had elected to play with four strikers from the start, two of whom were members of the current England squad. One of those, Clinton McLean, a tall powerful veteran of Caribbean descent, was Billy Regan's regular partner in the England team, and ironically, Harry's favourite player. Clinton and Harry had been good friends since the late 1980s, when the striker's illustrious career was just beginning. Now it was in its twilight, and Harry was still cheering his every touch of the ball.

Teesside also boasted an England regular, the goalkeeper Lloyd McGrath, and it was a duel between the two 'Macs' which became the focal point of the match. Nestled in his vantage point directly in front of the jumbo-sized cinema screen, Harry watched with fascination as the drama unfolded, as first McGrath somehow saved a McLean penalty, and then as the highly-rated 'keeper tipped over a seemingly unstoppable shot which his international colleague delivered from point-blank range. Indeed, it appeared that the vastly inferior Teesside team might actually make it to the halfway stage unscathed, until the forty-fourth minute, when McLean finally did score, heading in a fine cross from the manager's son, Luigi.

As the goal went in, the heavily-tattooed human contents of The Locomotive pub practically combusted with joy. And as they did so, Harry looked on in wonder. This game was occurring several hundred miles away, and no supporters of either team were in this room. The commentary was entirely in Norwegian. And yet, grown men – dangerous grown men even – were hugging each other at the sight of a goal. Previous to that, they'd been holding their heads in shock, dropping drinks in disbelief and swearing repeatedly in frustration. Harry almost laughed at them, but then he realised that he'd been doing the same, and so laughed at himself, too.

Through the smoke Harry could see an obsessive barmaid making a beeline toward him, and chose to use the half-time respite to get outside and breathe some real air. Propelling himself quickly towards the beer garden, he managed to evade Karen's grasp and found himself outside in no time. But while avoiding Karen was a secondary reason for getting some air, there was also a more pertinent motivation. He had a telephone call to make.

Turning on his phone for the first time that morning, he was first met with three answering machine messages from an increasingly angry Eddie Chung, who wanted to know 'What is the meaning of this?' 'What on earth are you playing at?' and 'Do you want to rot in the gutter without a penny to your name?' All of these made Harry chuckle, especially as he had no intention of replying, but after they had run their (considerable) course, he became more serious, punching in the number of his friend Tom. Tom was a scout for Ariel Hill FC, the local semi-professional team with which Harry had begun his own ill-fated footballing career. Today, just as ever before, they played in the Conference division, one below the football league proper, and there it seemed they were ever destined to stay. But while their players were decidedly average, their behind-the-scenes staff were far more impressive, and that included Tom, who was credited with discovering a whole host of players who'd gone on to bigger things, most notably including a certain Clinton McLean.

As was to be expected at this time, Tom was on the terraces at Ariel's sparsely populated 'stadium' when his phone rang. A little beleaguered after watching Ariel concede three in the first half of their game, he was still pleased to hear from his old friend.

'Harry, good to hear from you,' he said, before embarking on one of his infamous high-speed monologues. 'This game's terrible – Ariel are all over the place. We're 3–0 down, should be ten. We've got nothing up front, nothing in midfield, and still less at the back, Harry. Useless. I've tried to find them a striker, really I have, but there's just no talent about . . . .'

'I might be able to help you there, Tom,' Harry tried to interject. It bounced off Tom's ear.

'I told the wife the other day there used to be thousands of strikers waiting to be discovered by a club like this. Told her about old Clinton McLean – he was a real find. . . . '

'Tom.'

'You don't find 'em like that anymore. None of 'em have got the passion for it. All loads of mouth and nothing when they get out on to the pitch. . . . '

'TOM!' Harry's shout was deafening, and startled a few of his fellow fresh-air seekers. 'Will you listen to me for a minute? I've got a player that I want you to take a look at.'

'Oh. Striker is he?'

'Er . . . sort of. I'm not sure really.'

'Cos we could do with a striker. I was telling the wife the other day about when I first saw old Clinton McLean . . . .'

'I think he's a striker,' Harry bellowed instinctively. 'Can you come down and take a look at him next Saturday morning?'

'Alright. Where.'

'Ariel Fields, but it's probably best if you come to my place and we walk down together.'

'It's no problem, I can meet you there. Which pitch is he playing on?'

'Er . . . I'm not sure. Probably best if you meet me first. Be at mine for about 10 o'clock?'

'Will do Harry. Hope he's good though. We could really use a striker right now. It's not like it used to be here – I remember when we used to have Clin . . . .'

At which point Harry could take no more, and switched off his phone again. He didn't mean to be rude, but there was only so much of Tom that any man could reasonably take. And besides, the second half was about to kick-off, and no man, not even a friend, could come between Harry and his passion.

Five

'The plan,' explained Harry, 'is that you sit on the bench, and pretend you don't know me. Just stare into space. Watch one of the games. Do anything you like Tom – just don't let on that we know each other.'

'What is all this Harry?' asked the bemused-looking elderly scout.

'And put the notebook away. He might suspect something.'

'What?' Tom's head was spinning. Quite understandably, he'd assumed that he'd come down to Ariel Fields (once again, a marshland after the week's rain) to watch some fleet-footed teenager turn out for a pub team. Now the man who'd made the recommendation was telling him to stare into space and put his notebook away.

'But what if I need to write something down?'

'Just remember it. Once you've seen two minutes of this fella, you won't be able to forget.'

Tom looked around at the barren, boggy park. In the distance, he could see twenty-two fat men limping around and falling over sporadically. Ariel Fields was not generally a breeding ground for new talent, so his expectations weren't high anyway, but besides a few joggers, some truly terrible Saturday morning veterans and Harry, no one was anywhere to be seen. After a few minutes of silence, his patience wore thin:

'So come on, where is this kid of yours then Harry?'

'He'll be here,' said Harry, through tightening lips. 'Just give him a chance.'

'Give him a chance? Give him a chance?' Tom sounded slightly like a lunatic as he repeated himself, and Harry was a little concerned that he might suddenly pop. 'I've given him a pretty big chance just by coming here. I can't remember the last time I came to this dismal little place. Nobody with an ounce of talent would ever disgrace themselves by kicking a ball on this ground. It's claimed more broken ankles than I've had hot meat pies. And I've had a lot of pies. No – I don't think I've ever even offered a trial to a player I've seen here. I told the wife this morning that this was a waste of time – Ariel Fields indeed. Ha! And he doesn't even have the decency to turn up. I should be in the West End now, finishing off the Christmas shopping; instead you've made me come out in . . . .'

A firm shove in the chest from Harry forced the wind out of Tom and brought his monologue to an abrupt end. It also planted him squarely on the bench, which thankfully this week, was not covered in the evidence of the previous night's excesses. As he landed, not a little disgruntled, he caught sight of a young man in a cheap-looking track suit, dribbling a football towards them.

'From now on,' Harry whispered out of the corner of his mouth, 'we don't know each other.'

And for once, Tom sat back in silence.

The young man was, as expected, Harry's mysterious undiscovered genius. King of the keepy-uppy; master of the gymnastic, overhead, missile-propelled volley. And, judging by the way that the ball remained glued to his feet as he jogged and paid no attention to it – also dribbling dynamo. As he noticed Harry he waved warmly, again without suffering any loss of ball control. Then he sped up, although only into second gear, and arrived at his new friend's side within moments.

'Hi, Harry,' he said enthusiastically. 'Did you bring your trainers?'

From behind his back, Harry produced a plastic supermarket bag containing two museum pieces. As he slid one foot into each, he saw decades-old shards of mud splinter away and fall to the ground. He was sure he even spotted a couple of fossilised insects. 'I haven't worn these for a couple of years,' he said, although he really didn't need to state the obvious.

'I'll go easy on you if you're out of practice,' offered John magnanimously.

'No, no,' replied Harry, with a half a glance toward a now-intrigued Tom-the-scout, who hadn't seen Harry Foster kick a football for at least twenty-five years. 'Give it your best – I'm sure it'll come back to me.'

John threw his track suit top into the mud, which along with an adjacent tree made for a decent-sized goal. Harry retreated to his (far narrower) end – the scene of the original miracle – and hung his jacket on a branch.

'Ready?' asked John.

'Ready.'

At which point the (colossal mis-) match began. Harry started with the ball, almost fell over it with his first touch, and with his second rolled it too far ahead of himself. John eagerly collected the misplaced pass, and set off toward Harry with a menacing glint in his eye. Harry stuck out a leg to tackle, leaving a slight gap beneath him, and John saw it straight away. In a flash he had rolled the ball between Harry's legs, run around one side of him, collected it again and plopped it into the goal. It was 1–0 to John after twenty seconds. Harry chuckled a curse, afforded himself another quick look at Tom, who didn't yet look overly impressed, and retrieved the ball.

Just five minutes later, it was 4–0. A deft lob, a blasted shot from the other end of the pitch and an end-to-end dribble had all yielded rewards for John, while a couple of easily fielded shots were all Harry could offer in response. And then, somehow, Harry found his rhythm. John had admittedly relaxed to strolling pace, but he still should have done better when a man more than thirty years his senior came racing toward his goal. Using a trick that had been on ice since 1971, Harry fooled his opponent into making a rash tackle. Instead of winning the ball, John took an accidental swipe at Harry's leg. The puffing gent in the old muddy shoes came crashing to the floor, wheezing the word 'penalty' as he went. Immediately, the smiling John nodded and extended his hand, as if pointing to some imaginary dog-mess penalty spot.

'Penalty it is,' he agreed.

And then, quite suddenly, Harry found himself thrown into a vivid daydream of remembrance.

Harry took what seemed like an age to pick himself up, dust himself down, and claim the ball. Behind the goal, Moss Side's notorious home fans were screaming a thousand different slurs at him – each of which stung at him like angry insects, but which collectively were threatening to blow him back off of his feet. 'Cheat' was the most common word used, although it was clear to any neutral that he had not won the penalty by diving. From the edge of the area, Mile End's experienced captain, Robert Wilson, was offering as much calming encouragement as he could – although his words were barely audible against the deafening backdrop of the home supporters.

The referee signalled that he was not ready for the kick to be taken, and began stamping at some uneven ground in front of the penalty spot. To young Harry, this only heightened the anxiety. Turning around, he tried to smile at Wilson, but the expression dissolved into a look of sheer terror, and this only encouraged the Moss Side players to join in with the crowd. Now it felt like the whole world was against him.

But that realisation helped to clarify the picture for Harry. Suddenly he realised the importance of the next minute. On his first appearance for perennial top-division strugglers Mile End, he had the chance to score what would almost certainly be a winning goal against the top side in all of England. A month ago, he'd been playing in the semi-professional league. Tomorrow, if he made the kick, he'd be the main feature of every back page. Of course, if he missed, the consequences didn't bear thinking about. Despite much paper talk that this was an England superstar in the making, many at the club had already grown impatient with him. He needed this kick to silence not only the ferocious crowd spitting fire at him right now, but also the poisonous figures in his own team who were already plotting to send him back to the non-league.

This moment had played in the theatre of Harry's mind throughout his childhood. Penalty kick to win, final minute of the match, against one of the best teams in the world. As the referee blew his whistle, and the bellowing crowd suddenly subsided into hushed silence, the moment began to play out just as he had imagined it. Fixing his eyes on the ball, he strode confidently forward, decided to put it to the goalkeeper's left, and kicked as hard as his teenage legs would allow him.

The ball rolled lamely towards the Moss Side goalkeeper, who grabbed at it hungrily. The crowd threw a million spears of abuse at the hapless young striker who lay prostrate in the area, and team-mates shook their heads. The whistle blew for full-time, and Mile End knew they had missed their chance of a famous result.

But the hapless young striker didn't move. And the look of agony on his face did not just come from the penalty miss. In blowing his golden moment, he had also caused himself serious physical pain – his poorly aimed kick had taken one-third ball, two-thirds ground. Now he couldn't feel anything below his right knee, and he could see his blue sock turning purple as it became saturated with his blood. This was a bad injury.

He screamed out to his team-mates, but none of them could bear so much as to look at him. The embarrassed opposition, who were still going to be heavily lambasted for only managing a draw in the game, had already departed the pitch. So Harry, with tears moistening his face and his numbed right leg moistening the pitch, just lay back down alone, with his head in his hands, as everything he had ever dreamed about shattered into a million pieces around him.

When he snapped out of that quite hideous recollection, which had plagued him since the moment it happened, he was again sitting on his own in a penalty area, having been scythed down there by a reckless challenge. But as he picked himself up this time to take the kick, he realised that there was no goalkeeper. Spinning around, he saw John and Tom, talking briefly and then shaking hands. A moment later, Tom was walking away, and John was looking stunned.

'John?' said Harry, leaving the ball and his second chance at glory behind. 'Are you okay, son?'

'Yes, I think so,' replied John, although his eyes had glazed over.

'What was all that about?'

'That man – he said he was a scout from Ariel Hill Football Club.'

'No!' Harry realised that he'd probably overdone that a bit. 'What else did he say?'

'He said he thought I looked like a good player, and he wondered if I'd like to come for a trial.'

Harry resisted punching the air. Steadying himself, he asked 'And what did you say?'

'I told him I'd think about it.'

'YOU WHAT?' As soon as the words left his mouth (at considerable volume) he realised that he really shouldn't have delivered them with such ferocity that they were accompanied by a volley of spittle. 'I'm sorry. I mean, what is there to think about?'

John was a little surprised at the level of Harry's unease – especially since, as far as he was concerned, the arrival of this scout was a complete surprise to both of them. 'Well,' he explained, 'I'm not sure whether I'd want to play for a team. I've never done it before.'

'But you must have played in school?'

'No, not really. Everyone took it too seriously.'

'So you're telling me that you can do all these tricks, and you've never even played in a proper match.'

'I guess so.'

Before this Harry had been confused and intrigued by John. Now, he was completely baffled. How on earth could someone become this good at football by playing on his own once a week at the local bump-infested park? And how could any young man who loved the game turn down the chance of playing it for a half-decent team? Now, granted, Ariel Hill were no Moss Side, but they were a start, and as far as Harry was aware, they still paid a little better than the building trade.

John did a lot of shrugging. Now he shrugged again and said: 'I haven't got that much time to spare. I'm a very busy person – football takes up too much time if you start taking it seriously.'

'But . . . but . . . .' Harry was struggling for words, and breath. 'But . . . if you took this game seriously, imagine how good you'd be then.' From the look on John's face, he realised that this wasn't really getting through. So he changed his approach: 'John, you play football in the park, once a week, on your own unless you happen to meet up with a few local waifs and strays. From my experience, you barely play for an hour before turning for home. And yet I've seen you running along at top speed as if the ball is just another part of your foot; I've watched you juggle the ball like a circus showman; I've seen you score the finest goal ever to grace a recreation ground kick about. John, there are people in this country who devote their whole lives to trying to develop in themselves just an ounce of what comes to you naturally. They don't just get their football out for an hour a week – they go out running every other night, practise twice a week, play a game every weekend, watch two more besides, abandon their wives, form friendships purely on the basis of common sporting interest and lose all perception of what's important in life. And then suddenly, they hit 40 and look back over their broken marriages and survey their vacuous friendships, and realise not only that they never quite managed to develop much ability at all, but that they wasted half their lives trying. There are thousands of people like this John. Maybe even hundreds of thousands. And most of them would kill to be able to control a football like you.'

'So what are you saying?'

'I'm just saying that if this is what you're like when you don't take your football seriously, imagine how much better you'd be if you did.'

'But I don't want to be better.'

Harry looked heavenwards at this point, and drew breath. There was, of course, nothing ridiculous in what John had just said, and yet to Harry, it sounded like the ravings of a lunatic.

'Look John,' he said eventually, 'I like you. I really do – you seem like a nice enough kid. But I'm afraid I'm having trouble understanding where you're coming from here. You've just been offered a trial with a half-decent football club. If they were to take you on, even as a reserve-team player, you'd be earning . . . . How much do you earn right now?'

John picked up his football and began to step backwards again. This sort of personal question unnerved him. 'Nearly £200 a week,' he replied softly, before defensively adding, 'I know it's not great money, but the man I work for pays me even when there's not much work around.'

'You'd be earning more than that, trust me. And if you started to play well, and got into the first team, they'd pay you more. And then, if you caught the eye of a third division club . . . well, then you're talking about a comfortable living.'

'I'm not too interested in money,' John interrupted. 'And besides, I like my job. No, Harry, I've thought about it and I'm not interested. I don't think I'll bother with the trial. Anyway, I need to get home now.'

'ARE YOU MAD?' bellowed Harry, completely free now from self-restraint. 'YOU COULD PLAY FOOTBALL FOR A LIVING! Does that not even interest you in the slightest? What on earth is wrong with you man? I thought this was every young boy's dream!' He was going argument-with-the-editor red now, and stopped to compose himself.

John stood his ground, gave half a smile of understanding, and put his hand on Harry's trembling shoulder. 'Are you busy for lunch?' he asked.

'I thought you needed to get home,' answered Harry, slightly stunned by John's sudden willingness to move their relationship beyond the park.

'I do,' said John. 'But I thought maybe you could come with me?'

This was not the end of Ariel Hill in which Harry spent most of his time. In fact, this was not even a place in which he would feel comfortable leaving his car. Everything here was grey – from the high-reaching tower-blocks that dominated the foot of the hill like giant overgrown toenails, to the tired-looking people milling about between them. The prevailing expression among its fake-designer-clothed inhabitants was a one-size-fits-all scowl, although Harry wasn't sure whether they'd brought that out specially for him. The sun was shining now, but here it created only shadows.

The estate reminded him of the one on which he spent his own formative years. A few decades had advanced since both had been built but this one was in a far greater state of disrepair. It displayed the same unimaginative architecture; the same sense of bottom 'rung-ness'; the same shade of grey that had provided such a bland backdrop to his childhood. So he sympathised with the residents of this place – even if he did often blame some of them for 'bringing down the neighbourhood' – and yet at the same time his successful escape from this kind of landscape only heightened his desire never to revisit it. In short, he didn't really want to be there.

The passageways which John led him through were overflowing with a stench akin to that of a badly-serviced pub toilet. Holding his breath, he advanced at pace, accidentally knocking over a bicycle and incurring the foul-mouthed wrath of an incensed 6-year-old. There's no place like home, he thought, and prayed that he'd soon reach John's.

'Here we are then,' said John, stopping at a particularly unimpressive door. A swear-word had been carved into it, and it looked as if a platoon of rabid zombies had spent the previous night scratching their nails into its surface. 'Do you mind just waiting here while I go and talk to Mum? She's a bit funny about visitors.'

And before Harry could answer, John had disappeared, closing the door behind him. Planting his hands as deep into his pockets as the seams would allow, he glanced around and noticed that he had made an error of observation. Up close at least, grey was the least prevailing colour of all in this place. Of course, that was because, with less than a week to go until Christmas, the good people of the estate had spent every penny they could comfortably borrow or steal on the most elaborate decorative displays available. Every window was awash with little coloured bulbs, leaping reindeer and flickering snowmen. It was garish, it was tasteless; to Harry's mind it was hideous – but it did demonstrate that there was life behind these lifeless walls, perhaps even hope.

Harry was shaken from this happy thought by a short sharp pain in his leg. Before he could work out what had caused it, it was followed by another, this time in his neck. Then a pinging noise just by Harry's head revealed the reason for these sudden bursts of discomfort: he was being shot at, albeit with small green plastic pellets.

'Oi!' he shouted angrily. 'Oi!' He didn't really know what else to say apart from that.

An irrepressible childish giggle gave away the youth of the perpetrator – most probably this was the same swearing 6-year-old whose bike Harry had just unwittingly attacked – but his position was still a secret. Therefore he was well-placed to take pot-shots at the older gentleman in the ridiculous trainers, and the older gentleman had no idea where to go to take cover.

Thankfully, before any further pain could be inflicted, John reappeared, smiling and ushering Harry inside. He didn't wait to be asked twice.

The inside of John's flat was not only the most welcome sight Harry had seen in a while, it was also one of the most attractive. Although space was limited, good use of it had been made, and the tasteful colours and wooden floors gave it the appearance of an interior design magazine's 'after' shot.

'Hey, this is nice,' said Harry, rubbing his neck. He'd expected to say that anyway, but he hadn't expected to be telling the truth.

'Well,' said John, a little proudly, 'we're happy here. Mum and Becky are in the room at the end of the hall – I'll take your coat if you like, you go and introduce yourself.'

John disappeared again, and Harry ventured down the hallway, offering a fairly pathetic 'hello' as he went. After a few steps, he reached another small but beautifully-decorated room, in which two women were seated. One, a thin, frail-looking woman of about his age, smiled nervously but said nothing. The other was unexpectedly beautiful – tall and blonde with high cheekbones and carefully-applied (although not overdone) make-up – and at least half his age. As Harry tried to prevent his tongue from rolling out on the carpet in front of her, she greeted him:

'You must be Harry,' she said, in the velvet voice of a PR executive. 'I'm Becky, John's sister. He's told us so much about you.'

'H . . . hello,' replied Harry, transfixed, and far too obviously so, by her magnetic-field face. Then he realised that he'd been staring, turned pink and blurted, 'So, can you play football too?'

Chuckling, Becky looked at her mother, who was not. 'No, not really,' she replied. 'It's not really my game.'

John emerged again, this time clutching two wooden chairs which he had built, like most of the other furniture here, himself.

'I'll make us some lunch in a little while Mum,' he announced, before turning to Harry. 'Hope you don't mind Spam?'

Harry forced a smile, but his stomach churned at the mere thought and he couldn't hold the expression. Then there was a moment of silence, before John, then Becky, and even Mum began laughing hysterically. Realising that he'd been made fun of, Harry joined in too. The laughter kept coming for a little while, too.

The next half-hour was very pleasant. In the office, the study, the betting shop and even the pub, Harry didn't have this: the aura of a happy family to bathe himself in once in a while. Here he was in the company of people who had little, but shared everything, and seemed far happier than him as a result. As the conversation continued, Mum (also known as Marilyn) revealed the personality behind her shyness, and Becky demonstrated her wicked sense of humour. All the way through, John's face was radiant with immense pride as he showed off the things most precious to him in life.

After plenty of small-talk, in which he was forced to list most of the famous writers and sports-people he knew, Harry found the courage to mention football and John in the same sentence:

'You know, Mrs Christie, John is a very talented young man.'

John's face fell, and he glared at Harry, as if he'd just felt a betraying dagger pierce his skin.

'You mean his work?' She smiled benevolently.

'No – although I'm sure he's a fine electrician – I meant his football.'

'Really? Is he a good player?'

Harry was puzzled. 'Well – yes. Hasn't he told you about the newspaper article?'

'I'm sorry?'

'Leave it Harry,' a forceful voice cut across from John's direction, before adding, more softly, 'please.'

Harry persisted. 'Mrs Christie, John is a quite gifted player. I'm surprised you didn't know that. In fact, I think he could make it as a professional.'

'Harry!'

'Really?' Mrs Christie was shaking slightly. 'Our John, a professional footballer? Did you hear that Becky?'

Becky smiled, but not too much. She could sense her brother's unease. Then she did something to make Harry quiet.

Harry wasn't quite sure how he'd missed the empty wheelchair by Becky's chair. But when she lifted herself into it, made her excuses and left for the bathroom, all he could think about was his original question to her. Given that she was paralysed from the waist down, it was unsurprising that football 'wasn't really her game'. Harry felt stupid, and offensive, and at the same time angry with John for not warning him. All this was unimportant now of course – the look of silent-struck shock on his face as she'd made these movements was a lot more damaging. Suddenly his throat went very dry, but Mrs Christie was not ready to stop talking yet.

'But he doesn't even play for a team . . . does he?'

Harry shook his head and tried to compose himself. 'No, Mrs Christie. But he could do – in fact a scout from Ariel Hill Football Club has invited him for a trial this week.'

'Harry, please!' John tried, in vain, a third time to silence his friend.

'Well, you've got to go John!' she exclaimed, her face lighting up like the Christmas decorations of her nearest neighbour. 'You've got to go and have the trial. You could be a proper footballer, like on the television . . . like that Billy Regan.'

Harry bit his lip at that last comment, then felt John's firm hand on his shoulder.

'Perhaps I should make lunch now,' said John, seething a little. 'Would you mind coming to help me Harry?'

Moments later, a whispering row was developing in the kitchen.

'You've got no right to come round here and excite her like that,' snapped John. 'Don't fill her head with all these dreams – she's been through enough disappointment in her life.'

'John, I only want what's best for you.'

'You don't even know me. Do you know why I brought you here? I thought that if you saw where we lived, and met Becky, you might understand.'

'Understand what?'

'Understand why I can't go chasing some ridiculous dream like professional football. I've got responsibilities – I have to look after my family.'

'But if you made it as a footballer you could look after them a lot better than this John.'

'And what if I didn't make it? What if I gave up my career, joined a football team, and it didn't work out? What then? Then I haven't got a job, and suddenly the rent money dries up, and my family goes hungry.'

'That won't happen,' protested Harry, '– you're good.'

'Stop it Harry. Please. I'm really flattered by everything you've said to me. It was incredible that you wrote that article. It's like a dream come true – being in the paper and having all those nice things said about me. But that's enough fantasy now. I need to get back to reality. Please leave it alone now.'

Harry tried to muster more words of argument, but found none. Instead, he softly asked for his coat, bid a general farewell to the Christies and plotted a course for The Locomotive.

There he drank away the rest of the day, in monastic silence.

Six

Harry's New Year resolution had been to forget all about John Christie. So when he was asked to cover England's crucial World Cup qualification match in Iceland, he jumped at the opportunity. Through friendships with players he'd managed to get himself a seat on the team's own charter jet; now he was on his way to Reykjavik, in a plane that only catered for business class passengers, sipping fine champagne and surrounded by celebrities. This was a good way indeed to forget.

On the left of his more-than-ample leather chair/bed, the tall, noble striker Clinton McLean was snoring with gusto. On his right, the defensive cornerstone D'Alex Smith was diligently studying a Bible. Neither of them looked remotely interested in starting a conversation, and so with an hour left until landing, Harry decided to go for a walkabout and gauge the mood of the squad. He'd already taken note that Billy Regan was engrossed in a video game at the front of the plane; thus he wisely headed for the rear.

On the back row he found a nervous Lloyd McGrath, the first-choice goalkeeper, who looked as if he'd been having nightmares about the Icelandic forwards. In fact, he was simply terrified of flying, but had decided that to have navigated the choppy January waters below by ferry would have been the greater of two evils. Now he wasn't so sure. His face was a pale white, his jaw hung open and his breath was stale. When Harry crouched beside him, he began to mumble about the remaining flight time, as if engaged in some childishly long rendition of 'Ten Green Bottles'.

'So,' said Harry, trying to take his mind off the flight, 'how are you feeling about the match?'

Lloyd rolled his eyes and turned away.

'Not too good?' persisted Harry.

'Not too good,' Lloyd repeated. 'Not too good.'

'But it is *only* Iceland,' said Harry, a little more quietly. 'You are the favourites, surely?'

Lloyd's head spun back toward him at this suggestion. 'You know better than most Harry. I read your column. These days, we're *only* England.'

Back in his seat for the descent, Harry noticed that D'Alex Smith had put his Bible down. They'd never been formally introduced, but as he was both a player who Harry greatly admired, and a close friend of Clinton McLean, he decided that now would be a good time to say hello:

'I'm Harry Foster. I'm a good friend of Clinton's.'

'I know who you are,' said D'Alex, impaling him with huge piercing pupils that gave nothing away. 'You're the newspaper columnist.'

Harry always hated that comment. It was far too ambiguous. Did it mean D'Alex was a fan, or an irate victim of his writing, ready now to dish out his Old Testament-style revenge? In the library box at the back of his mind, he flicked back speedily through his last 200 articles. No, he was pretty sure he'd only been complimentary. He just grinned and nodded, and hoped for clarification.

D'Alex's blindingly white teeth burst through his lips, and he gave a hearty West Indian laugh. 'I like you,' he said, which was a relief to Harry.

'I'm a great fan of yours,' said Harry. 'I hope that comes across in my writing.'

'It does,' replied D'Alex, 'you've certainly always been pretty fair to me. Which is more than I can say about some of your colleagues.'

This was a less-than-subtle reference to the editorial team of the right-wing tabloid the *Mouthpiece*. A few years ago, they'd criticised a decision he'd made not to play in Sunday lunch-time matches because he wanted to attend church. The newspaper was widely berated for its standpoint by rival newspapers, but 'coincidentally', D'Alex announced soon afterwards that he would subsequently be available for all matches, including those on a Sunday. Despite his humiliating climbdown, the *Mouthpiece* sports team had remained on his back ever since. He was a fine player – widely-regarded as one of the best emerging defenders in the world – and yet whenever you heard the name D'Alex Smith, that story always came to mind. Harry wanted to ask him about it, but acknowledged that now probably wasn't the time. Instead, he wanted to know whether the rest of the team concurred with Lloyd McGrath, who was now filling a paper bag with his in-flight meal at the back.

'Can I ask you,' he said gently, 'how you think the game on Wednesday will go?'

D'Alex leaned back in his chair, fastening his seat belt. It was perhaps symbolic that he did so. 'Are you asking me as Harry Foster the journalist, or Harry Foster, Clinton's mate?'

'The second.'

'Then ask Harry Foster the journalist. He knows already.'

'Are you saying that you're worried about this game?' The England fan at Harry's core was rising up in terror. Alright, so he'd written in his column that England were going to lose (although Alex Knight made sure that there was at least some hope injected in the edit), but he didn't want to hear that from one of the players two days before the game.

'I'd say we should be worried,' he said, lowering his voice. 'But I don't think that many of us are. Some of the quieter, more sensible lads – me, the 'keeper, and maybe a couple of the older ones like Clinton – we realise that we're not the team we used to be, and we know we'll do well to get a win. Most of the rest just assume we've won before the match has even kicked off, just because we're England. And that's why I think we might lose.'

'Lose?' the fear and shock with which Harry uttered that word took him by surprise. Again, *he'd* written that they'd lose, but to get it straight from the horse's mouth was quite another thing.

'Why not?' replied D'Alex as the plane skidded to a halt on the runway, and Lloyd McGrath immediately began contemplating the return journey. 'They're at home, they've got a couple of decent players–'

'But England expects . . . .'

'Then England better get used to lowering its expectations,' D'Alex replied, without a trace of a smile.

Simple maths revealed that this was a game which England badly needed to win. Poor results (a home draw against lowly Moldova, and a defeat in Lisbon) had shunted them into an unimpressive third place in their qualifying group, behind both the Portuguese and the good folk of the frozen island on which they now stood. An English victory here would see the second and third-placed teams switch positions, and leave England only a point behind the leaders. A defeat, however, depending on other results, could see them free-fall into the unthinkable position of fifth in a group of six teams.

On Wednesday night, Harry took his shiny brand-new seat in Iceland's shiny brand-new 30,000-capacity national stadium a few minutes before kick-off. The temperature at pitch-side was such that his coffee had lost all heat before he'd even had a chance to taste it. His hat, his scarf, his gloves and the seven layers of clothing he'd wrapped himself up in all seemed to have no effect. And as the last of his body heat escaped in the unforgiving night air, Harry's heart went out to the eleven Englishmen in skin-tight, red-and-white shirts and shorts who were running out onto the pitch. As he wrote – with difficulty – in his notebook, he was certain he'd never before seen a team jogging on the spot during their own national anthem.

The English players' overwhelming desire to run around as much as possible, if only to warm up, made for an entertaining first half. They didn't score, but they had plenty of possession, and created a few chances that on other, warmer evenings, may have otherwise been converted. As predicted in Monday's *Foster's Eye*, Billy Regan found his way into the referee's book within the first ten minutes, and spent most of the rest of the game sulking as a result. Lloyd McGrath managed to take his focus away from his waiting aeroplane torture for long enough to make a smart save from Iceland's outstanding player, Thomas Bjarnason. And D'Alex Smith, whom Harry was growing more and more impressed with by the minute, was having another excellent match at the centre of defence. At half-time, although not ideal, 0–0 looked a satisfactory enough scoreline, and one on which to build in the second period.

But when that half kicked off, it appeared that everything that had gone before had abruptly been forgotten. England were suddenly sloppy, giving the ball away under the slightest pressure. Regan and McLean disappeared completely from the match, meaning that the defence and midfield came under siege from Icelandic attacks. And after fifty-nine minutes, and much persistence,

Bjarnason got his goal, weaving past three desperate tackles and firing past McGrath from near the penalty spot. 1–0 to Iceland, and the doomsday scenario had suddenly come into sharp focus.

After the goal England rallied, bringing the strikers back into the game and constructing several attacks. But when McLean missed what Harry later called 'a heartbreaking, career-shattering chance', the team in red and white looked as if they had all but given up. Then, as the second minute of injury time began – and Harry swore he picked up the sound of faraway screaming on a northeastern wind – England were granted a corner. With defeat beyond contemplation, the team piled every last player into the box, including McGrath, who gleefully leapt at the chance to finally warm himself up. Paul Kerridge, the midfielder, took the corner, but just as he did so a freak blast of icy wind blew the ball way off course, and out towards the middle of the pitch. There, Thomas Bjarnason was both delighted to receive it, and overjoyed to discover that there was no England player within 20 yards of him. He scampered toward the abandoned English goal, got to within 30 yards, set himself, and then with trademark style lobbed it straight in. 2–0 to Iceland, and eleven Englishmen literally frozen with shock.

Conversations on the plane had partly prepared Harry for this eventuality, but it still rocked him like a nuclear explosion. As much as he criticised this team in his writing, he still cared about it deeply. To Harry, the England team was like a rebellious child, and right now he was watching that child being sent off to a young offenders' institution – possibly for four years; maybe for longer than that.

The players trudged back to the changing room while their opponents danced and revelled in the stadium's carnival atmosphere. Although Harry had access, he didn't really want to be around for the manager's end of game debrief. Instead, he headed straight for the press office, and hoped that his laptop hadn't frozen up. On his way there he heard a stadium announcement that turned England's terrible evening into a total nightmare. Poland and Moldova had played out a 2–2 draw, meaning that both sides moved above England in the group table. Now only lowly Tajikistan lay between them and rock bottom. Harry sighed even harder than he had previously, and warmed his hands in preparation for the inevitable literary slaughter he'd now have to wreak upon his team.

Harry was about to start typing when his mobile phone, which had apparently survived the conditions, began to ring. The specially-set ring-tone, 'God Save the Queen', now seemed hideously inappropriate, as confirmed by the sniggers of several local journalists with whom he was sharing the press office. He needed to e-mail his copy back to London within an hour, yet he was not looking forward to writing it, and was glad of the opportunity of a distraction. He answered as chirpily as he possibly could, which still made him sound like he was at a funeral.

'Harry?' said a voice.

'Yes?'

'It's Tom here. From the club. Did you see the England game? What a disgrace. Those boys shouldn't even bother getting back on the plane. I watched it with the wife and one of my boys and I said to them this is the worst England team I've seen in my life. Absolutely useless I say, the worst I've ever seen. If we'd sent our first team out there they wouldn't have done any worse. In fact, as I said to the wife, if we'd sent her out there she probably wouldn't have done any worse. And poor old

Clinton. Poor Clinton. I think he'll probably call it a day after this. I mean, I'm not saying he's not a great player . . . I discovered him myself you know. I remember when I first saw him–'

'I'm at the game,' said Harry, losing his patience. And then to emphasise the unwelcome effect that these ramblings were going to have on Tom's phone bill he added, 'in Iceland.'

'Are you? Oh! I didn't realise. Silly me – I thought you'd be watching it at home like you normally do. Did the paper send you, or did you go of your own accord? I'd like to go to a few more international games you know, but I never seem to get the time–'

Clearly he didn't get it. 'I'm at the game Tom. In Iceland. Where it's very expensive to call someone on a mobile phone.'

'Oh heavens!' exclaimed Tom, as the penny, or rather the large bag of pound coins, dropped. 'I'd better be quick then. Listen, I just rang to say, we've signed that lad you showed me. John Christie. We did all the contracts this afternoon. Alright, see you Harry, bye.'

Harry took a second to process what Tom had just said, then screamed a tremendous 'Wait!' But it was too late, Tom was gone, and subsequently refused to answer Harry's repeated return calls, fearing that it might cost him something to do so. It didn't seem possible to him that John Christie had changed a mind that had seemed so decisive, and yet Tom was not the sort to make things up. It didn't make sense, and yet regardless of that it elated Harry. Suddenly the world didn't seem so bad after all.

The England report which appeared in the next morning's *Daily Reporter* was markedly more positive than the one in every other newspaper. Something had clearly put Harry Foster in a good mood.

Seven

Tom had already filled Harry in on most of the details. John's trial at Ariel Hill FC had been awful; laughable even. And John's trial had been magnificent too – depending on what it was that you were assessing.

It had become apparent early on, for instance, that John's claim of never having played in a team was almost certainly truthful. He'd been asked to play in attack, but had spent the whole of the practice match following the ball, all over the pitch. He had no notion of what 'attack' meant – he simply went where the action was. This alone would have been enough for the manager to reject him – were it not for the fact that he kept this up, without any loss of pace, for an entire ninety minutes. Every other player – be he trialist or squad member – was practically on his knees with exhaustion by the end. John, who'd covered every inch of the grass and never stopped running, finished by seeing how many keep-ups he could do.

Yet despite having the positional discipline of an excited puppy, John's skill had spoken far louder than his flaws. In a ninety-minute trial, featuring seventeen members of the Ariel Hill first team squad, John had scored twice (in a game which finished 2–0). He had also, according to Tom's notes, won thirty-eight headers and thirty-five tackles, lost possession only twice, had eight shots – all on target, completed nine dribbles success-fully, and thrice set up shooting opportunities for his team-mates. As Tom put it, if Billy Regan had come down to the same trial, he probably would have been made to look second best.

But things weren't all as good as that. Despite plenty of encouragement from the other players, John had barely spoken throughout the trial. He also had a gap-toothed understanding of the rules – to the immense frustration of his colleagues, he'd been caught offside twelve times, foul-throwed at least as often, and handled the ball innumerably. Basically, it was clear to all that John did not understand how football worked.

Which was one of the reasons why Harry was now waiting for him in the lounge of the best restaurant in Ariel Hill. The club had signed John on the strength of his performance – they knew they had no other choice after he'd dominated the trial so incredibly – but he was still a great enigma to them. How could a man be so good at something he knew nothing about? Was it all some kind of big joke? For a slap-up meal and as much good wine as he could fit into his expanding guts, Harry had agreed to find out.

Gluttony wasn't the only reason behind Harry's decision to come though. Since returning from Reykjavik a week ago, he'd repeatedly had to closet his inquisitiveness and prevent himself from wandering around John's estate in the hope of finding him again. The questions that had buzzed around his head like angry mayflies since the first moment he'd seen John had multiplied exponentially ever since. After John had first turned down a trial and then mysteriously attended one (dominating it and signing as a result), the mayflies had gone ballistic. The man made no sense at all, and perhaps that was exactly what made him the most intriguing person that Harry – who'd spent much of his life chasing interesting people and their stories – had ever come across.

There was an obvious problem though. John was hardly a contender for the world's most talkative man. The first time Harry had tried to speak to him, he ran away. The second time, he'd given one-word answers, then run away. At his own home, he'd been a relative mute as his mother and sister had chatted happily. Apparently, he'd barely spoken at the trial. So there was nothing on which to base much hope that this evening would be any different. Harry had a simple plan though, one which had worked time and again with many decades of footballers.

'A bottle of your most expensive red please,' he barked at the immaculately dressed *maître d'*, just as John shuffled into view. He was wearing an embarrassingly cheap suit that was turning the head of every other customer as he passed by.

'Hello Harry,' John almost whispered as he offered a hand to shake. 'Nice to see you again.'

The head waiter arrived with two glasses, but John held up a hand. 'Not for me please,' he said, a little assertively. 'I don't drink.'

Harry sighed and grabbed the bottle. Suddenly it looked like being a long night.

It took quite a while, and the telling of plenty of his own story, but midway through a main course of moules marniere and steak frites, John did eventually lower his guard. Harry wasn't quite sure why, but after one particularly considered mouthful he simply said:

'You probably thought my family a bit odd.'

Defensively, Harry knee-jerked a rapid 'No!', but John indicated that it wasn't necessary.

'It's OK,' he went on, 'my sister's in a wheelchair, there's no father figure around; we live in a very troubled area. I'm sure you had your questions.'

Harry's face lit up with the realisation that at last, he might get somewhere. Terrified though that he might say something to ruin the moment, he simply smiled and tried to maintain eye contact.

'We didn't always live on the estate. My father ran a car business and he and Mum were quite wealthy. Then, about twelve years ago, he met this other woman – a friend of Mum's actually. The three of them used to go out all the time together, or she'd be over at our house; sometimes she'd even baby-sit for Becky and me. That went on for a year, and I think that for most of that time Mum suspected that something was going on between them. But she didn't say anything – she just ignored it; wanted to believe that it was all in her imagination. Anyway, it wasn't. One day he didn't come home, and a month later, she had the bank on the phone asking her how she was going to pay the mortgage. He'd sold the business, taken all the money, and run off to Spain with Mum's friend. So we had nothing.'

'You must hate him,' Harry gasped, unable to stop himself.

'No, I don't hate him. I'm sad that he did what he did. I wish he hadn't. But you can't live like that, holding on to the past, never forgiving–'

'Forgiving?' shrieked Harry, 'Why on earth would you want to forgive him? He ruined your mum's life.'

'No he didn't. He broke her heart, but he didn't ruin her life. She's still got Becky and me, and she's got some good friends through her church. She's happy enough now, it's just that things are different.'

'But how can you sit there and be so gracious about him? He took all your money, he lost you the house – heck, what about your sister? How could he leave her in the lurch?'

'Eh? Oh, no. She hasn't always been paralysed Harry. That didn't happen until a few years ago. She was in a road accident – got hit on her bike by a driver who was high on drugs....' He tailed off as he spoke, and took a long slow sip of mineral water.

'You forgiven him as well?' asked Harry, sensing that he knew the answer.

John looked into his dinner plate, and sighed.

'Do I take that as a no?' Harry persisted.

'I'm working on that one,' replied John quietly. 'I'll get there in the end.'

A period of silence followed, during which Harry felt he'd gone too far and John barely touched his steak. It was the latter who spoke first though, turning the subject conveniently to the very reason for their meeting:

'So, I'm a footballer now,' he said, hardly dripping with enthusiasm. 'Gave up my job last Friday.'

'So I hear,' said Harry. 'I have to admit, it came as a bit of a shock to me.'

'I'm sure it did. After all, the last time we spoke I asked you to leave my flat at the very suggestion. Sorry about that, by the way.'

'So what changed?'

'Nothing. I still think it's a stupid risk. I'm still terrified that it might all go wrong and we'll end up with nothing.'

'Right. That doesn't make a whole lot of sense.'

'No, but then you don't know my family. After you left, all I had was three days of constant nagging from both of them. They kept saying that this was the chance of a lifetime, kept telling me that I had to go to the trial or I'd regret it for the rest of my life. They kept begging me – and in the end I couldn't say no to them.'

'I heard the trial went well,' Harry offered, encouragingly.

'I suppose it must have done.'

'Yes. My friend at the club said they're very excited about you. Two goals in your first ever match – pretty impressive stuff. Although they did mention that you had a few difficulties . . . .'

'There were a lot of rules to remember,' John replied, smirking a little. 'When I play in the park, I don't usually worry about offsides and handballs.'

'Hmm,' agreed Harry, also smirking. 'About that. When you're in the park, on a Saturday morning . . . ?'

'Yes?'

'Why *do* you just play with the local tramps?'

'I told you Harry. Other people just take the game too seriously. I didn't have time to worry about that – my job took up most of my week. Those guys are always too drunk to worry about commitment – you just turn up and play. Anyway, you probably turned up on a bad week; often there are five or six decent players down there.'

'Maybe we could get them trials too.' Harry chuckled at his own joke. Then he looked more thoughtful. 'John, you just said you *didn't* have time – does that mean you're going to take it seriously now?'

'Of course. Now it's my job. You've got to take your job seriously.'

Harry smiled and chewed a mussel. 'Yeah,' he agreed, taking a moment to get excited once more about John's potential.

'The thing is,' said John, again lowering his voice, 'I'm a bit embarrassed. I don't know a lot of the rules.'

'Surely you know that you can't handle the ball?'

'Yes, I know that one. I guess it was just force of habit. But I'm talking about the more complicated stuff – like offside.' He looked at Harry, dead in the eye. 'Maybe you could help me?'

The next twenty minutes were spent ruining an extremely expensive tablecloth in a lavish and over-priced French restaurant, as several of Harry's defunct mussel shells became players on a three-dimensional chalkboard of explanation. As they kicked around a football (or, pea), John's eyes began to flicker with understanding. By the end of the demonstration, quite a crowd of waiters and other service staff had grown around the table.

'So,' said Harry, as the disappointed throng dispersed, 'I've got to ask you one last question. How did you get so good at this game? I mean, you didn't play at school, you never joined a team outside. Did you teach yourself?'

'My dad used to teach me. He used to take me out in the garden every chance he got; it's the only thing I really remember about him. Mum says he was completely obsessed with football – he used to say he was going to train me to be a professional. I think he probably had me kicking a ball as soon as they first got me back from the hospital.'

Harry leaned back in his chair and plucked a cigar from his pocket, as if he had just uncovered the answer to a particularly taxing mystery. 'I get it,' he said, with more than a shade of self-satisfaction. 'So you were trained from birth. That explains why your touch is so good, and–'

'Not really,' John interrupted, 'because he got fed up with me. I was coming along well enough for the first six or seven years, but then I kept making mistakes.'

Harry's cigar went back into his pocket. 'What kind of mistakes?'

'I wasn't a fast enough runner, for one thing. And I couldn't do keep-ups.'

'What? But you're brilliant at both of those things. . . . '

'When he stopped training me, I started taking myself outside to practise – then, when I was a little bit older, I started going up to Ariel Fields. I practised it all, but especially the running and the keep-ups. I just wanted to show him that I'd got better. But I never got a chance.'

Harry reached across and put a hand on John's shoulder. 'You never know,' he whispered. 'You might just get one yet.'

Eight

The next few weeks went quite well for John Christie. By mid-January he had shrugged off his difficulties with the rules to make a first-team debut. The manager initially used him as a second-half substitute, playing him in the centre of midfield to rejuvenate the team when it tired. His first five games yielded no goals, but fans and teammates alike quickly warmed to him thanks to the hard work he always put in. He was asked to play defensively – sitting just in front of the centre-backs – and his pace and natural timing helped to break up many opposition attacks. Of those first five games, Ariel Hill, a small and un-fancied team which perennially struggled at the bottom of the league, lost none, winning three. Almost immediately, the talk in the club bar and the local newspaper was circling around the new player.

Skinny and stretched-looking, with unkempt blonde hair, John hardly cut an impressive figure when he arrived into each match from his regular spot on the bench. An intensive gym programme was going to help in the long term, but at first John's emergence from an Ariel Hill track suit consistently drew sneers from opposition supporters. They were silenced quickly enough.

Silence was a trait that soon became essentially associated with John. He both commanded it from those he played against, and was a chief exponent of it. Just as in his trial, John was always a man of few words. In training, he only spoke when spoken to. In the heat of a game, he responded to abuse, violent tackles and the occasional sneaky punch (unfortunately prevalent at such a level of football) with nothing more than a shrug or a disappointed glare. It wasn't that he was afraid to talk – this theory was regularly disproved when other players suggested as much – it was simply that he didn't open his mouth unless he had something to say.

His sixth appearance brought with it a first start. February had arrived with a burst of ice and snow, and the resulting conditions at training had claimed the ankles of two of the regular starters. Although he remained unconvinced that John was ready for ninety minutes of football, the manager was beginning to listen to the chatter from the stands and the changing room, and when injuries struck, he found an opening in defence, at left back. For the visit of Kingston Town, John was on the pitch from the outset.

Although reporting duties had until this point kept Harry from attending any of Ariel Hill's matches, he'd managed to negotiate with Knight that this weekend he'd be excused. So when he scanned the crudely-produced photocopied team sheet, he was delighted to spot John's name next to the number 3. At the same time he was a little disappointed that John's striking abilities (which he'd been the first to uncover) were being overlooked, but that was relatively unimportant. Harry was about to watch John Christie – the player who he had discovered, who would still be a local electrician were it not for his involvement – start a competitive match. Pulling the lapels of his jacket up and tucking his scarf inside them, Harry carefully selected a seat (from the 400 empty in the 600-seater stand) and waited patiently.

At 3 o'clock, a referee's whistle sent twenty-two tin-helmeted gladiators into a battle against each other and, more significantly, the elements. A freezing wind lashed relentlessly across the pitch like an icy whip, continually knocking players off balance and passes off course. Because of that factor, this was always going to be a hard game on which to make an impression. No one had told John Christie that, however.

Kingston had scored almost straight away. It hadn't been John's fault – the aging and overweight goalkeeper behind him had simply palmed a sedate shot into his own goal. Then, after he had done so – as if to rub salt into Ariel Hill wounds – the already poor conditions took a turn for the worse. The game progressed to half-time fairly painfully, but there was no notable goal-mouth action.

The second half followed a similar pattern, and so with time running out, the manager decided to make some changes to his team. When he beckoned John across to his position on the touch-line, the player naturally assumed that he was about to be substituted. He was mistaken. Instead, John was to get his first chance as a striker, as the team threw more men forward in the hope of finding a goal. With a hint of a smile on his face, he charged to the other end of the pitch to join the two regular strikers, a 39-year-old cart-horse named Brian Labant, and a precocious teenager who preferred to be known only as 'Paulo'. They were both as bad as each other – selfish, arrogant and bereft of true talent. The fact that one was the manager's brother-in-law and the other was his own son had nothing to do with the fact that they persistently played of course, despite rarely finding the goal. John, arriving now from the back with a look of determination in his eyes, certainly couldn't do any worse.

As Harry realised what was happening, it almost – although not quite – thawed his stiffening body with excitement. John's performance in defence, solid and dependable as it had been, had encouraged him, but he'd never been a great watcher of left-backs. Kingston had a pretty average right-midfielder who would have posed few problems to a cardboard cut-out, let alone a real defender, so John had been offered few chances to impress, simply because the ball had not often travelled to his corner of the field. Now perhaps he'd have a chance to fulfil his real potential.

With five minutes left on the referee's watch, he inevitably did just that. A long ball from one of his former defensive colleagues landed directly on his chest, and with a clever twist he was able to confuse an opposition defender into missing the ball and toppling to the frozen turf. As he advanced toward Kingston's goal he glanced around in the hope of spotting some support. It was nowhere to be seen. 'Paulo', envious at John's skilful dispatch of the defender, had stopped on the halfway line in a sulk. Brian Labant was attempting to sprint up to join the attack, but this kind of physical activity was beyond him nowadays – especially in these conditions – and so he, too, was forced to stand and watch. John was on his own. Upon realising this he seemed unconcerned. From some way outside the area, he took a full swing at the ball, which arrowed towards the far corner of the Kingston goal at breakneck speed. The goalkeeper, untrained to combat such ferocity, slipped comically into a half-dive after the ball was already well past him.

The crowd, such as it was, went wild with appreciation. Even the visiting supporters, who seemed to heavily outnumber their rivals, offered conciliatory applause. John beamed, happy to have brought such pleasure and, with naïveté and innocence pasted across his face, gave them all a humble wave. His team-mates, with the exception of the moody striker with the pretentious moniker, mobbed and hugged him. And in the stand, Harry roared like he hadn't done in thirty years.

When the celebrations subsided, there were still three minutes left to play. Kingston, having led for so long against what appeared to be a toothless team, were now suffering from severe shellshock. Sensing as much, John again made a darting run towards their goal the very next time he was given the ball. Fearing the worst, a lumbering oaf of a defender made a crude lunge at him just he was about to let fly again – and less than 10 yards from goal. It was a clear penalty, and the end of the game for the oaf, who lumbered his way into the stand with a customary curse or seven in the referee's direction.

Having been fouled, John naturally picked up the ball himself in preparation for the penalty. Before he could place it on the spot though, it was being wrenched from his hands by a petulant teen.

'Paulo takes the penalties at this club,' he snarled.

John didn't blink. He simply released his grip on the ball, and walked away. 'Forgive me,' he said gently. 'I didn't realise.'

'Paulo' sniggered to himself as he placed the ball on the spot. He stopped sniggering when he watched his penalty bounce back off the crossbar. And his facial swagger buckled completely as John Christie floated the rebound back into the centre of the goal.

This time the crowd went completely mad. There was a pitch invasion. There was hoisting of players onto shoulders. There was infectious chanting.

'Christie, Christie, Christie.'

To the very short list of Ariel Hill legends, a new name was already being added.

Afterwards, Harry waited patiently outside the ground like a schoolboy desperate for an autograph. Evening was drawing in, and the ground had emptied itself of cheering locals. When John finally emerged, with a duffel bag hoisted over one shoulder, Harry couldn't stop himself from running over. He slipped on the icy tarmac of the car park, landing on and bruising his posterior, but bounced back up to his feet without a care, and threw an arm around his hero.

'That was incredible!' he enthused. 'I can't believe it!'

John smiled unassumingly. 'It went well I thought,' he said, understating the obvious.

'Went well? You won the game single-handed. You're their new hero.'

An elderly figure emerged from the shadows behind them as Harry continued to lavish praise. It was Tom, Ariel Hill's chief scout. Without saying a word he simply laid a hand on both men's shoulders, squeezed, patted, and then with a grin fixed on his face, departed.

Harry was shocked. 'Do you know,' he whispered to John as the old man meandered off into the evening, 'that in all the years I've known that man, I've never seen him do that. He didn't say a word. He was speechless. You did that John – what you did out there today stopped him moaning. You stopped him worrying – you stopped him chattering away without a purpose. Look at him: he feels fulfilled.'

They both watched Tom as he practically danced his way to the bus stop.

'Isn't that a bit of a shame though Harry?' asked John, straight-faced and wide-eyed. 'Don't you think it's a bit sad that the only thing that can make him happy is a football going into a net? When I scored that first goal, I looked up and saw all those grown men jumping around, screaming in ecstasy and hugging each other – shouting only good things. And yet they can't do that normally. Only two minutes earlier they'd been cursing, abusing each other, even heading for the exit. I wonder how they would have treated their wives and children this evening if I hadn't scored?'

'Don't get too philosophical about it John. Just keep playing like that, and try to enjoy yourself. It can't be that hard.'

'Oh, don't get me wrong – I am enjoying all this. I'm just not sure I really understand it. I've got my head around offsides now. But football's a lot more complicated than its rules.'

A deflated Harry half-heartedly offered John a lift home, but it was politely declined. John said he wanted some time to think.

'You ever fallen in love, Harry?' he asked as he backed away.

'Once,' mumbled Harry, without looking up.

'I haven't. When I do, I want it to feel better than that did.'

Around thirty years had passed since Harry and Jessica had last met or spoken. Both had taken place in a pub in East London, a meeting which itself occurred a full two years after their last. They'd agreed to meet one last time, just to talk through what had gone wrong, and so that Harry could finally obtain closure.

They'd met and started dating, at least according to their parents, far too young. He was from a poor estate background, but his blossoming career in football had begun to offer an escape route. She was from a far richer family, born and raised in fashionable Chelsea, and she first saw him as a 'bit of rough', about whom her friends would cry 'Ooh look – you've got a real one!' Her feelings quickly and unexpectedly changed though – his wizardry on the sports field had given him a confidence which she found commanding; his difficult upbringing had forced him to mature early, which made her feel safe around him. By the time they were both 18, they were already talking – although only talking – about marriage.

At 19 he'd earned his first contract with Redwood Spartans, a semi-professional team at the same level as Ariel Hill. In his first season he'd scored 27 goals. Then, midway through his second season, he got a call to say he was being transferred to a large First Division team, Mile End.

Throughout this period of increasing success and acclaim, Jessica repeatedly asked Harry a simple question: when would they marry? His answer was always the same:

'When I get a contract with a big club. Then we'll have enough money.'

In 1970, the line at which football history is divided in two, Harry travelled to the magnificent, 60,000 capacity Mile End stadium. There he was offered his 'contract with a big club', and there he duly signed. It was the greatest moment of his life – the realisation that his dreams were being achieved. The pretty, upwardly-mobile girl at his side was equally excited that soon the same would be true of her own dreams.

She gave him two weeks to ask, but he did not.

'I've not played in the first team yet,' he argued. 'I need to settle here first.'

She gave him another week, and another week passed. At the end of the month, which brought with it a fairly hefty pay cheque, quite large enough to finance the purchase of a ring, she decided she'd had enough.

'Harry, are you ever going to ask me to marry you?' she bellowed.

'Not now,' he snapped defensively, 'I've just been told I'm in the team tomorrow. Can we talk about this another time? This is my first big chance. I've got to get my head right for the match.'

'Another excuse!' shrieked Jessica, bursting into tears. 'I can't take this any more. I love you. I've always loved you – but you never want to talk about planning our life together.'

Harry looked away. 'I've got the biggest game of my life tomorrow.'

Jessica cried and cried, while Harry looked out of the window of his tiny one-room flat. She asked him if he loved her, and he stayed quiet. She asked him if she mattered to him even half as much as football, and again he was silent.

She rose to her feet to leave. 'I'm sorry Harry, I think your silence says enough. You've made your choice. I'll never be the love of your life.'

The door slammed, but Harry did not react. He was too focused on his true passion.

The following night, in the darkness of a hospital bed in central London, a young man with a brutal leg injury lay awake for several hours, sobbing over his losses. It was then, as everything else fell apart around him, that he realised the true weight of what he'd done. His leg was agony. His mind was crushed, along with all his hopes. But it was his heart that gave him the most pain. In that moment of total exposure, of complete vulnerability, Harry realised that the beautiful, witty, clever girl who he'd taken for granted, was not by his side. Perhaps she never would be again.

He tried to call her for several weeks. Her parents never allowed them to speak. 'For her own good', they were protecting her. Soon they had arranged for her to begin dating a more respectable young man of their own class. 'You're just a distant memory to her now,' her mother told Harry during one of his last attempts to make contact.

The wound in Harry's leg healed after a year, but those in his confidence and his heart did not. In training with Mile End, he bewildered the coaches sufficiently to earn himself a transfer back to football's lower echelons. At his next club he impressed even less. Then, as he slumped further and further down the football ladder, his talent seemed to wither more and more until there was none discernibly remaining.

In 1974, a friend from his Mile End days suggested he try a career in the football media instead. At just 24, he took that advice and retired from the game.

Harry and Jessica met up from time to time. At first he would always attempt to patch things up between them, always without success, but then another man's engagement ring made that conversation a lot more difficult. Eventually they agreed that it would be best not to see each other again.

Two years after that final meeting, they did share one more drink. Jessica laughed that she was still wearing the same engagement ring – yet another man was having trouble committing to her completely. On that occasion, he managed to say all the things that he'd been too proud, or distracted, or tongue-tied to get out before. He insisted that he had loved her, and that he had never met a woman since who matched up. He told her that he was sorry for the stupid and thoughtless way in which he'd treated her, and wished her the best in everything she went on to do.

As they hugged to say goodbye, Harry promised that his feelings for her had at last been laid to rest. He was as much promising himself as he was her. And for many years, he even believed his own words, throwing himself back into his other passion – a glorious association with football. That had worked for a long time, until this new 'wife' began to grow ugly and money-obsessed. Suddenly it became impossible for Harry to truly love the game any longer. His heart was torn, and inevitably, thoughts crept back towards the love he'd lost. A long-forgotten photo album was recovered from a loft. One photograph in particular, of a 19-year-old girl on Blackpool pleasure beach, kept finding its way into daylight.

In the last year, Harry had kissed that photograph at least a thousand times.

Nine

England had five qualifying matches left through which to rescue their World Cup chances. Two of those arrived within four days of each other, in early March. On the Saturday, England would travel deep into the rarely-charted territory of Moldova, against whom they had only managed a draw in the home tie. Then, on the following Saturday, they would face an experienced but unspectacular Polish team at home. A defeat in either game would mean the end of their automatic qualification hopes; if they were to lose both, it would be almost impossible for them even to make the play-offs.

Fortunately for England, and contrary to the negative-as-ever predictions of a certain newspaper column, they managed to win both games by the same margin – a heart-failure-inducing 1–0. In both games, Billy Regan scored the only goal, and by the end of the second, even Harry Foster was forced to offer him a little grudging applause. The following Saturday, *Foster's Eye* noted:

> . . . a change in temperament for Regan, a change in tempo for England. The chilling shock of the Icelandic nightmare seemed to have shaken the whole team into life, and just in time. The odds are still against England, but at least the horse is now facing in the right direction.

Meanwhile in the heady realms of non-league conference football, another young striker was also making a name for himself. Ariel Hill had dropped Brian Labant, the old war-horse, to the bench, replacing him with the still-improving former left-back, John Christie. Just as Harry had surmised, attack was indeed his natural position, and once stationed there permanently, he grew into the role with every game. By the time he'd played there five more times, he'd scored eight further goals, taking his tally for the season, and the month, to ten. The defenders in the conference did not know what had hit them.

Meanwhile, halfway between the gutter and the stars, the one-time club of Harry Foster was not having a good season. Lingering in 19th position out of twenty in the league table, Mile End were contemplating the horrific possibility of their first relegation in twenty-six years. Desperate measures were required and duly executed, as, in a manner of speaking, was the club's manager. His replacement, the former England boss Frank Crumb, was charged with turning their year around lightning-quick. With the 31st March transfer deadline looming, after which no player could be bought by the club until the summer, he was handed a measly sum by the chairman, and told to bring in a couple of fresh faces.

Crumb's first purchase, on 25th March, raised eyebrows all over the football world. Helmut Mahel, a 35-year-old former German international midfielder, had already announced his intention to retire in the summer, and it was widely-felt that this was a good idea, such had been the deterioration of his form at Dynamo Berlin. His German team were only too glad to accept the token £100,000 offered by Mile End for his services. And sadly, even that token amount had represented over half of Crumb's emergency rescue budget.

In the days that followed, what seemed like hundreds of out-of-contract journeymen made their way to Mile End for a trial or a pleading interview. Crumb took none of them on. As he told Harry Foster in an exclusive *Reporter* interview, he already had plenty of dead wood on board, without taking on any more. What he'd really been looking for, he revealed, was a striker who'd never had his chance, someone who'd perhaps been forced to wait in line behind big names and foreign imports. He'd hoped that in some reserve team somewhere, he might discover a man with a point to prove. But his talent search had proved fruitless. Mile End would have to fight their way out of this corner with just the ten pieces of dead wood and the German pensioner.

Harry turned off the tape as the interview came to an end, thanked Crumb for his time, and went to leave. But as he got to the door, the words that had been on the tip of his tongue throughout their conversation burst free from his mouth.

'I know someone you should sign,' he blurted.

Crumb looked up from his desk, smiled the smile of a man with very few options left, and bid him to sit back down.

The name on Harry's lips was, of course, John Christie. At the same time, however, alarm bells were ringing in his head. Issue number one: John was a reluctant hero even at conference level – there was no telling what his reaction to such an idea would be. Issue number two: Harry was becoming increasingly aware that John's life was beginning to mirror his own. He'd already sent him from a council estate to the conference – could he really send him on to the very club at which Harry himself had played and self-destructed?

The answer, rightly or wrongly, was yes. Within two hours, John had been summoned from his usual training duties, placed in a taxi and whisked over to the Mile End stadium, where an instant trial had already been arranged. Four members of the first-team squad and a handful of youth-team players were assembled at a nanosecond's notice, and by the time he arrived, still wearing his Ariel Hill track suit, a ready-made five-a-side match had been organised specifically for his benefit.

John's face was, for the rest of the day, a contorted mix of fear, awe and bemusement. He'd seen Premier Division stadia on television, but he'd never been inside one before. In fact, he'd never even been outside one; just turning in to the shadow-flooded car park of Mile End's William Hinkley Stand made him gasp. The taxi pulled up outside the red carpeted director's entrance, and a smartly-suited porter rushed to open its door and pay the driver. As usual, John was distinctly quiet as activity buzzed all around him. At the huge panelled door, he was met personally by a figure who again he knew only from television – Frank Crumb himself.

'John Christie?' he grinned.

'That's me, sir.' John swallowed hard, disorientated by his frenetic afternoon so far; even more so now by his encounter with a major celebrity.

'You come highly recommended. Ten goals in your last six games I'm told. That's the sort of firepower we could do with right now at this club. Why the sudden burst of form, do you think?'

'Well sir, I was playing in defence before.'

Crumb chuckled, presuming this to be a joke, but noticing John's dead-straight face, realised it was not, and laughed even louder. 'Ha ha – good! Very good! Well then, let's see this prodigious talent in action.'

'I'm sorry sir?'

'The trial. It's all arranged for you laddie. And please stop calling me sir, at least until I've been knighted.'

'Sorry si– I mean, sorry. But I don't know anything about a trial. And although I'm sure I'd love to join your team, I really wouldn't be able to. You see, I'm already signed to Ariel Hill.'

Crumb looked at John long and hard, again gauging whether this was an attempt at some kind of 'alternative' humour. The naïveté in John's eyes told him that it probably wasn't. He asked, 'You do know why you're here, don't you son?'

'Not really. The manager just told me that I needed to come here straight away. He just pulled me off the training pitch, gave me my bag, and put me in the cab. So I really must apologise that I'm looking so scruffy–'

'Right,' said Crumb, utterly confused and assuming that this supposedly gifted footballer must have all his brains in his feet. 'Well then, I'd better explain. At the moment, Mile End aren't doing so hot. They've called me in to try to turn things around, and I've noticed that we're a bit thin up front – so I'm looking for a new striker. I've got until tomorrow, and everyone I've looked at so far just hasn't been right for us. But I was talking to someone today who told me that you might just fit the bill. I called your club, and they're prepared to sell you to me for about £100,000. Now–'

'WHAT?!' bellowed John, knocking Crumb backwards and surprising himself a little in the process. 'How much money? That's ridiculous!'

'I'm sure you're worth much more than that,' Crumb tried to reassure him, 'but the market's not what it was.'

'How can you justify spending that much money on me? I'm not worth £100,000!'

'We'll be the judge of that.'

'But it's immoral! Think of all the people in the world who go hungry every day – people without clean water, people who freeze to death because they've got no proper housing – and you want to spend £100,000 on a footballer?'

Crumb stared at him in utter shock. Then, after a few seconds, something clicked in his head and he began to laugh. 'Oh, so it's a joke! Good one son. Very good. You almost had me there for a minute. Come on then, let's get this trial started.' And without giving a once-again confused John a moment to respond, he beckoned to his entourage and disappeared through the big doors. A hand was thrust into John's back, and he was made to follow.

Harry had just turned around a feature article in record time. His interview with Crumb was transcribed, written, edited and sitting in the sports editor's in-tray within about two and a half hours. After that, he was on the next tube back to Mile End, where he hoped and prayed he'd see them unveil their latest signing – and not the old German.

Instead, he arrived to find John Christie, still in full football kit, sitting on the kerb outside the ground. His head was in his hands, and he wasn't moving. Harry was immediately overcome with guilt. This was his fault. He'd pushed him too far, too quickly. Knowing that he was probably the last person who John wanted to see at this point, he edged up to him nonetheless.

'I'm sorry John,' he said softly. 'I'm sorry it didn't work out.'

'It wasn't your fault,' came the reply, muffled by the hands.

'Well,' Harry began, cautiously, 'maybe it was my fault. You see, it was me who suggested your name to the club . . . .'

John's hands dropped away from his face. He laughed. 'Ah. I see. Well, in that case, I'm sorry to disappoint you.'

'How could I be disappointed? You gave your best in there.'

'Yes I did.'

'But it's a massive leap up. A couple of months ago you didn't even know the rules. Maybe after time, a club this big will be desperate to have you on board. I know I made the leap up to this level too early. It's probably for the best that they turned you down this time. Give it a couple of years, score lots of goals in the Conference, and then perhaps–'

'Harry stop,' John commanded, putting a finger to his lips.

Harry stopped.

'They didn't turn me down. They asked me to sign.'

Harry's face broke into an uncontrollable beam. Then he looked at John, this crumpled heap on the floor of the car park, and realisation filtered through him. He knew that he was not looking at Mile End's new signing. His face fell again. At that point he wanted to shout and scream, and tell John what an idiot he was being, but it felt like he'd already done that once too often. Instead he bit his tongue, and sat down on the kerb next to his friend.

For ten minutes, they sat in absolute silence, save for a moment when three angry players walked past on the way to their sports cars and launched a battery of abuse at John for wasting their time. Then, when he could stand it no more, Harry spoke:

'It feels like I should say something like, "You remind me so much of myself at your age" at this point. But to be honest, you don't. When I was your age, I was obsessed with this game – so much so that I couldn't see anything else. You asked me the other day whether I'd ever been in love. Well I was once, but I was so immersed in football that I never realised until it was too late. That's what it can do to you. But it's not like that with you John. You barely seem to know or care anything about this game. You enjoy it, but you don't take it any further than that. You don't have that passion that every other footballer I've ever come across has. You play your heart out in every match, and you certainly don't want to let your team-mates and supporters down, but from what I've seen, there's no obsession there.'

John nodded slowly. 'I do love playing football Harry,' he whispered.

'Yes, I know. And that's what I don't understand about you. If you love it, why did it take three of us to coerce you into even turning up for a trial? Why now are we sitting outside a massive football stadium, when we could be inside sipping champagne with the chairman?'

John turned to look up at the gigantic structure behind him. 'It scares me,' he said, almost too quietly to be audible. Harry picked it up though.

'What are you scared of?' he asked.

'Just because I don't say an awful lot, it doesn't mean I don't think. I've thought about a lot of things over the last few weeks, Harry, and they're frightening me. Being a footballer isn't like being an electrician – there's no steadiness to it. Things have gone well for me at Ariel Hill so far – I've scored a few goals, the fans seem to like me – but I know how quickly things like that can change. What if it all goes wrong suddenly – what if I lose my confidence and stop scoring for a few matches? Suddenly they all hate me. Suddenly my job is on the line.'

'That's not going to happen,' Harry assured him. 'You're far too good for that level.'

'Maybe. But who's to say that I'm not just a Third Division player? Harry, I turned them down today because I don't think it's sensible to make this sort of a jump. At the moment I play in front of 500 people if we're lucky. This club gets 35,000 to every game. At Ariel

Hill I'm in a squad of nineteen players. The shirt number they were offering me here was 47. I could go on Harry. One of the coaches here told me that nobody ever goes straight from the non-league to the Premier Division. There are probably a lot of good reasons for that.'

'So you're a little overwhelmed,' said Harry. 'It's understandable. But have you even stopped to think about what this club would offer you? I mean, apart from anything else, John, a couple of seasons at this level will make you rich.'

'I don't want to be rich.'

'No, somehow I knew you'd say that. And maybe, for whatever bizarre reason, you really don't want to be rich. What about your mum though? What about Becky? Surely they don't want to stay on that estate for the rest of their lives? You could buy a nice house to live in with them – they give footballers pretty big mortgage allowances you know.'

'I – I don't know,' John looked away. 'There are other things to think about.'

'Like what?'

'I don't want to be famous.'

'John, they're offering you the number 47 shirt. Let's not get carried away.'

John giggled like the youngster he was. He was able to make eye contact with Harry again.

'You know,' said Harry, sensing that his words were at last having some effect, 'once your mum hears about this she'll be going on at you until you come back here and sign.'

John giggled some more. 'That's true,' he sighed.

'Look John,' said Harry, rising to his feet. 'It's not too late. If I go in there and talk to Frank Crumb, and explain that you're just a little bit overawed, I'm sure he'll give you the evening to think it over.'

'OK Harry,' said John, 'if you really think it's for the best.'

'I know it's for the best,' replied Harry, before disappearing into the stadium.

The next morning, six hours before the transfer deadline, Mile End called a press conference. On one side of Frank Crumb, attracting a myriad of flashbulbs, Helmut Mahel was giving royal waves and wearing a look of childish excitement; he hadn't expected to receive this kind of attention again in his career. On Crumb's other shoulder, a nervous-looking lad with wild blonde hair and newly-developed muscles was trying to make himself look invisible. He might as well have been – none of the journalists in the room (bar one) had ever even heard his name before.

In the official photographs a little later on, he held aloft a scarlet red Mile End shirt with 'Christie – 47' on the back. He smiled. Harry, standing in the shadows at the back of the room, hoped that smile was genuine.

Ten

After impressing Frank Crumb and the coaching staff sufficiently in his first full week of training, John found his name in the squad list for a Premier Division match. He wasn't in the starting line-up, and seemed only to have narrowly squeezed his way onto the bench as the last name on the team-sheet, but he was in the squad that would travel to Yorkshire that night. And that meant a telephone call home after training. To the amazement of his new colleagues, he produced a little packet of coins from his bag, and used the generally-redundant club pay-phone.

'Hello Mum?'

'John!' cried his mum with a pride that had lingered and grown for weeks now. 'Is everything OK?'

'Everything's fine Mum. But I've got some more news. I'm in the squad for the Pennines game tomorrow.'

He heard sobbing and muffled conversation on the other end of the phone. Then his mother returned, stricken with joy. 'Oh John,' she spluttered, 'you'll be on TV!'

'Mum, we're going down tonight, to stay in a hotel. Will you and Becky be alright if I don't come home?'

'Don't be so silly son! They need you. If you get on, score a goal for me.' There was a pause while she fielded a shout from the background. 'And another one for Becky.'

'I love you, Mum.'

'I love you, too, John. And I'm so proud of you.'

The other players, who'd listened intently, sniggered in

the background. John, in his innocence, wasn't sure why. Harry found out John's news through an e-mail from the Premier Division news service. Instinctively he reached for his mobile phone, before realising that John didn't have one. Desperate to offer his congratulations, he called the club direct, but was told that John had already left the ground. As Harry later discovered, he'd had to go to the nearby house of one of the youth team in order to borrow some clothes for the morning.

Harry was not easily beaten. He found out that the *Reporter* was sending Bill Harris to the Pennines vs Mile End game, contacted him, begged a favour and duly called Alex Knight to explain that he'd be covering the match instead. He would offer his good wishes to John in person.

The evening was difficult for John. He had not yet made any friends at Mile End, and a few of the other players had already made derisory remarks toward him, noting that he was a 'non-league nobody' and a 'scruffy tramp.' The next morning, a lavish breakfast at a five-star hotel, was a lonely experience. No one, save the manager, felt that he had much right to be there, and he agreed with them. He sat silently in one corner of the huge boardroom table and hardly touched his food.

Mile End's star player was Carl Barton. A short, stocky midfielder on the fringes of the England team, he was generally regarded as their only player of true class, and was feeling the weight of expectation on his shoulders particularly heavily that morning. He too was quiet and short of appetite, and sat in the same corner of the breakfast table as John.

John mistook Barton's silence for benevolence toward him, and tried to make conversation. Icy glares were all he received in return.

Frank Crumb's team talk was straightforward enough. Keep it tight at the back, hit it long to the strikers. It was the classic tactic of the struggling British team. Helmut Mahel, who was used to a little more culture, tried to protest but was shouted down by his new team-mates. Again, John sat quietly in the corner. As he looked around him, it suddenly became obvious to him that he was purely in this squad for the sake of experience. Mile End's two first-choice strikers, both of them internationals, were starting, and a third, an exciting product of the youth system, was also on the bench. There was little chance he'd see action in this game, but at least he'd be able to relax a little in that knowledge.

John watched his first ever live professional football match from the comfort of the away-team bench. He wondered, as he sat there proudly in his monogrammed club track suit, whether that was some kind of world first. He gazed around the magnificent Pennines stadium, a terrifyingly tall affair with a capacity of over 45,000. For a moment, he thought of his father, a long-time Southwark Albion season-ticket holder, and imagined him sitting in one of the stands. For all he knew, he could even have been there.

The match kicked off to a deafening roar from the highly partisan crowd. Only 2,000 tickets had been sold to Mile End fans – more had been available but supporters were currently deserting their club like rats from a sinking ship – and they made up a tiny island of scarlet in one stand, surrounded completely by a sea of Pennines green. The crowd, whose team were still on course for a place in European competition if they held on to fifth position in the league, viciously booed every Mile End touch. As this occurred – and many of the away team's passes went astray as a result of it – John realised that he was probably living out another footballing first: he'd never seen his own team play before, even on television.

Perhaps if he had done, he would have waited around for a better offer. They were sloppy, disorganised, ill-tempered and well-short of ideas. Carl Barton, who had once gained a reputation for inventiveness and glorious long passes, just kept whacking the ball up field as if it was highly explosive and placing him in danger. The two strikers never looked like scoring, but that was hardly their fault since none of their team-mates were playing the ball remotely near them. The goalkeeper, meanwhile, was certainly earning *his* money. A string of fine saves were all that stood between Mile End and total obliteration. In the first half, Pennines scored once, and at half-time, Frank Crumb admitted that he couldn't believe his good fortune that they'd been restricted to a single goal. That comment was the only light point in an otherwise painfully aggressive half-time rant, during which John's hair actually stood on end.

An attacking substitution was made, but, just as John had predicted, it was the more established young striker, Mark O'Donnell, who came on. It was his introduction which turned the game on its head. On fifty-five minutes, the young Irishman scored his first goal, bursting through the stationary Pennines defence and rocketing a well-placed shot to the goalkeeper's right. A further twelve minutes into the game, he scored again, heading in a cross from a rejuvenated Mahel. A minute after that, he looked set to score his hat trick when put through again by the German, but a heavy challenge from a lightning-quick defender changed the picture. Concerned team-mates waved for a stretcher – it was clear to all nearby that O'Donnell's match was at an end.

John's first thought was one of concern for the youngster. It was only when he felt Frank Crumb's hand on his shoulder, and noticed the collective glares of 2,000 travelling supporters, that the penny dropped. For the last twenty-two minutes, he was on.

Up in the press box, Harry was screaming for John's introduction. His peers looked at him, perplexed and disdainful. When he saw his friend emerge from the sidelines, he was dancing for joy.

Down on the pitch, John was less excited. His heart was beating so fast that he feared it was going to explode. He was visibly shaking, and his face was burning red from the scorching glowers of 43,000 angry supporters. A couple of the Mile End players spoke to him for what seemed like the first time ever, telling him to calm down, keep it tight and not do anything stupid. He hoped he could obey at least some of those instructions.

A footballer's first appearance can often shape his career at a club. Strikers who have scored in their first game have often gone on to glittering careers during which they're always near the top of the goal charts. On the other side of the coin, players who've started off with a nightmare have sometimes never recovered.

John prayed that his first touch was not a sign of things to come. Looking up immediately after the restart, he saw a long ball from one of the centre-backs coming towards him. He'd made a good run, and had managed to catch his defender sleeping. If he could control this pass, a decent second touch would put him in on goal. But he needn't have thought that far ahead. The ball did come to him, and the defender was indeed lacking in concentration, but as he stretched out his still-quivering leg to trap it, he only succeeded in kicking the ball directly out of play. The resultant jeer which emanated from the crowd very nearly knocked him off his feet. So far, so bad. And there was much worse just around the corner.

After his first contribution, John's team had decided against passing to him, and subsequently he'd decided that he would be doing them better service if he helped out at the back instead. The pendulum of the match had swung back heavily after the injury to O'Donnell, and Pennines were virtually encamped in the Mile End half in their search for a goal. Without receiving any instructions to the effect from his captain or manager, John decided to revert to his old Ariel Hill position in defensive midfield.

What he failed, in his simplistic understanding of football tactics, to realise, was that his voluntary withdrawal from the front-line only served to tighten Pennines' grip on the game. Now they could send yet another player forward in their search for a goal, and it was at this point that the visiting defence, which had already been buckling under the pressure, capitulated completely.

The final score – unsatisfactorily for both sets of fans – was 2–2. Considering the position at half-time, it would have been reasonable to expect a certain degree of acceptance from the Mile End team and supporters that this was a fair result. But a scoreline can never fully tell a story, and the truth behind this one was that, had one of their players not pressed the self-destruct button, they probably would have escaped from Yorkshire with a priceless win.

With a minute and a half remaining, another long Pennines ball was pumped through the air and into the Mile End box. There it was met and repelled, for what seemed like the hundredth time, by the ultra-dependable head of Allan Strong, the giant Scottish centre-back. As it floated out to the relative safety of the edge of the penalty box, a stampede of players mindful of the offside rule charged away from the goal. Trying again, the Pennines player who'd collected the ball lofted it back towards the goal, to precisely the area where seven of his team had just been standing. Now only one remained, and he gleefully accepted the pass. The entire Mile End defence stood with their arms in the air, screaming for offside, but the linesman's flag stayed by his side. On the far side of the box, still lost and rembling, John Christie had forgotten himself. His position meant that the striker was still onside. The stadium exploded. With the goalkeeper completely exposed, Pennines equalised. The home side, jubilant in celebration, didn't care how it had happened, or whose fault it was. John Christie's team-mates felt differently though.

Harry had not expected it to be like this. Of all the scenarios that had gone through his mind that morning, none was as worst-case as the one that occurred. When he found John, an hour after the game, he was a broken man, huddled into a tiny ball on the changing room floor and leaking tears like a burst water main. All around him, disgruntled members of the Mile End coaching staff were casting dark glances in his direction. In the wake of his first match as a professional footballer, John was not experiencing the elation, glory or joy, but the icy shivers of alienation.

Harry approached him slowly, took a seat on a wooden bench opposite his, and said nothing. John sighed. They sat that way for five minutes.

In the corridor outside, John's disgruntled team-mates were trickling onto the coach home. Each of them was murmuring about the result. Each one mentioned John's name in irate tones as he stropped past the doorway.

'Bus is leaving in two,' came an angry shout offered in John's general direction. 'If you want to come with us, you'll have to come now. Feel free to walk back though.'

John composed himself, tried and failed to smile, rose to his feet and picked up his bag. He shuffled towards the door, trying to avoid contact with every pair of eyes.

'John, wait,' called Harry. 'You don't have to go back on the coach. You can come back in my car if you like.'

John looked back at Harry with wide eyes, as if he'd just been offered a reprieve from the gallows. 'Yes . . . please,' he answered, in an unsteady voice.

The long drive back to London was made longer by the silence. Though there was quiet, there was no sense of calm in the air; just an overwhelming feeling of hopelessness; of despondency. John clearly had not come to terms with his error, and the level of cost which it carried with it. He knew, for the manager had told a television crew immediately after the game, that his poor positioning, and the two points that it had cost his team, could be the decisive factor in their failure to avoid relegation at the end of the season. They were still in 19th place. For a moment, before John's passive intervention, they'd been hoisted to the Promised Land of 17th.

They were well into the Midlands before John finally said:

'This is exactly what I was afraid of.'

Harry felt terrible, hearing this, but it only confirmed what he already knew. During the hours of hush between the ground and here, he'd gone over the conversation they'd had a little over a week previously a thousand times in his mind. John had been scared, Harry pushed him on. His only respite from this stuck-record-memory was another recollection, of an earlier dispute between the two of them. This one was even more of a dagger to him: John had never wanted to be a footballer, even at semi-pro level. Now he'd been pushed out onto a grand stage far too soon, had suffered a terrible bout of fright at exactly the worst moment, and was to receive the most vicious punishment as a result. And while nobody but John knew, it was all Harry's fault.

He was desperate to find a way to make things better. He blurted out hopeful sentiments like 'everybody makes mistakes', and 'this won't seem so bad in the morning'. But he knew he wasn't having much effect. John might have been naïve, but he wasn't stupid.

About half an hour from home, John seemed ready to talk. His body was still slumped in the passenger seat, and his lips barely moved as he spoke.

'I don't know what happened to me Harry,' he began. 'I just wasn't myself out there.'

'You got nervous John. It happens to everyone. There were 40,000 people and more in that stadium all baying for your blood. It's not a surprise that you made a couple of mistakes.'

'What are they going to say about me? In the newspapers?'

'I don't know,' Harry lied.

'What did you say about me?'

'I . . . ' Harry choked a little, 'I didn't mention you. I said that the defence got it wrong.'

'*I* GOT IT WRONG!' screamed John suddenly, jumping out of his seat and causing Harry to swerve across two lanes of motorway. 'It was no one else's fault. You should have written that I got it wrong. Ring them now and tell them to change it.'

'I can't do that John. The paper's already gone to press.'

John's face expressed a rare anger. It was almost as if he was having to use new muscles in order for it to do so. 'You shouldn't have done that,' he fumed. 'It wasn't true. And it's just going to make it worse for me.' His mind had clearly already drifted toward Monday morning's training session.

'I'm sorry that this has happened John,' sighed Harry, 'I'm devastated for you. But believe me, I know how you are feeling better than most. If you let it, this day can destroy you, just like it destroyed me. Or, if you can find the strength of character somewhere in that quiet head of yours, it can be the making of you.'

There was a pause.

'This is exactly what I was afraid of,' said John again, followed by nothing more.

The morning papers were merciless. The tabloid the *Daily Spark* went as far as suggesting that Mile End had been the victims of a hoax, and that Christie wasn't really a footballer at all. Its major rival the *Mouthpiece* even insinuated that he might have been paid off by the opposition. The *Reporter*, which featured Harry's article, was the only national newspaper not to feature a photograph of a dejected John Christie on its back page.

'A week ago,' wrote a reporter in the broadsheet the *Morning News*, 'I stood in a press conference where Frank Crumb announced his new signing from the non-league. Not a single one of the journalists I spoke to at the time had ever heard of this John Christie fellow. Well, I guess we've all heard of him now.'

Eleven

On Monday morning, the vultures were circling at Mile End's training ground in a fearsome swarm. The gate was blocked by bloodthirsty reporters, all hungry for a word with the club's new anti-hero, and the fences on one side of the pitch were being rattled by a band of irate supporters who'd come to demonstrate their disgust at the team's current form and latest performance. But in the changing room, a far more malicious group was assembling. Each of the players – who to a man blamed John for Saturday's disaster – had individually lobbied the coaching staff for a chance to play against the new signing in practice. They all wanted their chance to give John his reward.

Several wagers were lost when John arrived, on time, at the ground. His eyes were bulging, with heavy bags underneath, and his face was red and puffy. It was clear to all that he hadn't enjoyed much sleep since the game. He drew stares from all quarters as he staggered into the changing room, set down his bag and began to change into his kit. A few initial salvoes of abuse were fired in his direction. He didn't react to any of them. Instead, he shocked everyone in the room by speaking loudly:

'I just wanted to say that I'm very sorry about Saturday. I made a terrible mistake and it cost us the game. All I can promise you is that it won't happen again.'

'You're right there mate,' sneered Mark O'Donnell, who was now hobbling around on crutches, 'because you won't be playing again.'

There was laughter from all quarters. John stood absolutely still, before giving a gentle nod, although not of agreement. He changed quickly into his full training gear and left the room without a word. He was keen to begin again. This was a very different John Christie to the one who'd left Harry Foster's car in tears late on Saturday night.

As training began, some of the other players immediately noticed a difference in John. He was still quiet, unassuming and aloof, but the look in his eyes had changed. Where before there was fear, now there was determination. Where there was inadequacy, now there was confidence. After ten minutes of a training five-a-side match, during which John scored again and again like some out-of-control machine-gun, Allan Strong took him to one side.

'Lad, what tha heck's happened to ye?' he asked, in thick Glaswegian.

John looked at him with this new, arresting air of his. 'I did some thinking on Sunday. Took some advice from a friend. He made me realise how strong you've got to be if you're going to succeed in this game. So I decided, either I give up and go back to being an electrician, or I stick with it and learn to grow stronger.'

'An ye chose the latter, aye?'

'Not for me though,' insisted John, with the authority of honesty about his voice. 'I don't care if I succeed or not. It's for the manager, who paid all that money for me – and for them, over there.' He indicated towards the fences, where the once-angry mob of supporters had now been placated, and had begun to cheer his every touch in training.

'Aye lad. Well if you carry on playin' like you are now, there'll be nay a problem with the club or the fans.'

John indicated his agreement, then returned to the five-a-side and picked up from where he'd left off – scoring at will with both feet, his head and even his chest. And suddenly, no one wanted to be playing against him after all.

Saturday night had been long and restless. His mother and sister had tried their best to offer comfort, but John's disappointment ran deep, and although he was a man of little anger, that emotion was emerging too. All night he lay awake, listening to the drunks, then the wind, then the birds. When Sunday morning arrived, it brought with it a pain behind the eyes that was hard to bear. Contrary to Harry's promise, it certainly felt as bad in the morning, if not worse.

His mother appeared around 8.30, with a breakfast tray and a sympathetic smile. Her arrival was a reminder that he needed to get himself ready for church, which, despite lack of rest, he managed to do without fuss. As he showered, without his seldom-missed morning song, the women of the household held each other tightly, unsure exactly of what they should do or say.

In church – a fairly pathetic congregation of twenty or so people all much older than Becky and he – John found a small voice for the hymns. During the sermon he listened intently, as he always did, as the minister praised virtue and slandered sin. At the end he remained silent, his head bowed in thought and prayer.

When he'd stayed that way for five minutes, his mother, assuming that he'd finally been able to fall asleep, gently nudged him. But John was not sleeping. Instead, he explained that he just wanted some time here to gather his thoughts. He agreed to catch up his mother and Becky later, and they left him, the only remaining figure in a church built for 400.

The minister returned to lock up the building ten minutes later. He was startled to discover the figure slumped in the front pew – even more so when he realised that it wasn't one of his elderly female 'fans'. A short, slim and disappointed-looking man in his late thirties, he had seen little incident in his eighteen months in the parish beside a gradual numerical decline. To find a young person in his church fifteen minutes after the service's end, for whatever reason, was unusual indeed, and slightly concerning to him.

'Er . . . hello?' he offered, a little nervously.

The slumped figure rose, which was of some relief to the minister. Then he recognised the messy blonde hair, and strode to the front of the church.

'You're Marilyn Christie's son!' he announced. 'John, isn't it?'

John nodded, trying hard to conceal his fatigue. 'Yes Reverend. That's me.'

'Hello!' he paused. 'Er . . . can I ask . . . ?'

'Why I'm still here, fifteen minutes after the service?'

'Well, it had crossed my mind. You see, we don't generally get people staying around after the service, especially not of your generation. I mean, sometimes they actually *can't* leave, but on both occasions, if you speak to the police, I was cleared of any possible culpability.'

John managed a smile. 'I needed some time to think,' he explained. 'I'm having a few problems at the moment.'

'Understood, I'll just leave the place unlocked. Not like there's anything worth stealing anyway. Don't know why I lock it at all to tell you the truth – the bishop tells me it stops us from looking desperate. Anyway, if you find you need someone to talk to, I've got a window in my diary just about all the time, so–'

'Actually,' said John, grabbing the minister's arm, 'that'd be great.'

'Oh!' The minister – whose name was Paul Miller – couldn't hide his surprise when this offer *wasn't* thrown back hard in his face. 'Well, in that case, let me go and make a cup of tea. Oh, no, what am I thinking – you won't want tea. I'm afraid I can't really give you alcohol in the church, but if we were to go out into the graveyard I–'

'Tea would be great,' John interrupted.

'Right.' The minister disappeared, slightly flustered, tripping over a pile of hymnbooks as he went. He returned a few moments later, with two crumbling mugs full of hot brown fluid and worrying floaty bits.

'So,' said Paul, finding it hard to conceal his excitement at this rare counselling opportunity, 'what was it that you wanted to talk about?'

'Do you like football?' asked John.

Paul gave an honest smile. 'I'm not really a big sport man,' he replied.

'Oh, well actually, that probably helps a little. You see, I'm a footballer. I've just signed for Mile End, which is one of the bigger London clubs, and–'

'You what?' Paul leapt out of his pew with excitement. 'You play for Mile End?'

'Yes – I thought you said you weren't a big sport man?'

'I'm not – but I'm just thinking, with you opening the church fete, we could get hundreds along! You are free on 19 June aren't you?'

John glared at Paul through puffy eyes. The minister remembered himself:

'Ah, sorry about that. It's just that we've never had a celebrity in the congregation before.'

'I'm no celebrity. That's what I was about to explain to you. Yesterday afternoon, I made a mistake which cost my team the game.'

'Everybody makes mistakes, John,' said Paul robotically.

'It was my first game. I'd only come on for the last twenty minutes.'

'Oh. Well I suppose that's worse then. And that explains why you're looking so tired, and so unhappy? Yes, I can understand that.' Paul wriggled his fingers and tapped his feet. He thought for a while about an appropriate piece of advice to give.

'It's more than just that though,' John continued, 'it's the whole thing. They paid a lot of money for me – a ridiculous amount – and it really weighs on my shoulders. Then there's the fans; they all spend £30 to come and see us play, and it's the most important hour and a half of their week. When I got out onto that pitch yesterday, I couldn't stop thinking about those two things. It was like I froze under the pressure.'

'That sort of thing does get easier John. I know it's not the same, but I remember the first sermon I ever preached here. I saw all these people – thirty of them maybe – who'd all hauled themselves out of bed to listen to me. They hadn't spent any money – the average church collection here is £2.50 and a button – but I guess for those people, too, it was the most important hour and a half of the week. I'd been a curate before, but never a full-blown vicar, and the pressure nearly flattened me. I preached the worst sermon in the world. I think it was even theologically inaccurate – I'm almost certain I said that Jesus killed Goliath. But in the end it didn't matter. Do you know why?'

'Why Reverend?'

'Perseverance. It's a biblical virtue. I came back the next week, preached again, and did a little better. Then the next week, I'd improved a little more again. A year and a half later, I'm still here. Although admittedly, some of the congregation aren't.'

'But I might not get a chance to play again,' said John. 'There's no way they'll put me in the team for the next match.'

'Then you'll just have to find a way to make them put you back in the team.'

As Paul said those words, it was as if something clicked inside John's head. He began to nod vigorously, lost in thought. 'Do you have a football?' he asked, without looking at his minister.

'There might be one in the vicarage garden,' came the reply. 'I could go and have a look for you. Why?'

'Perseverance,' said John, rising to his feet.

John spent the last eleven hours of Sunday in the far corner of Ariel Fields Recreation Ground. There, under varying degrees of sun and moonlight, he practised his skills with a level of intensity that he'd never reached before. And when he was finished, he returned to the flat, slumped into his bed and went straight to sleep.

He awoke again six hours later. He could have used at least twice as much rest, but it was time to report at the training ground, and time to begin again.

John was like a new man in training, and his performances there were beginning to win him the hard-to-earn respect of his colleagues. For the first time, he began to feel part of the group, receiving (and declining) several invitations to join them socially, and building formative friendships with Allan Strong and Helmut Mahel. The squad began to reclassify his naïveté as humility, and their collective contempt soon morphed into respect.

One man was not sufficiently impressed to change his mind about John, however. Frank Crumb, the man who'd paid just shy of £100,000 for him, often admitted in interviews to having three little boxes in his mind. One was marked 'yes', another 'no', and a third 'maybe'. They were where he placed the names of his squad, and referred to whether he thought they were of sufficient quality to play in his team or not. On arrival at Mile End, John had been placed immediately in the 'maybe' box. After his performance against Pennines, he'd been given a free-transfer to 'no'. There, despite his obvious improvements, he remained.

A week after the nightmare, Mile End had a home fixture against Littlehampton, another team threatened by the possibility of relegation. John did not even make the bench. Mile End were defeated 4–2.

In the week after that, he was overlooked for two more games, both of which his team lost. By mid-April, Mile End were rock bottom, and had only a mathematical chance of remaining in the Premier Division.

Then, if such a thing seemed possible, things got worse for the club. In the space of two days, both their international strikers were struck down by a fearsome virus that left each of them bedridden and ruled out for at least the next game. Mark O'Donnell was still on crutches. Discounting youth team players, John knew that he'd suddenly been elevated to the position of first-choice striker.

But he'd have been foolish to discount the youth team. When the team list for the next match – against North-East giants Tyneside – was pinned up on the noticeboard outside Crumb's office, John and the rest of the squad were shocked to discover that his name was not to be found in the first eleven spaces. The ninth player listed, and the only striker, was a 16-year-old who had rarely trained with the first team. When François Rieux had signed for the club, just before Christmas, for the most nominal of fees, the then-manager had insisted he was 'one for the future.' It appeared that his future, and not John's, had just arrived.

So, despite being consistently the best player in training, despite the protestations of many other players, despite Rieux having even less experience than his twenty-two minutes, John would watch the Tyneside game from the warmth of the bench.

When, in the office late on Friday, Harry noticed John's name in the Mile End squad, he instinctively hugged his nearest colleague, who just happened to be Martin Burke, the goblin. He didn't care – he would have hugged Billy Regan at that moment. John's career was not quite in tatters yet; instantly a huge weight lifted ever so slightly from Harry's shoulders.

A few phone calls later, Harry had organised three tickets for the game. This time, he decided, he'd make himself useful.

When he left the flat the next morning, John had no idea that his family were coming to the game. Harry deliberately arranged to pick them up after he was due at the ground. He didn't see them in the crowd as he ran out to warm up before the game; he didn't spot them as he took his place on the bench and looked around the magnificent stadium. But they were there, hoping for victory and praying he'd get his shot at redemption.

Fortunately for John, François Rieux suffered a torrid debut. In the first forty-five minutes he touched the ball three times, and on all three occasions he lost possession instantly, demonstrating all the resilience of a bath bubble. The third time he did so, it cost his team dearly: his poorly-placed pass started off the move which ended in an opening Tyneside goal. After thirty-two minutes – at which point that incident occurred – Rieux had already been deposited deep into the 'no' box in Frank Crumb's mind.

With half-time approaching, Crumb ordered all four of his outfield substitutes to warm up. He was, he promised, going to make a change to the side during the interval, and it was pretty obvious to all inside the stadium, and especially the substitutes, who was going to be replaced. Driven by the possibility of an appearance, John tore up and down the touch-line like an express train. He ran so fast, in fact, that he almost missed the screaming voice of a girl, sitting in the front row in one corner of the stadium.

'John!' shouted Becky, her voice supported by two quieter shrieks from Harry and Marilyn.

John stopped in his tracks as he spotted his sister, then his mother, and Harry. He waved, beaming with delight. A tear ran down his cheek. Just as he was about to run over to them and hold brief conversation, the whistle blew for half-time. Instead he pointed towards the players' tunnel, smiled and waved again. As he disappeared, Harry realised that he'd never seen him look so relaxed.

Frank Crumb's team talk held a nasty shock, however. Rieux was being replaced, but not by John. Instead, the midfielder Mark Rankin was coming on as an 'emergency striker' – even though he'd never played in the position before and had scored only once in his last three seasons. Again there were dissenting voices; again John's name was loudly mentioned, then ignored. To his credit, John took the news with dignity. Although when he reappeared for the second half, still clad in the track suit, the same could not be said for his friend and family.

Harry had successfully roused his corner of the ground into a chorus of 'Crumb out' by the time the sixty-third minute arrived. At that point, Helmut Mahel went down clutching his ankle, and didn't get up again. Once more, Crumb's hand had been forced by an injury to one of his first choice players. On receiving the thumbs down from his physio, Crumb took a stroll along the bench, eyeballing each of the four remaining substitutes like a staff sergeant at roll-call. Aside from John, there were two young defenders and a goalkeeper. Common sense, not to mention Crumb's assistant, insisted that Mark Rankin should be moved back into midfield, with John coming on to take up the striking role.

'Can you play in midfield?' he asked one of the suddenly-petrified defenders, who instantly shook his head.

'What about you?' barked Crumb to the other. 'You ever played up front?'

Again, the response was negative. They both retreated, indicating in John's direction. Crumb thought for a moment, then growled.

'Fine,' he snarled. 'Christie, you're on. But if you let us down again like the last time . . . ' he gave a cursory glance towards the cowering François Rieux ' . . . then you can forget about ever pulling on that shirt again. Now get out there!'

John removed his track suit, to muffled cries of despair from the home fans, and a tiny patch of confident screaming in one corner. The referee signalled for him to enter the game. As he reached the side of the pitch, he crossed himself and whispered a single word:

'Perseverance.'

John no longer seemed to carry nerves around his neck like a string of weights. Instead of fearing the crowd, he suddenly seemed now to find his confidence in them. From his first touch – a thudding but fair tackle which set up Mile End's first chance in nearly an hour – those who'd hurled abuse at him before were now eking back onto his side. Within ten minutes, and a barrel full of neat passes, they were all rooting for him. But then, something happened that had the potential to blow it all into the sky again.

A quick through-ball from Carl Barton put John one-on-one with the Tyneside goalkeeper. There were no defenders in sight, and with his recent displays in training, every one of his team-mates expected an equalising goal. What they saw instead, was a goalkeeper who decided to tear up the rule book and aim a diving kick directly into John's primed-to-shoot foot. The ball rolled out of play. John was tossed up into the air. The physio sprinted out to help him. And the goalkeeper didn't even stay around to wait for the referee's card, running off to a mighty wind of boos.

In amongst the mangled screams of anger at the tackle and delight at the resultant penalty, Harry stood in stunned silence. Suddenly, his worst nightmare came flooding back to him. But this time, it wasn't him taking the penalty. How was this possible, he wondered? The same situation, against the very same team? John did seem resurgent, but if he missed this, would he ever recover? Harry turned and faced the rest of the crowd – still hurling abuse in the direction of the disgraced goalkeeper. He could not watch.

After a few anxious moments, the physio gave a thumbs-up. John was OK, and furthermore, the rest of his team were in agreement that he should take the penalty. John indicated, much to Frank Crumb's distress, that he was happy to do so.

The substitute goalkeeper had taken up his position. John placed the ball on the chalky-white marker spot. The referee blew his whistle for the kick to be taken.

Harry bit his lip. Becky and Marilyn hugged and screamed. Frank Crumb held on to his preconceptions. The crowd held its breath. John Christie scored.

As soon as the ball hit the net, John was running at full pelt towards the corner of the ground. There he buried himself in a four-way hug in which only pure joy existed. And pulling away from that slightly, he realised that the same feeling had spread all around three corners of the stadium. Thousands upon thousands were cheering, jumping and embracing. He'd done this.

And three minutes later, he'd done it again. A clever exchange of passes with Barton, a deceptive back-heel from Mark Rankin, and he was right in front of goal. The poor replacement 'keeper got his second touch of the ball, but again it was only when picking it out of his net.

The reaction was like the hell of the Pennines game thrown into glorious reverse. This time it was the Mile End fans who were chanting, singing and dancing. This time he was no longer a villain, but a hero. And when the final whistle blew a few minutes later, the old Ariel Hill acoustic chant of 'Christie, Christie, Christie' had been reworked as a symphony by his legion of new admirers.

This was, as the next morning's newspapers rightly pointed out, 'a different John Christie'. He was 'electric ... riveting ... full of ideas' (the *Mouthpiece*), he 'turned the game, and the league table on its head' (the *Spark*), 'burying a thousand clumsily-wielded insults with a swift one-two, and proving we'd all judged him both prematurely and incorrectly' (the *Morning News*).

John Christie had been reborn.

Twelve

Harry had suggested a meal at a nice restaurant or a drink at a swanky wine bar. Becky had declined both offers. Instead, she'd asked him to take her to her favourite place, a nature reserve in the countryside twenty minutes' drive from Ariel Hill. On the phone, Harry had been at pains to assert that he was not asking to meet with her out of any kind of dirty-old-man amorous intent, despite her radiant beauty. He – who by choice had few friends, but was feeling a strange magnetic draw toward the Christie family – insisted that he simply wanted to get to know her better. And what's more, he was telling the truth. The John Christie roller-coaster had completely enslaved his imagination now, and something within him, perhaps the journalist at his heart, wanted to experience the story as three-dimensionally as possible. Beyond that though, he had also noticed that the two women with whom John had spent most of his life were almost as interesting and unique as him. Marilyn, the quiet, resilient woman who commanded such devotion from an immaculately-raised son, and Becky, the beautiful butterfly with clipped wings. All close-knit, all churchgoers, all bunkered away in the bowels of that hideous estate. Partly through intrigue, partly through a tinge of pity, Harry just wanted to know them more.

After calling both John and Marilyn to pre-empt any misunderstanding, he picked Becky up after work on Tuesday evening. She had a job as an assistant in a small chemist in Ariel Hill, a few doors down from The Locomotive pub. She enjoyed herself there, though it was a far cry from a first-choice career as a conservationist. Just like the rest of her family, however, she refused to dwell on her misfortune, and worked hard and with a smile.

Despite the rush hour traffic, they were out at the sanctuary by 6 p.m., with plenty of daylight left. Harry was a little awkward at first in his handling of her wheelchair – realising that he'd never had to push one in his life before – but he soon got the hang of it and managed to follow directions to her favoured, secluded hilltop. There they found a bench which she preferred to her chair, and with plenty of space left for him. Not being as fit as he was in his heyday, Harry was glad of the rest after the climb.

They looked out together over an impressive landscape, where the slowly descending sun illuminated wooded slopes and created golden ripples on a perfectly circular lake. In the exact middle of the water was a tiny island, complete with two trees about the width of a goal mouth apart.

'That's John,' whispered Becky, looking out across the water, and breaking a comfortable silence that had lasted several minutes.

Harry replied with a quizzical expression. 'I'm sorry?'

'The island in the middle. It's John. I always say that to him when he brings me here. It just makes me think of him – all cut off there in the middle of the water – it's like how he always keeps himself at a distance from everyone else. Those trees out there are me and Mum: the only people John lets close. So it's his island. It's him.'

'What does he say about that?' asked Harry, intrigued.

'He says he'd like to get out there – and score a goal between those two trees.' She giggled, as did Harry. 'Mind you,' she continued, 'we might need to plant a new tree there now, for his friend Harry.'

Harry couldn't help smiling at the suggestion that he warranted a place on John's island. He wasn't certain it was deserved though. 'I'm not sure about that Becky,' he said, genuinely. 'We've not known each other too long, and most of the time I've only caused him problems.'

'Are you joking Harry? Before he met you he was a junior electrician. Now he's a Premier Division footballer. A couple of days ago he was on every news bulletin and back page.'

'Well, obviously I think that's great, but I'm not always sure that *he* does. I think he was happy being an electrician.'

Becky threw back her head and laughed wildly. 'Oh Harry! You really haven't worked him out at all have you? He's wanted to be a footballer all his life. It's all he wanted to do since he could stand up. Sure, he enjoyed his job, but only in the same way that I enjoy mine. We're positive people, but that doesn't mean that we don't have dreams beyond what we already smile about. He's living his dream now.'

'But he seemed so torn about it. He didn't want to sign for Ariel Hill, let alone Mile End.'

'That's only because he feels such a sense of duty towards Mum and me. When we heard about his first trial there was no way we were going to let him miss it. He kept saying that if it all went wrong he might not have a job at all – he was so worried about not being able to look after us. Anyway Harry, you definitely deserve a place on John's island – he talks about you all the time when he's at home.'

'Does he?' Harry warmed with pride.

'Constantly. That's pretty significant you know, because he's never had many friends. He wasn't unpopular at school, but he never found much in common with the other lads.'

'And what about the girls?'

'There were one or two I think, but it was never anything serious. I've asked him about it – I mean I'm his sister for goodness' sake, it's my job – but he always says that he's waiting for the right girl. I think when he meets someone, he'll just marry her and that'll be the end of it.'

'I've got to say,' smiled Harry, 'that John is probably the most unique and interesting person I've ever met.'

'I expect he probably is.'

'You know, a lot of people are going to ask you this question if he keeps on progressing at this rate, but how on earth does someone that good at football get to 22 without ever even playing for a team? I mean, if it wasn't true you'd have a hard time making people believe it was possible.'

Becky thought for a moment, took a long, lingering look out at John's island, and sighed gently. 'I guess . . . I guess it's all to do with our dad. I think that when he left, John felt he had to take on all the responsibility as man of the house, and that meant there was no time for things like friends and football. Plus, Dad was a mad football fan from what I remember, and maybe John didn't want to remind himself, or more likely remind Mum, too much of that.'

'I see. I suppose that does make rather tragic sense.'

'But it's not tragic now is it?' Becky beamed suddenly. 'Now it's all going great. It might have been a bit difficult at first, but Saturday was incredible. There were tens of thousands of people shouting his name. Plus, he's got another game tomorrow night, and he told me this morning that he might be starting.'

'That's great Becky. You must be very proud.'

'We are,' she said, as she gazed again at the island, a tear appearing in her eye.

The following evening, Harry settled down alone in his living room to watch the next chapter of his friend's life unfold. Mile End's game against fellow bottom-of-the-league strugglers Minehead was being televised, and John was a confirmed starter. Harry was more excited about this game than he had been about any for years. It wasn't a title decider or a key cup game – just a fairly important relegation battle between two strikingly unattractive teams – but he was veritably pulsing with energy at the thought of it. Already drunk on excitement, he decided against his trademark stiff whisky (triple measure) before kick-off, and instead created a little shrine in front of his television, complete with large packet of crisps, salsa dip, cold bottle of cola and print-fresh copy of *Goal!* magazine, which this week included a photo-special on John's weekend demolition of Tyneside. If he hadn't been sitting in the middle of all of it, one would have guessed that this was a teenager's bedroom.

All the TV-talk before the game was about Saturday's two-goal hero. The anchorman and his guests laughed as they discussed their lack of information about the player; his mysterious ascent from the non-league at a relatively late age; the persistent story that he'd never played for a team before this season. They assured the viewers that this last rumour couldn't possibly be true, and promised to get to the bottom of it once and for all in the post-match interviews. Jesper Klein, the former Danish international defender-turned-pundit, tipped John as his man to watch in the game. 'I've got a feeling this lad's going to set the world alight,' he told the camera.

He certainly set the game alight. Again he scored two goals, again he won Mile End a game they had otherwise looked likely to lose. Both strikes were close range finishes; neither was spectacular: together they were priceless for Mile End. And had there been any doubters left – inside or outside the club – that John Christie was made of the right stuff, they were converted by this performance. After the game, which finished 2–1, Frank Crumb openly hugged John in front of the watching television cameras: an unusual display of affection, recognition and confirmation that John's name was now plastered to the bottom of his mental 'yes' box.

As he left the pitch, John was grabbed by an enthusiastic reporter, begging to ask him a few questions. Bedazzled by the moment, he misunderstood the request, and began to talk, unaware that this was a television interview, and that a camera was relaying his profile into millions of homes around the country.

'John, fantastic performance, your third and fourth goal for the club, in only your first full game, you must be thrilled?' blurted the animated little man, in perfect football house-style.

'I can't believe it to be honest with you,' replied John warmly, 'it's just all happening so quickly at the moment.'

'And let's talk about that John, because I'm sure the viewers at home will want to know: is it true that you hadn't played for any kind of team before this season?'

'I'm sorry?' John shuddered as he processed the first part of the sentence. 'Did you say viewers?' He turned to his left, noticed the camera and jumped. 'Am I on TV?'

The reporter looked slightly embarrassed. 'Well, of course you are. The whole game's just gone out live.'

John began edging quickly out of shot, and the camera panned round to follow him. 'Sorry,' he hollered, nervously, 'I've got to go now. Th– thanks.' Then the camera followed him as he turned and darted into the players' tunnel, before the broadcast switched hurriedly to the studio, where an unprepared bunch of ex-professional footballers were hastily refastening their ties.

'Er . . . John Christie there . . . ' spluttered the anchorman, 'in obviously his first ever television appearance. . . . '

An hour after the game had finished, Harry was surprised to hear his telephone ring.

'Hello?' he answered, intrigued by such a rare occurrence. When a piece of writing *wasn't* due, Harry seldom received late-evening calls.

'Hi Harry, it's me,' chirped a familiar voice.

Harry wanted to say a thousand things at once but managed 'John! Congratulations! How are you doing?'

'I'm OK, I suppose. A little bit embarrassed.'

'The TV thing?'

'You saw it then. Did it look as bad as it felt? It wasn't really my fault – the man didn't say anything about it being a television interview – I just thought he was a newspaper reporter or something.'

'I don't think they'll crucify you for it John. People understand that you're very new to all this. You're bound to be a bit nervous. Great game anyway. Are you happy?'

'Of course I am. We won again. That means we can still stay up.'

'I've got good money on you doing so John. Don't go letting me down now; you were 1–3 to be relegated when I put that bet on.'

'I think I'm flattered.'

'You should be.'

'Anyway, Harry, I've got to go. I just rang to say hi.'

That meant a lot to Harry. 'OK John,' he said choking just a little. Then he remembered what he'd been meaning to say for a while. 'Hey, John.'

'Yes Harry.'

'I'm proud of you John. I've been in this game a long time, and I don't think I've ever felt so proud.'

'Thanks Harry.'

In the next two games John drove Harry's pride to uncharted territories. Despite their wins against Tyneside and Minehead, Mile End still required maximum points from their last three games to be assured of footballing salvation. Two wins and a draw would make survival a mathematical possibility if other teams around them dropped points, but anything less than that would spell their certain demise. Saturday; Wednesday; Saturday – three short matches would take them into mid-May, and, in all probability considering the opposition lined up for them on the final day, the First Division.

Their first game was the easiest of the three, against the one team that was below them in the league. Shackleton County had been doomed for nearly a month already, and most of their players were too busy trying to arrange their passports out of the club to worry about fulfilling the futile final fixtures. The team they sent to Mile End's stadium was a ragtag mix of young prospects and gutsy old pros who'd spent most of the season on the bench. Thus, while they lacked great talent and skilful polish, they did at least possess the spirit for a fight, and gamely battled for the full ninety minutes. They were no match for John Christie, however, as the striker, who the *Morning News* said was 'maturing by at least one year in every match', turned into a provider, setting up Helmut Mahel for his first goal in England. The old German's celebration was as excited and exotic as any seen in the league that day – again this was something he hadn't expected to experience this late on in his career. The whistle blew twenty minutes later, and Mile End were still alive. Two games left, two wins needed.

The second game was a much tougher proposition. They travelled overnight to the far north of England, where Teesside – a team still battling to win a place in next season's European competition – were waiting for them; licking their lips in anticipation at playing the 19th-placed team in the division. This was Mile End's wild card, their game in hand: a victory would put them into 17th place, out of the relegation zone and holding the future in their own hands. In a pre-match interview, Frank Crumb insisted that he expected nothing less than a win from his players, and more goals from John Christie.

On the pitch, John found it tougher going. While the goalkeepers he'd faced so far had been good, none of them were in the class of Teesside's Lloyd McGrath, the England no.1. This man had experienced a quite extraordinary season of form, during which he'd single-handedly kept out some of the world's best strikers, and inched towards a new record for the fewest goals conceded by a goalkeeper in the club's history. The record was 29; so far he'd only let in 26 – the fewest of any goalkeeper in the Premier Division. If Teesside could only score goals at the other end – it was often said their attack was as toothless as an old sugar addict – they'd have been league title contenders. Again in this game, while the strikers barely got a shot on target, the man at the very back was playing like a man possessed. First, John tried a shot from 20 yards when the defenders stood off him. It appeared to be arrowing into the top right-hand corner, but McGrath leapt like a man on a pogo stick to divert it to safety with his palm. Then, John used his pace to puncture the Teesside defence, and headed towards the 'keeper, one-on-one. McGrath timed his counter-run perfectly, and met the ball just as it was about to leave John's boot. John tripped over the top of the prostrate goalkeeper, but it was no foul. At half-time, although the scores were level, it was McGrath 2, Christie 0.

With only fifteen minutes left on the scoreboard clock, the Mile End party was beginning to run out of good music. There were still no goals in either column, McGrath looked equal to everything John and his contemporaries were capable of throwing his way, and Frank Crumb was screaming so hard that those around him feared his head might fall off. Then John conjured up another miracle, and everything was right in the world again.

He'd noticed through the course of the game that Teesside's weakest defensive link was their left back, and so moved himself quietly into the right wing position. Carl Barton spotted his run, and swept a majestic 40-yard pass across the pitch and directly to his feet. John controlled the ball with a single, devastating touch that left two defenders sliding around him, and cut inside towards the goal. He looked up, and in an instant came to exactly the same realisation as McGrath – the goalkeeper had been caught off-guard, and was standing 10 yards off his line. That realisation came too quickly for McGrath to recover. Within a second, the ball was looping away from John's boot, over the goalkeeper's head and into the vacant net. McGrath 2, Christie 1 perhaps, but the only score that mattered stayed 1–0 until the end.

After the game, McGrath made a point of finding John in the locker rooms. He shook his hand, recognising a worthy opponent, and spoke one short phrase:

'You'll play for England one day son.'

Which was exciting, but not quite as pressing as the final game of the season – against the best team in Europe.

Thirteen

It had started reasonably enough. The club's press office had begun to receive two to three interview requests a day in the lead up to the Teesside match, mostly from local journalists interested in the brewing miracle of relegation avoidance. But after its chief conjurer had proved, against one of the world's best goalkeepers, that he intended to see the whole trick through to completion, the phones turned suddenly and violently hot. In just five games (four if the debacle at Pennines was to be forgiven), John Christie had notched up five goals, and almost completely raised Lazarus in the process. On Thursday morning, England's most popular newspaper, the *Mouthpiece*, referred to him as 'The Messiah of Mile End'. And after that, they and forty other national, regional and student newspapers wanted to talk to him, as did various television and radio stations and even a couple of interested local politicians.

They all tried the clearest route to goal first of course. The press office phone-line became permanently clogged with journalists trying to call in a favour from the PR people there, and although some initial requests were met with favourable responses, there were soon just too many bowls for the soup to go around. Midway through that Thursday morning, the idea of a press conference, at which John would appear with Frank Crumb, was pitched. It was rejected by almost everyone. Nobody wanted to share him – they all wanted the exclusive with the Premier Division's mysterious new superstar.

Who, incidentally, was totally unaware of this flurry of activity. He, like the rest of the squad, undertook light training on Thursday morning, and spent the afternoon in the gym doing arm work, as he did on most days. Six months ago, John's upper body was skinny and brittle-looking; now he had developed the muscular arms and torso not quite of a bodybuilder, but certainly of an athlete. His training, which was always just a touch more intense than the session that preceded it, was interrupted by the influx into the gymnasium of a press officer and assorted club marketing people.

'John!' exclaimed the press officer, a young, tubby, excited-looking man. 'So glad we've found you!'

John released the pressure on his weights machine, wiped his brow with the sleeve of his T-shirt, and looked up. 'What's going on?' he asked, alarmed by the number of inanely grinning suits staring back at his sweat patches.

'Everyone wants a piece of you John,' replied Tubby, 'All of them – the *Mouthpiece*, the *Spark*, the *Reporter*, the *Herald*, Channel One News, Sport One, ten different radio stations . . . '

'What?' John replied, frozen to his seat with shock, 'What do they want?'

'To talk to you – ahead of Saturday's big game. You're the new hero of the club; now they all want an interview!'

'But . . . but I can't. I don't want to . . . I've got nothing to say.'

'You must – it's all for club morale. We've got to create a buzz before Saturday – make the fans believe.'

'I can't. I'm sorry.'

The abundance of suits looked at one another, shrugged collectively and disappeared from whence they'd come. John sagged into his padded seat. On the next machine along, Allan Strong allowed a booming laugh to escape his throat.

'No use givin' 'em that sort 'a answer laddie,' he said. 'You don't know these journalists yet, but you will, soon enough. They cannae understand the word "no".'

Across London, an irate sports editor was grilling his chief minion.

'What do you mean, we can't speak to him?' bellowed Alex Knight, holding a golf putter in a particularly threatening stance.

'Th-they said we might be able to,' stuttered Burke, retreating further under the desk with every word. 'But they've had a lot of requests . . .'

'I DON'T CARE IF THEY'VE HAD A DINNER INVITATION FROM THE QUEEN!' Knight swooshed his putter before calming slightly. 'We're the *Daily Reporter*, the most respected daily newspaper in the country, nay the world. They speak to us first – always us first.'

'But, Mr Knight, they say he may not even speak to anyone.'

'Oh really? He won't speak to the rats from the tabloids who knock on his door in the middle of the night? Not to the relentless hacks who camp outside his house?'

'But we don't do things like that Mr Knight.'

'No Burke. But it makes me sick that we miss out on these things because we play by the rules. Look, you've got to think of something – this is the story I want for the front page of Saturday's section. Do we have any links into Mile End?'

'Not that I know of,' lied Burke.

'Wait a minute – wasn't that Harry Foster's old club as a player?'

'Er . . . I don't think so.'

'Foster,' shouted Knight, launching himself out of the door of his office. 'Can you come in here for a second?'

'I'm sure he doesn't have any contacts there now Mr Knight,' weaselled Burke. 'This is probably a waste of time.'

A rapid conversation, a telephone call and a taxi ride later, Harry was standing outside the Mile End Stadium. There he met three of his press colleagues, encamped outside the ground with cameras at the ready, and promptly incurred their displeasure by sailing through them, past a security guard who had been briefed on his arrival, and into the ground. He, John and the Mile End Press Office had struck a deal, as he informed his rivals on the way past: he was to conduct *the only* pre-match interview with John Christie.

Inside, John was waiting for him with a warm hug.

'Thanks for letting me do this,' said Harry.

'No – thank you,' John replied. 'They told me I had to do at least one interview; I was terrified I'd have to go on TV before you called.'

'Where are we going to do it?'

'We thought it might be good to use the chairman's office,' replied the tubby press man, who appeared from the shadows just behind John. 'Our photographer will take some pictures for you as agreed – and you'll keep the sponsor's name in them, as agreed.'

Harry laughed gently. 'Whatever you say,' he said, and then under his breath, 'good to see my editor hasn't lost his sense of editorial integrity.'

They moved up to the chairman's office, the most majestic room in a mighty building, with spectacular views across the pitch. As they entered, the sweeping windows were being defaced by the addition of large plastic boards carrying the sponsor's logo. Despite the ugly commercial invasion, however, this was still a mightily impressive space, lined with paintings of former chairmen and playing greats. The photographer, a big-haired woman with delusions of grandeur (she usually worked as a community development liaison, but had taken evening classes in photography) suggested that the interview should take place at the chairman's mighty wooden desk, with John in the main man's seat. She thought that this would be helpful to the headline-writers; Harry wasn't so sure but didn't have the energy to argue.

Harry positioned his dictaphone on the desk, pulled out a sheet of questions, and looked on as John pulled unnatural smiles for the camera. After a few minutes, the flashing subsided, and they were left alone, at which point they both relaxed and exhaled deeply.

'I don't know how you want me to do this,' Harry began, 'but I thought I'd try to tell a bit of your story, do a little on the last few weeks and how they've felt, and maybe sandwich all that around a few of your thoughts on life – your philosophies and so on.'

'Philosophies?' repeated John. 'I'm not sure I have any of those.'

'Oh, I think you do. Maybe you've never thought about it, but you don't live your life like many men of your age. You don't smoke, you don't drink, you don't chase women around. You speak little, you think a lot. You seem to have no interest in money – that sets you apart from practically every other footballer in recent history. You've certainly got philosophies in that head of yours.'

'Well, I suppose I have reasons for behaving in that way, if that's what you mean. . . . '

Harry pressed record on the dictaphone, and sat back into an extremely comfortable leather chair.

Saturday morning saw the publication of the *Daily Reporter: Sport*'s big interview. Two broadsheet pages, including a huge photograph complete with gigantic and conspicuous sponsor's logo in the background, were devoted to 'Harry Foster meets John Christie – World Exclusive'. It was all, predictably enough, very positive and pleasant stuff. The other newspapers, meanwhile, had no such exclusive. That was not to say that they ignored the new superstar, however. Far from it in fact. . . .

'Hero Christie Still Lives in Slum' read the back page of the multi-million circulating *Mouthpiece*. 'Mile End Star's Secret Heartbreak' hollered the *Spark*. With their left hand they caressed him; with their right hand they unleashed an unexpected pair of body blows. When he heard about it – a concerned call from Allan Strong just beat off others from his manager, press officer and Harry – he was struck by an instant devastation. One newspaper had denigrated his community, attributing entirely fictional quotes about the 'appalling area which I can't wait to leave for ever' to his lips, while another had got even dirtier, drawing on an unidentified local 'source' to get the inside story on Becky's crippling road accident. They'd crossed a line – they'd attacked his family, and for no good reason.

'Why have they done this?' he cried on the telephone, his voice breaking with tears. 'What did I do wrong?'

'You cannae stop it, John' replied a similarly shocked Allan. 'They'll always do this kindae thing. They're scum, and that's all there is to it.'

'But they can't do this sort of thing – surely there's a law or something.'

'They can do it John, and they will. It's partae the job. But listen – you better forget all about this now. Just until after the game. That's all that matters now. At quarter to five, that's the time to think about nasty stories in the press and lawyers and movin' hoose. Until then, it's only football.'

John Christie, even more subdued than usual, arrived at the stadium at 11 a.m., where the players met for the lightest of lunches and a short coach trip (in distance at least) across London. Their destination: the mighty City Stadium, an almost-mythical 75,000-seat lions' den and home not only to the national team, but also to the most feared club side in English and European football, London City. In a week's time they would face Billy Regan's Moss Side in the EFF Cup final. A few days after that they would take on the mighty Club De Paris in the European Cup final. But today, they would, according to their manager, 'devour the minnows of Mile End and send them hurtling through the trapdoor to the First Division without a shred of sympathy.' And, while others were kinder with their words, nobody had predicted any other result. London needed only a single point to be crowned Premier Division champions for a third successive year. Their opponents needed a win to be sure of their relegation escape. Even with the Messiah in their ranks, their seemed little chance that Mile End could become the first team in a year and a half to win at this ground.

London boasted so many international players that barely half of them could fit on to the pitch at one time. Only two of those were Englishmen – both full internationals, both ever-presents in the London team – the midfielder and England captain Simon Brazier, and the defensive rock D'Alex Smith. The other nine at any one time always comprised a mix of fleet-footed Brazilian geniuses, revered French flair players, well-groomed Italian superstars and the occasional Dutch master. No other nationality ever got a look in –

the club seemed to have an unspoken ethos that only these five nations could ever be represented in the interests of maintaining footballing purity.

Their team sheet for this match, passed around the Mile End changing room an hour prior to kick-off, would have been enough to make the greatest teams of all time shiver, let alone a side in 17th place. Helmut Mahel, a veteran of two European Cup finals and three World Cups, further decreased confidence within the camp by announcing that it was the strongest team he had ever seen in his career. 'It is like a dream,' he announced, almost delirious with nerves, 'like all the great warriors of history have been sent out to fight us at once.'

His analogy seemed fair to John as, an hour later, he emerged from the players' tunnel into an arena of truly gladiatorial proportions. As far as he could look up, he saw only stand upon stand of animated fans, all chanting imperiously; all clad in the London blue; all rooting for the other side. The noise was deafening – like standing next to a 40-foot speaker at a heavy metal concert. The pitch, which seemed unsteady under his feet, was lush, and green – as unlikely an end-of-season service as could be imagined. This was the most incredible place that he had ever been, and yet right now, it seemed an awful lot like Hell.

As he stumbled onto the pitch, John was thrown off-balance by the flashing of a hundred photographer's bulbs. Despite the presence of all these superstars, it was his face that the press were interested in now. This match, which would decide matters at both ends of the league table, which was being beamed live across the world in more than twenty countries, was in many ways the biggest of the season. And, despite his inexperience, despite the fact that no one knew his face a month ago, despite the way his body was involuntarily folding under all the crowd-induced pressure, John was the centrepiece, the focus, the man of the moment. He was the one figure in whom Mile End's fingernail-chomping fans could place their last scrap of trust; the one small threat to the clinical execution of the inevitable London victory. The newspapers had each picked him out as the key player, the television company had a dedicated camera that would be fixed on him for the duration of the match. Every one of the 75,000 people was looking at him either to produce the one moment that turned the football world on its head, or else to fall flat on his face and return quickly to the obscurity from which he'd arisen.

Terrified, angry and alone, he took up his position as single striker, cut off from and unsupported by an ultra-negative nine-man defence. Five defenders lined up behind four defensively-minded midfielders, specially selected for their shared love of tough tackles, sideways passing and punting the ball as far away from their own goal as humanly possible. Attack-minded players like Rieux, Mahel and Barton were kept warm in their track suits on the bench. Barring John, whom he felt he simply couldn't leave out, Frank Crumb had opted for the most negative, defensively-minded shield of players that it was possible to send out. So John not only felt isolated by the media's sudden and unprovoked attacks on his life, but he also felt friendless on the pitch. A good striker converts a decent percentage of the chances provided to him by his team-mates; a player in John's current form could score even more. But every header needs a cross to come before it; every one-on-one requires a preceding through-ball from an attack-minded colleague. Without a single fellow attacker to assist him, John would roll around the pitch like a head without a body.

The cauldron reached boiling point as the whistle blew to begin the match. The incessant crescendo of sound became even more intense than it had before the kick-off, causing the fair hairs on John's arms to stand erect. The unrelenting noise on four sides made him dizzy – so much so that he remained rooted to the spot as the action began around him. It took the vociferous cry of a team-mate to wake him into action – just as the Brazilian wonder-kid Pretedinhio danced past his stationary frame with the ball glued to his foot. Grinding slowly into action, he turned and saw one of Mile End's 'midfield of steel' carve through the teenager's leg and earn himself a yellow card. Pretedinhio rolled on the floor like he'd been attacked by an axe-wielding maniac. The crowd got even louder. Only half a minute of the game had elapsed.

A shaken and disoriented John got his first touch of the ball – a clumsy tackle which sent another player crashing to the ground and resulted in a London free kick – after five minutes. His face had drained of colour, such was the combined weight of the pressure being applied to him from within and without, and his concentration was drifting between the tearful sister he had left at home that morning, the tens of thousands hurling abuse at him and the impending downward journey that his team looked certain to make. And it really did seem certain – after only a few minutes the gulf in talent between the two teams was becoming painfully apparent. The French striker, Jean-Paul Cottard, had already fired three warning shots at the Mile End goal, and it was surely only a matter of time before one of them found the net.

After twenty-one minutes of persistent pressure, one of them did. A swerving drive from the edge of the area, at which the goalkeeper made a quite hopeless dive, was enough to get the scoreboard ticking. Cottard, full of his trademark arrogance, refused even to celebrate, simply retrieving the ball and returning to the centre spot with it. There he threw it at the feet of John, who continued to wear his bamboozled expression.

Allan Strong, already drained from twenty-one solid minutes of pure defence, ran to join him as the rest of the team argued and attributed blame. He gripped John by the shoulders, shook him violently, and shouted:

'What's wrong with ye laddie? Ye've gotta wake up and get playing otherwise we might as well pack oor bags for the First Division now.'

'I'm sorry,' replied John, refusing to look Allan in the eye. 'I'm sorry.'

Allan slapped him around the back of the head, and swore under his breath. Then he jogged back to join the rest of his defensive legion, and prepared for another onslaught. 'Damage limitation,' he told himself. 'Let's keep this score respectable.'

'I'm sorry,' said John again, to no one in particular.

Half-time was reached, somewhat miraculously, with no further addition to the score. John sat in silence, his eyes glazed, as Frank Crumb tried unsuccessfully to find some kind of rallying cry. Despite plenty of prodding and shouting, he responded to no one, until he heard a familiar voice amid some commotion outside the changing room.

'I have to get in there,' shouted Harry to the security men with whom he was struggling. 'I've got to speak to John Christie.'

He was about to be ejected from the ground when John stood to his feet and called across to them. 'No, let him in. He's a friend of mine.'

Frank Crumb was outraged by the interruption. 'What the – Foster?' – he yelled in disbelief – 'Get out of here man! What on earth do you think you're doing?'

'I'm sorry Frank, but I've got to speak to John,' replied the breathless journalist, who'd just hurdled a considerable number of seats to get there. 'Please – he's out of the game. Give me two minutes.'

Crumb was so shocked by Harry's audacity that he was rendered speechless. He tried to yell again, but there was no breath within him. Finally, he looked away and said, 'Make it one.'

Harry nodded to the red-faced Crumb, before grabbing John's arm and leading him back into the corridor. The ten other players simply reflected their manager's look of incredulousness.

'John,' whispered Harry, at the colourless slouching heap before him. 'You've got to snap out of this.'

'They wrote all those things. I didn't say I hated the estate. I never said that.'

'I know John. But that's what happens in this game – people want to read about you, and if the papers have got nothing true to tell them, they just make something up.'

'But why? How could they write those things about Becky – it's nobody's business–'

'Listen John, this isn't fair, I know. But now is not the time to be thinking about it. You've got forty-five minutes to keep this team in the Premier Division. Focus on that now, and when it's over, I promise I'll help you through everything you're worried about. We'll move you and your family into a house with a ring fence if we have to. We'll go on TV to tell the real story. Whatever you want. But not now. Now you've got to think only about the game.'

'Time's up,' screeched Crumb, his voice re-discovered. 'Get in here Christie!'

Harry patted his friend on the shoulder, and watched as he returned to his bemused team-mates. As he walked away, he heard Crumb threatening him: 'You've got ten minutes to start playing. Otherwise I'm taking you off.'

Meanwhile, in two similarly simmering cauldrons in different parts of the country, the Mile End story was being forcibly reshaped from several different angles. The 19th-placed team, on 35 points, was Minehead, who had a home fixture against Pennines. The score there was 0–0 at half-time, meaning that they were looking doomed. The team above them, in 18th place with 37 points, was East Coast. They were currently winning 1–0 in Littlehampton. If the scores remained the same, East Coast would leapfrog Mile End, currently one place and one point above them, sending them back into the dreaded relegation zone at the last moment.

All this was relayed to the Mile End players in no uncertain terms by Crumb, who sent them back out into the arena with eleven lit fireworks placed strategically in their posteriors.

Harry's pep talk had done the trick. Suddenly, John was able to shut out his concerns about the morning's media. After he'd done that, he was in turn able to block away the crowd. And with those two worries lifted from his shoulders, the pressure of the situation suddenly seemed manageable.

With his first touch of the half, he sent a long ball back towards his own penalty area, and set off running towards the opposite end. Allan Strong, who received his pass, immediately understood the plan, and fired a huge kick back up the field. There it nestled comfortably on John's chest, came under his control, and set in motion the first genuine Mile End attack. Despite heavy pressure from an extremely 'friendly' Italian defender, John managed to shield the ball for long enough to allow a team-mate to join him in the mid-point of the opposition half. He waited for his colleague to stroll past, then feigned to flick the ball to him with his heel. The defender moved to block the pass – but John had not really passed. Instead, he turned towards goal, running with the ball at his feet, and advancing with a pace that caught London by surprise. In a sudden panic, two defenders launched themselves towards him around 25 yards out. They were both aiming at the same point, and John saw them coming. Just as they reached him, sliding and snarling with studs raised, he flicked the ball calmly beyond them, leapt into the air, and avoided them both. They did not, however, manage to avoid each other. There was a crack of bones behind him – part of him wanted to stop to see if they were OK – and he was unopposed on the remaining journey to goal. He didn't wait for the goalkeeper to advance – he simply struck a powerful shot upon entering the penalty area, and placed it well out of reach. One goal each, and six in six for Christie. The crowds' silence was the most lavish praise he'd received all season.

The rest of the Mile End team mobbed him, while in the stand Harry shed more than a couple of tears. But Frank Crumb knew that only half the job had been completed. While London had allowed themselves – through sheer complacency – to be pegged back for the draw, there was no way that they'd give away the win, and the title. He screamed to his players to reform into their positions. The task they were about to attempt – to win in this fortress – was nearly impossible.

On sixty-five minutes, John got another chance to silence the assembled masses. Another long ball came his way, again he had it under control a little way outside the penalty area. But this time, the mighty frame of D'Alex Smith stood between him and the goal. John faked to go one way, then turned back to go the other. D'Alex read it like a poorly-written book. The chance had died.

On eighty-one minutes, Mile End won a corner. It was floated in towards John, who for a moment found himself unmarked. Again, D'Alex appeared to block his path, materialising in front of him to clear the ball just as he was gearing up to pounce. The same occurrence was repeated four minutes later. Again D'Alex won the battle – and now it seemed inevitable that London would win the war.

Then, with scarcely a minute left on the referee's watch, D'Alex was left standing as John collected another long ball from the defence. This time, it was just him against the goalkeeper. This time, there was no powerhouse defender ready to leap in to save the day. Taking a second to check that he really was in such an incredible position in the final minute, he took careful aim from the same spot as before, just inside the area. He let fly with all his might, and watched as the ball sailed towards the corner of the net. His arm reached skywards in celebration . . . and then returned to his side. The goalkeeper had plucked the ball out of its trajectory. No goal, and still 1–1. The final whistle blew a few moments later. London City were champions again – and Mile End were relegated. John, like each of his team-mates, sank to his knees with the realisation. It was as if someone had plunged a dagger directly into his heart.

And then someone pulled it out again. It started with loud chatter on the touch-line, barely audible above the victorious chants of 75,000 London fans. But it soon grew as the tiny contingent of Mile End supporters realised what had happened through their terrace radios. In the final minute of the other match, Littlehampton had equalised. Now East Coast only had a 1–1 draw – the same as Mile End – meaning that they were short of the points needed to move out of 18th. The chatter then turned to wild screaming – the final whistle had gone there, too. Bizarrely, every fan in the stadium was cheering and smiling, although for slightly different reasons. Mile End had been saved at the last.

Some players danced in jubilation, others broke down in tears. John Christie simply laid down in the centre of the pitch alone, and looked up at the heavens. 'Thank you,' he whispered.

Fourteen

Most of the Mile End players spent Sunday in bed, recovering from life-threatening hangovers. John was not among them. Instead, in the morning, he accompanied his mother and sister to church as always, and in the afternoon, he met with Harry for a 'problem solving session'.

Harry had arranged to pick his friend up at 12, from outside St Peter's Church in Ariel Hill. When he arrived there, he found John sitting on the wall, idly swinging his legs like a 10-year-old child. He didn't look carefree – the media-generated concerns of yesterday had not simply evaporated in the heat of victory – but there was still a naïveté about him. It occurred to Harry then that John still had no concept of what had happened to him in the past few months. He was still the same, quiet, simple-living young man he'd first met playing football in the shadows. And yet, to the sports media, he was a volcanic household name just waiting to erupt.

He jumped from the wall at the sound of Harry's horn, and nimbly leapt into the passenger seat of the car, showing no signs of post-match fatigue. The two men exchanged a handshake, and set immediately to work. John had managed to calm down and put the previous morning's newspapers to the back of his mind, but only because of Harry's promise that matters would be rectified today.

'Right,' Harry began abruptly, 'first things first. We've got options to do television interviews at Channel One and Sport One later this afternoon, where you can talk about yesterday morning's press, what you thought about it and what the real stories are. Are you happy to do both?'

'Will you be there?' John asked, in a flash.

'Of course.'

'Do you think it's a good idea?'

'Definitely. And those are all the interviews you'll need to do. The newspapers will see what you've said, then tomorrow they'll all lay into each other for making up lies about you, and the negative stories should disappear. You have to understand John, yesterday you were big news because of the importance of the match you were playing in. They all wanted a John Christie story, because it was a John Christie news day. But in a few days that will all have gone by, and it'll be a Clinton McLean news day, or a Billy Regan news day. There are World Cup qualifiers coming up – it's incredible how quickly this weekend will be forgotten, no matter how important it seemed at the time.'

'So you're saying that there won't be more stories like the ones they made up?'

'Well, no – I can't promise that. But unless you were to become, say, a regular England player, they shouldn't come around very often. And when they do, you just have to learn to be strong, allow them to bounce off you, and strongly deny them. So that's what we're going to do now – agreed?'

'Agreed.'

'Great. Second then, we're going to need to look at getting you a new place to live.'

'But we're happy in the flat,' protested John.

Harry looked back at him despairingly. 'John, you're a Premier Division footballer on . . . . How much are you on?'

John went instantly red. 'It's embarrassing,' he said. 'I told them it was ridiculous.'

'Come on John, I know the game. How much are we talking about here – five, ten grand a week?'

John burst into instant hysterics. 'No! Are you mad? It's £500 a week!'

Harry slammed on the brakes, jolting himself and his passenger toward the windscreen. 'Are you serious?' He yelled, brimming with sudden anger.

John nodded. 'What's wrong?' he asked, a little warily at seeing Harry's change of colour.

Harry turned away from him, grabbed an address book from his coat pocket, and with his stubby fingers jabbed a number into his mobile phone. He growled as he waited for an answer, like a lion waiting to pounce on its prey. Then a click signified that someone had picked up.

'Crumb?' he almost shouted. 'Harry Foster . . . . Yes, I know it's Sunday lunch-time – I'm sure your wife will understand. Listen, I'm with your star player. The bloke who single-handedly saved your club from relegation and bankruptcy. . . . Yeah, that's the one. I understand that you're paying him the same as the boot boys. . . . Don't try and lie to me Crumb – he's told me himself. Now you know you're taking liberties here; the guy's just scored six goals in his first six games, and you'd have been dead and buried without him. Nobody gets paid that sort of money in this division. . . . I don't care if he hasn't got an agent – that's hardly his fault. . . . Well then I'll be his agent. . . . Yes of course I'm serious. And we want ten times what you're paying him now, or this'll be in the *Reporter* tomorrow morning. . . . You know you've done wrong Crumb, come on now. . . . Good, thanks, enjoy your lunch. Love to the wife.' He hung up the phone, and started driving again.

'What was that?' asked John, his eyes wide.

'Just solving your first problem. They'll call us tomorrow to re-negotiate the terms. They won't dare pay you under £5,000 a week from now on.'

'But that's stupid. There's no way I deserve that kind of money.'

'Fine John – give it to me if you want. But considering that your goals saved them from millions of pounds of debt, I'd say you're being a little hard on yourself. Oh, and by the way, that stuff about being your agent, that was really just for effect, I don't really expect–'

'No,' John broke in, 'please – I'd like that. Really I would. Ever since I started getting into the first team there have been all these strange men approaching me, offering to be my agent. They scare me. I don't want anything to do with them. Why can't you do it? You've just organised two interviews and re-negotiated my salary. Isn't that what agents do?'

'Well, I'm not qualified, but I suppose I could do it.'

'Good – then it's agreed?'

'Er . . . agreed, I guess.'

'Then what next?'

'Well,' said John's new agent, 'as I was saying, you need to find yourself a new place to live. Now I know you like the flat, but I'm sure your mum and Becky would appreciate a bit more space.'

'They wouldn't want to leave Ariel Hill. We've grown up here.'

'Fine,' Harry replied, 'but could I suggest we look at the other end of town?'

Just five minutes later, Harry's car pulled to a halt in a large driveway. They both got out, walked up the path, and pressed their faces against a window of an expansive house.

'What do you think?' asked Harry with a wry smile. 'Would this sort of thing suit you?'

'It's huge,' answered John, his eyes popping out. 'Could I afford a place like this?'

'With your new wage, I'm pretty sure they'd give you a mortgage. Do you want to take a look inside?'

'Yes . . . but – wait a minute – how?'

'It's my house,' grinned Harry, waving the key in front of his face.

After a grand tour, John and Harry sat in the front room and sipped cola together. John expressed that he really would like to live in a house like this, and Harry promised to call an estate agent in the morning. And a financial advisor. And he'd sort out John's new employment contract, too. Being an agent looked like being an eventful business.

A little later they were back in the car, heading for the central London studios of Channel One Television. As Harry waited in the wings, an interviewer fired pre-approved questions to a nervous John, who swallowed his nerves, and, after being told that the recording wasn't live, managed to set the record straight effectively, albeit on the third take. John and Harry were in another studio on the other side of the city two hours after that, recording another interview with Sport One, the dedicated football channel. This one went more smoothly, requiring only a single take, as John eased past his early camera fright. Both interviews hit screens that same evening, and by 7 p.m. the cries of screaming sports editors could be made out clearly throughout the land.

The next morning, after sifting with a smile through handfuls of newspapers now more intent on shifting blame and attacking one another's integrity than in digging dirt on innocent families, Harry picked up the local phone directory and turned to 'estate agents'. There he found a list of numbers, which he worked his way along steadily for the next hour, at the end of which, a grinning John appeared at his door.

By 1 o'clock that afternoon, John and Harry had earned their lunch. On the fax machine, the ink was still drying on an improved contract offer from Mile End, which would now pay John £10,000 a week – twice what Harry had asked for. On the computer screen, a long list of suitable local properties was displayed. And behind a desk, half a mile down the road, a financial advisor was rubbing his hands with glee at the thought of being let loose on a footballer's accounts.

Harry would have liked to have spent the whole week engaged in this sort of activity. A fondness for John had softened his hard heart, and helping him made Harry happy when normally such activity would feel like a chore. Unfortunately, he still had a job to do, which, although not 9 to 5, still made great demands upon his week. Thus on Tuesday morning, with several matters unresolved, he had to leave John, Marilyn and Becky in the hands of estate agents – a fate he'd have been reluctant to impose on his worst enemy. He rushed through his work as quickly as possible – putting together his traditional 'end of season review' for the *Reporter*. He ploughed through as rapidly as his wrists would allow, but it was a two-page broadsheet feature, and a flagship article for Friday's paper. By the time he'd finished – and included a healthy chunk of pro-John Christie sentiment – it was mid-afternoon.

He arrived home around 5 p.m., to find John sitting on his front step. John had a reinforced-concrete smile on his face, and didn't wait for him to leave the vehicle before leaping upon him.

'Guess what?' he yapped, jumping up at Harry's side like an excited puppy.

'What?' asked Harry, slightly worried that his parting 'don't sign anything while I'm gone' might have been ignored by excitement.

'We found a house. It's perfect.'

Harry's concern levels rose sharply. 'Really? Where?'

John smirked, but said nothing.

'You've not bought a flat above an Indian restaurant have you? They're always trying to get rid of those. I told you not to sign anything without me–'

'Relax Harry,' interrupted John. 'I've not signed anything. And it's not a flat above an Indian restaurant. It's a house, in a very desirable area of Ariel Hill.'

'Where?'

Again, John said nothing, but this time extended both his arms.

'You can't have this house. It's mine.'

'No, but I can have the one next door.'

Harry spun to his left, and noticed the estate agent's board outside the house of his least favourite neighbour. His face broke into an irrepressible smile. 'Are you serious?'

'Of course – if you don't mind, that is. We agreed we wouldn't put an offer in until we'd talked it through with you.'

Harry didn't need more than a moment to think about his answer. In his suggestion, John had flattered Harry more than any admiring fan of his writing ever had. To his associates – he couldn't really call many people 'friends' – he was known as grumpy, antisocial and rude. His drinking and heavy gambling had driven most of those who had once been close to him away. To all of them, the prospect of living next door to him would have been as appealing as a painful maiming. Now a young man and his family, who knew him fairly well, were prepared to move in to the very next house from his. If he hadn't been so desperate to say 'yes', he would have been speechless.

'Yes John,' he said, almost instantly. 'I'd love that.'

John had promised to take Becky to her nature reserve for another viewing of his island. He didn't therefore join Harry for a non-alcoholic toast, and didn't follow him through his front door. Had he done so, he would have seen his friend collect the second post, open it, and fall to the floor in shock.

In his hand was the following:

Harry –
Got this address from a former friend of yours, so not sure whether you still live there. Hope this gets to you, but in view of the fact that it might not, I'll keep this brief. Not sure how you're doing these days, but things with me are not so good. Been reading your articles when I can – it's funny, you were practically illiterate when we were together. Anyway, I decided after reading one that you did a few months ago that I'd write to you, but never plucked up the courage. But here's that letter, at last, so: would really like to see you if you've got the time.
Call me – 7555 2512.

Jessica

Fifteen

They'd not been in the same room as each other for thirty years. Or even, as they were now, in the same market square. The bustle of tourists and street entertainers helped a little to allay the awkwardness between them, but not even Covent Garden had enough noise to fill such a gargantuan silence.

Harry and Jessica sat across a small metal table from one another, and each simply stared back at the other. Both were transfixed, taking in the effects of time – which had been kinder to her than to him – and sorting through a scale of memories that ranged from love to heartbreak. Their coffees went cold. Beggars and jugglers and women selling roses went ignored. When thirty years and more have passed since your last conversation, it's hard to simply start another.

In Jessica's face, Harry saw many things. He saw the payback of his decision to put her second: three missing decades which might have brought him children and even happiness. He saw a justification for his loneliness – a reason why he often woke up in the middle of the night groping around at nothing at all; sometimes drank himself to sleep; often wept over a crumpled old photograph. And he saw the girl in that photograph, still every bit as beautiful as she was on the day it was taken. How he could articulate those feelings, however, whilst retaining both his pride and his dignity, he did not know. So he articulated nothing. Instead he simply stared at her, ignoring his drink, the time – even the air he was breathing.

She wasn't silent for the same reasons. Instead, she felt a little ridiculous for reconvening them after so long, a little regretful that things hadn't turned out differently, and a little frightened by *his* continued silence. There were many things that she wanted to say, gnawing away at the insides of her cheeks and trying to burrow toward freedom. But until he spoke first, she would keep them captive.

And then, after the café clock had performed at least one full rotation, he finally found a handful of words. They weren't the magnificent words he'd hoped for, but they did at least bring colour back to both their faces.

'It's been so long Jess,' he said, softly. 'So much has happened in my life – I'm sure in yours, too. . . .'

'Yes,' she affirmed, putting her hand on the table.

'And yet,' he continued, growing in bravery, 'I've never forgotten you. I know that probably sounds stupid.'

She shook her head and smiled warmly. 'I've never forgotten you,' she echoed. 'How can you forget the love of your life?'

He smiled. Shyness forced her gaze away from him. There was further quiet. Then he spoke again, raising his own hand to the table, and edging it towards hers:

'So – are you still married?'

'No. Never was. I spent ten years with a man who kept promising we'd get married next year, and then he eloped to Las Vegas with a barmaid. Kind of ironic really, but it was probably the right thing in the end. I'm told you never did either.'

'No.'

'You got kids though?'

Harry paused and looked down, before announcing the other great regret of his life. 'No. No kids. No wife. Just football.'

Jessica's body involuntarily convulsed at the word. 'Ah yes,' she said, smirking but unable to disguise her displeasure. 'Still with the same mistress.'

'Yeah. But you knew that if you read my column in the paper.'

'I knew,' she sighed. 'And you turned out to be quite a writer – I'd never have guessed you had it in you. What are you again? Five-time sports journalist of the year?'

'Six, but I'm not really counting. Four of those times I've only won it by default because all the other writers were so bad.'

'Well it's not my subject, as you know, but you always seemed pretty good to me. I've been reading your stuff on and off for about twenty years now.'

'Really? All that time? But how come you never got in touch?'

She looked away, a little nervous that she might offend him. 'I guess . . . I guess because your writing showed me that nothing had changed, Harry. You were still as obsessed with that game as ever – still going to all those matches, still writing with all that pent-up passion and frustration that you couldn't still be out there playing yourself.'

'Guilty as charged I suppose – but then how come you contacted me now?'

'Something changed in your writing. Maybe three or four years ago. There was something new in your voice – maybe anger. The greed, the money, the commercialism – it all seemed to be eating away at you. You started rebelling against the game; you started seeing all the cracks. Then I started to think – this is a Harry Foster I can get along with again. So I decided I'd write to you.'

'Three or four years ago?'

'But I never did. Something stopped me. I realised that the change in your voice might not actually mean that you'd grown, but that'd you just capitulated – turned into a bitter old hack, with nothing good to say about anyone.'

'Hmm,' said Harry. 'Maybe you weren't so far wrong with that. But again I've got to ask the question – why did you contact me now?'

Jessica hit a sudden tangent. 'This is weird isn't it?' she said, with a rush of girlish excitement. 'You and me sitting here, talking together? You know, I honestly never thought we'd be here again.'

'So why are we?' asked Harry, a little frustrated now. 'Why did you get in touch with the bitter old hack?'

Her face froze over and became more serious again. 'There was this one article you wrote, about a player who you didn't like.'

'Billy Regan.'

'Maybe. You were talking about what a state the game was in and all that – the usual stuff. But then, suddenly, you changed your line. You started talking about this thing you'd seen – a young man scoring a goal in the park – and how it was so beautiful, so affecting; how it had restored your faith in the game. That article, Harry, it was like ambrosia. You wrote with such affection; such grace. And then I knew you weren't the burnt out hack after all – you just couldn't be if you wrote those words. So that's when I decided to write to you. It took me a few months, but, well, here we are.'

'Yes. Here we are.'

England were playing that night. For the first time in forty years, Harry didn't watch. What's more, he didn't even remember that he was missing it. England beat Iceland by a single Paul Kerridge goal to nil, and put themselves second in their World Cup qualifying group in the process. But, after turning a coffee into a drink into a meal into a drink into a long walk to the taxi rank, Harry was too content even to bother finding out the result until the morning.

Six weeks after making his offer, John received the keys to his new house, signifying his rise not only to the top end of the earnings scale, but also to the top of Ariel Hill. From his new garden, in which he now stood with his proud family, he could see the estate – a faint grey mass in the distance.

'Can you see our block?' asked Marilyn, peering through her glasses.

'I think so, Mum,' replied John, who'd been quite hyperactive since completing the first major purchase of his life. He put an arm round her shoulder, and directed her gaze to a particularly prominent dirt-coloured eyesore. 'That's it there.'

'I'll miss that place,' she said.

'Will you?' asked Becky disbelievingly. 'You'll miss a graffiti-soaked hole where they spit at your feet and swear through your letterbox?'

'Well, no, not really to be honest. But I just can't believe we're here. I don't want to say anything too nasty about that old flat, in case I wake up and we're still there after all.'

John smiled and hugged her. 'It's OK Mum. It's not a dream. This is really your house now. Things are different.'

Marilyn turned to him with tears in her eyes. 'I thank God for you every morning you know John. I always knew you were special, even when you were a boy.'

John was suddenly bashful. 'Mum. . . .'

'And don't think I'm saying this because of what's happened now. I'm not. I've always thought it – so has your sister. The way you've always cared for us, put us first. . . . Being on that estate showed me a side of life that I didn't much like, but seeing all those out-of-control kids never made me sad, even when they did swear through my letterbox. Do you know why? Because every time I saw how normal children behaved, it just reminded me what a special young man you were. Even despite everything that you'd had to go through – losing your dad, moving in to that estate – you were still always just that good lad you'd always been. That's why I'm proud of you; that's why I'm saying you're special. What's happened now is just the Lord's way of rewarding you.

'I've lost a lot in my life – my husband, my house, my possessions. But there's one thing I've always held on to – the Lord let me keep the most precious things of all: you two. And I honestly don't know what I'd ever do if I lost you as well.'

'That won't happen Mum.' Becky reassured her. 'I reckon we're the closest family in the world.'

'Yes Becky,' said Marilyn, suddenly solemn. 'But you never know what's waiting around the corner, do you?'

Waiting around the corner for John was a return to training, a glut of potential sponsorship deals and a much-improved squad number – 9. The end of a two-month break saw the squad come back together with revised perceptions of him. Last season it had been hard for them not to view him as number 47, the raw fringe player brought in from the non-league in the last months of the season. Now time had moved on – the Mile End jigsaw had been broken up and reassembled – and it was easier for them all to see him afresh. The negative preconceptions had diminished through time and experience. This year he would be number 9: the first-choice attacker who went into the new season with a track record of a goal a game.

While the rest of the squad had spent their summers on Caribbean beaches or in Balearic nightclubs, John had decided against such a break from exercise. The club's training complex had virtually shut down since mid-May, but of course, no such restrictions had been placed on John's favoured practise pitch. He had returned, on every day of the break bar none, to the corner of Ariel Hill Recreation Ground, where he had kicked a ball around – sometimes alone, sometimes with the local homeless, and sometimes even with Harry. As a result, he lost none of his considerable fitness over the summer, and returned to dominate the first week of training like a giant among Lilliputian men.

They trained hard all week, subjected by the fitness staff to lung-bursting runs of 5 miles and more, put through endless drills and punished with never-ending press-ups and ab-crunches. By Friday even John, who'd bled and choked considerably less than his peers, had well earned his weekend. When he came to sit down in the training ground locker room, after the week's last torture session had finally reached a merciful end, he did so with a great sigh of relief, and to an ensemble of encouraging words from all around him.

'Well done today,' said Carl Barton, who last season had spoken to John only twice. 'You looked really sharp out there. You have done all week.'

'Thanks very much,' replied John, a wave of acceptance surging through his body.

Carl sidled closer to him, and lowered his voice. 'You ran yourself into the ground. By my reckoning you earned the right to let your hair down a bit this weekend. Listen, one of the England boys is having a big bash up in Essex tomorrow. I'm going up there – thought you might want to come with me. I'd ask some of the other lads, but you know, they only want the real class acts there.'

'I don't really understand what you mean Carl. Are you talking about a party?'

'Yeah. Big thing. Lots of pop stars and celebrity chefs and stuff. Strictly no press.'

John thought for a moment. Then he said, 'I'm sorry Carl, I don't think I can go. I'm supposed to be redecorating my new house this weekend.'

Carl looked hurt. 'Oh. Well then, I suppose I'll have to go all the way up there on my own. But it is quite a long way, and I don't really want to arrive on my own. Maybe I won't bother going then.'

Again, John thought. He could see how badly Carl wanted to go, and felt sorry for him. 'I guess I could go, as long as we didn't stay too late. It might be fun meeting some pop stars.'

'Really John – do you mean we can go after all?'

'Why not. As long as we can leave at around eleven.'

'You have my solemn word of honour.'

'Great. Pick me up tomorrow evening then?'

'You can count on it matey. See you about seven.'

John beamed as he picked up his bag and headed for the door, glad to have so obviously made Carl's day. He was sure his mum and Becky would understand if he took a little break from the decorating. Now his only problem would be finding something to wear to the party. He'd ask Becky, he thought. She'd know about that sort of thing.

Carl watched John leave, then strode into the showers with a wide grin across his face.

'All sorted boys,' he shouted through the steam. 'I'm taking mister no-sex-no-drink-no-naughty-words up to Paul Kerridge's party tomorrow night. If that don't make a man out of him, nothing will.'

Sixteen

Paul Kerridge's home wasn't quite a palace, but calling it a house was certainly not sufficient. Four storeys high, set in acres of private land, and fenced off from the outside world by the sorts of fortifications normally reserved for keeping people in rather than out, it was a lavish and envy-inducing property – the sort that every city banker aspires to buy and every estate agent would give his right arm to sell. Towering redbrick walls gave the place a stately air; a renaissance-inspired fountain in the centre of the vast gravel driveway hinted towards the artistic; a fleet of security guards in black suits and sci-fi movie earpieces demonstrated its exclusivity.

Carl Barton's Litalia – no lesser car would have even made it through the gates – was attended on arrival by a gushing valet, desperate to park it and usher them inside. As he stepped out into the courtyard, in a slightly cardboard tuxedo hired from The High Street Suit Co., the desperate flashes of paparazzi cameras, pinned helplessly behind the distant front gates, caught John's eye. He felt like he was arriving at an awards ceremony.

In fact, he was arriving at a party for only the most elite of Premier Division footballers. As he trotted up the red-carpeted steps of the mansion, he noticed Hugo Veiga, the Moss Side player, complete with famous model on his arm, just inside the door. As Carl Barton handed over their gold-leafed invitations, his vision was distracted by the sight of a dinner-jacketed Pretedinhio –

London City's Brazilian, who'd recently been voted Premier Division player of the season – quaffing canapés while decked out in his official international cummerbund. There were no labouring cart-horses, or lower division journeymen here – every player who passed by was a genuine, bona fide, superstar. These were the players whose names sold the shirts in their club shops. These were the *crème de la crème*.

But it wasn't just footballers. Emerging from the next deluxe sports car along after Carl's was the current darling of the music world, Dina McGee – at number one for three weeks already, according to the heavy-nudging Carl, and a cert to remain there for at least a fourth. And inside – once Carl and John had finally negotiated the stringent security process – the former announced that, in the corner, a film director was stood chatting to a famous lingerie model, the two of them leaning on a statue of distinctly antique appearance. Had he been a reader of celebrity-spotting journals (like his sister), or motivated by a need to feel like he'd arrived in the world (like most of his team-mates), John would have been in heaven here. Instead, he just felt dizzy and out of place. Almost immediately, overcome by his awkwardness, he tried to find somewhere to take a seat. But Carl wouldn't allow him to – grabbing his elbow and hauling him back up even as he was stooping towards a bench in Kerridge's magnificent hallway.

'Come on Johnny-boy,' he rasped. 'Let's get ourselves a drink.'

They body-swerved their way through twenty people – every one of them at least on the B-list – and arrived in the drinks room, a vast space with crane-high ceilings and a gigantic and heavily-staffed bar. Every spirit known to humankind was encased within it, and thirty times over; twelve wines were only a cellar away. The beer – four varieties of it – was flowing like a natural spring into a production line of thirsty glasses.

'Lager,' shouted Carl to a waiting barman. 'No – two lagers. I don't want to have to come back. What about you John?'

'Orange juice please,' said John gently.

Carl looked horrified, leant over the bar, and mouthed 'with a double vodka' to the barman, who nodded obligingly. The drinks were produced and handed over. John took a sip, looked puzzled at the glass and said nothing. Carl smiled – one little victory ticked off – and put a shepherding hand in his team-mate's back.

'Come on,' he said, slipping a wedding ring off his finger and into his pocket. 'Let's go check out the talent.'

'The talent?' repeated John, unsure.

'The birds. The ladies. You know.'

'Oh, right. But I thought you were married,' said John straight-facedly, but unable to hide his disgust.

'Keep it down mate – *they* don't know that,' he said, before swigging deeply from one of his plastic pint glasses, tossing the empty back in the direction of the bar, and increasing the pressure in John's back. He skipped alongside him, and moved towards the rear doors. 'Anyhow,' he laughed, after an awkward pause, 'you told me you haven't even got a girlfriend. We can't have you crying yourself to sleep at night alone – you're one of the big boys now.'

John had no time to catch breath and protest – for he was whisked through a set of double doors and into the sprawling garden, in which a temporarily-erected miniature fun fair caught him by surprise. Out here there were at least another fifty people – all of them recognisable to any *Mouthpiece* reader – dallying on the Dodgems or sprawling their cliques and entourages across an array of ornate tables and chairs. The Dodgems looked attractive to John, but again, Carl had other ideas.

'Look!' he said. 'It's Paul Kerridge. We'd better go over and thank him for the invite.'

John half-smiled but agreed, and the two of them strolled across to where the skinny England winger was holding court. A small crowd parted slightly to allow them in, and the conversation paused to allow for introduction.

'Paul,' said Carl, a little over-enthusiastically. 'Really appreciated the invite. This is John – the lad I was telling you about when we were on England duty. You remember don't you?' He gave a sinister wink at that point, but John was too busy looking bashfully downwards to spot it.

'Yeah, course ah do,' said Kerridge, in the guttered manner of speaking for which he was infamous. 'A goal ev'ry game wernit? Good lad. We like 'ot shots like you.'

John did his best to look both flattered and humble, while the gang of attractive girls around him laughed and made eyes in his direction.

'How many of the other England boys are here Paul?' asked Carl, stepping away from John and leaving him flanked on both sides by glamour models.

'Clinton, Ben, Webbo, Si Brazier. Er, the goalie's 'ere somewhere, but he keeps goin' on the Dodgems. Oh, an' Regan's 'ere.'

Carl smiled and looked him in the eye. 'Bathroom?'

'Frequently.'

They both smiled knowingly. On the other side of the circle, John was becoming unsettled. A girl who he'd never met, with bleached hair and collagen-pumped lips, was stroking his arm and grinning at him. He really didn't know what to say to her.

'I like footballers,' she said, licking her artificial lips at him, and edging closer. 'Especially strikers. I just love strikers. When you boys score a goal, it just drives me wild.'

She was enunciating excessively, and John didn't like it. He didn't like her forcefulness either, as he found himself backing into a walled corner, nor did he much like her plastic-enhanced features. He tried to spin away from her, but was thrown by the realisation that Carl and Paul had disappeared. Eventually, her close-proximity cigarette breath suffocated him. He slid down the wall; out of her grasp, and without a backward glance sped back towards the double doors.

Back inside, he scrambled around the downstairs rooms, desperately searching for Carl. But he didn't want to be found. He wasn't in the drinks room, the sprawling lounge, the kitchen or the celeb-heaving dining room. Music was beginning to pour from a DJ's sound system, and the lights all dimmed in unison. Now it would be even harder to find him. In desperation, John even knocked on the door of the downstairs bathroom.

'Carl?' he called. 'You in there?'

The door creaked ajar, and a pair of unfocused eyes gazed crazily through the gap. Below them was an uneven grin, zigzagging across a half-open mouth.

'Whatyouwant?' asked Billy Regan, far too fast, his eyes everywhere but straight ahead.

'Er . . . I'm sorry,' said John edgily. 'I was looking for my friend Carl.'

'Charles?'

'No, Carl. Carl Barton.'

'Ohyeah. PlaysforEnglandsometimes? Notinthebig gamesthough.'

'Anyway,' said John, suffering now from a steady accumulation of unnerving experiences, 'he's obviously not in there, so I'll leave you alone, sorry.'

'IplayforEnglandtooyouknow. DoyouplayforEngland? No . . . youdon'tplayforEngland.' Without warning, Regan retreated again and slammed the door shut. John's head spun even more.

As he drifted – lost now in frightened thought – through the giant hallways of the mansion, girls tried to catch his eye and television presenters tried to grab his hand. But, with a modicum of politeness, he shrugged them all aside, and found himself a quiet spot at the foot of a minor staircase. This place, with its synthetic women, and its kooky-eyed bathroom inhabitants, was too much for him. The music – although it had not been pulsing through his head for long – was already making him ache. Coming here had definitely been a mistake. Gone by eleven, had been Carl Barton's promise. John prayed silently that he'd keep it.

He looked at the plastic glass in his hand, still untouched since his first sip. He ran his nose around the rim, and the alcoholic scent proved his initial guess correct. With a flick of the wrist, the contents were deposited into a nearby plant pot, which instantaneously appeared to wither.

The party went on around him. Occasionally another guest – bored or curious or both – would aim a nudge or a nod in his direction. After an hour, during which the music got more oppressive and the other guests got a lot more drunk, he was disturbed by a member of waiting staff, who seemed concerned that he was not having the prescribed amount of fun.

'Would you like a drink, sir?' asked the girl, a prettyish raven-haired mouse who looked as uncomfortable in her smart attire as John did in his. 'Perhaps some champagne?'

'No thanks,' said John wearily, without looking up. 'I'm just waiting to leave.'

'Oh. Right you are then sir. . . .' She didn't hide her surprise – this was the first person all evening to turn down an offer of a drink from her – but after a moment's pause she scuttled back out of sight, resuming her position down the hall as an imitation statue hors-d'œuvre dispenser.

But a minute later she had tiptoed back again, and peered from behind the vodka-and-orange saturated pot plant at the morose figure slumped on the stairwell. She didn't recognise him, so presumed that he must be either the boyfriend of another more famous guest, or else involved in football, about which her knowledge was microscopic (she had no idea, for instance, that the vomit which she had just cleared up in the downstairs bathroom had been ejected from the stomach of the England no. 9).

John looked up at a clock on the wall and exhaled deeply. It was still only 9.30. As his gaze returned downward, he caught sight of his observer.

'Hello?' he called quietly.

Embarrassed, she side-stepped into his view, her face turning poker-hot. 'Hello again,' was all she managed.

'Oh – you're the drink lady aren't you?'

The drink lady nodded.

'I'm still not thirsty I'm afraid. That plant could probably do with some clean water though.'

She managed the first formations of a delicate smile. 'Are you a footballer?' she blurted, all of a sudden, and every word at once. Her expression relaxed a little more again, revealing a touch more of her beauty.

'Yes. Only a baby one though.'

'What team do you play for?'

'Mile End, in London.'

'I've heard of them. You'll have to excuse me though, I don't know too much about football. I can't really hold a conversation about it, to be honest. Hmm. So, you don't like parties like this then? They're not my sort of thing either, but–' She paused. John was staring at her. 'Is something wrong? I shouldn't even be talking to you should I? I'm so sorry, I forgot myself.'

Instantly he realised what he'd done. 'No! Not at all. Sorry – it's just that . . . .'

They were disturbed by a meandering and heavily inebriated Carl, who appeared around the corner with a young woman under each arm. 'Johnny-boy – there you are, at last!' he called. 'I've brought your girlfriend back.'

The plastic-pouting blonde from outside blew a kiss in John's direction. Once again, she didn't speak, but just slid her hand down her side and attempted to look alluring. In fact, to John, she looked positively repellent.

'Carl – she's not my *girlfriend*. I don't even know her. Please, I was just talking to–'

'Yourself?' sniggered Carl. The waitress had vanished.

Having finally located Carl – who was now snoring on the same disused stairwell on which John had been sat waiting for him – a suddenly-rejuvenated John was now involved in another manhunt. Though they'd met and spoken for barely a moment, that nameless girl's face had sparked off a chemical reaction within him that he'd never experienced before. Thanks to his 'friend', he'd not even had a chance to learn her name. But he was adamant that this evening would not be a total write-off. He would find the girl, and learn her name, and see if the chemicals went off again when he did.

It took him an hour, by which time he had also realised that Carl Barton would be in no fit state to drive them home at 11, but he finally located her, cleaning imaginary dust in a sparkling upstairs bathroom. Even when he called to her, with a non-threatening 'hey', she was too self-conscious to acknowledge him. He had to move forward until he was actually overshadowing her before she stopped scrubbing the shiny taps.

'I'm very sorry about before,' she said, checking the sinkhole again. 'I shouldn't have been chatting to you – I interrupted your evening.'

'What are you talking about? That was the *highlight* of my evening. I was so bored that just before you came along I spent five minutes counting my teeth with my tongue.'

She giggled, and looked at him. She realised he was smiling, and so she smiled too. It was then that the chemical reaction hit John again. He almost slipped as the rush hit him, and put an arm against the wall to support himself. She was beautiful to him.

'I'm Elaine,' she said, offering her hand.

'Pleased to meet you,' he said, shaking it. 'I'm John. This bathroom's probably clean enough now, you know.'

'Yes, you could be right there,' she agreed, running her hand through her short dyed-black hair. His knees went weak again as she did that, and his pupils dilated. She noticed.

'I'm finished now,' she said, looking at her watch. 'They only hired the help until 11, when they thought everyone'd be too drunk to notice if we were still there or not. So I can leave now. Do you want to walk with me to the gate?'

'Yes,' said John. 'I'd like that.'

They went downstairs together, retrieved a rucksack and some more comfortable shoes which she'd hidden behind the bar, and made for the door. As he tried to follow her outside, however, his path was blocked. Carl, who had managed to stagger back to his feet and arm himself with another lager, had seen them together, and was incredulous. 'Oi – Johnny Boy – what d'ya think you're doing? She's a flippin' spotty silver service girl. I line you up with a right tasty sort – and you end up with that.'

That upset John. He looked away, composed himself, and tried a gracious reply. 'Carl, you're out of order. It's not nice to talk about women like that.'

Carl laughed, in the grating, prolonged way that's reserved for the very drunk. 'All the boys said you was weird John, but I reckoned you'd be alright once you had a couple of drinks inside you. But they was right – you are weird. She's ugly as, mate, and you ain't even been drinking.'

John snapped. He thrust both hands into Carl's chest, and catching him both off-guard and off-balance, sent him sprawling to the floor. He didn't bother to see if he was alright. Instead, he strode outside to join Elaine, who'd been oblivious to the commotion.

They reached the gate after a long, meandering walk that came close to covering the longest possible distance between two points. Along the way she'd been astounded by the story of his incredible year – assistant electrician to Premier Division football star in only a few months – and shed a tear as he'd told her about Becky's accident. He'd learned that her background shared similarities with his: the broken family, the council home; the general happiness in spite of it all. He'd also discovered that she liked clouds, warm bread and children. They got on well.

When comfortable silences punctuated their rambling conversations, John took a good look at her. The glittering moonlight showed him how pretty she was. Carl's junk-food idea of beauty had clouded his judgement. He'd been very wrong – Elaine wasn't 'ugly as'. She wasn't even spotty. True, her make-up wasn't the most expensive, but at least that was the face she was born with.

The security men on the gate called to John, asking if he wanted them to open it. He raised his hand to indicate for them to wait. He turned back to her. Even though it was the middle of summer, he noticed that she was trembling. But she wasn't cold.

'It was really nice to meet you tonight,' she said.

'Yes,' he replied, his heartbeat beginning to quicken with uncertainty. 'It really was.'

She looked at her watch. 'My dad's picking me up,' she said. 'He should be here in a minute.'

'OK then.'

'Hmm.'

'Er . . . Elaine?' he stuttered.

'Yes?'

'Do you think you might like to go out sometime? Maybe for a meal or something?'

Her eyes widened. 'I'd love that.' She rooted around in her bag and produced a pen and paper. She scribbled. 'Look, here's my number. You could give me a call.'

'OK then.'

'OK.'

They both looked at each other, then away, then back, then at the ground. Neither really knew what they were doing. He patted her softly on the arm. She returned the favour.

A car horn disturbed their clumsy flirtation. It was Elaine's father.

'Well, I guess I'll have to go then,' she said, pirouetting back and forth on the tips of her toes. 'Give me a call.' She waved to the car.

'I will. I really will,' he said. He really intended to.

Then she got really brave. She checked over her shoulder, and saw that her father was busy spinning the car around. 'You know,' she whispered, 'you could give me a kiss goodbye.'

He said nothing. He simply swallowed, then wrapped his arms gently around her. They both closed their eyes, and their lips met, only for a few moments. Then they stepped away, and took one last lingering look at each other. Both of their faces were illuminated like a Las Vegas casino. The horn went again. The gate swung open, and Elaine disappeared into the night.

John stood still for a few moments to catch his breath. Then he walked back along the same abstract route they'd followed from the house, and tried in his mind to process what had just happened. But then the chemicals took over, and suddenly he was dancing like a madman in the middle of the grass.

And it felt better than scoring a goal.

Seventeen

The new season started with a flourish, and so did John Christie. In ten Premier Division games on August's opening weekend, an above-average 39 goals were scored, and in one, a 4–3 win by Mile End over Suffolk County, three came from John's boot. It was his first hat trick, and the first time he got to keep the match ball. He didn't have to wait a long time for a repeat though – in the very next game, a 3–2 victory on the Isle of Wight, he was again responsible for all of his team's goals. And with Harry, Becky, Marilyn and now Elaine often cheering him on from the stands, he endured a quite remarkable month. At the end of August, after five games, Mile End were top of the league for the first time in forty-three years. John Christie had twelve goals.

The newspapers, which had all but ignored him over the summer, came racing after him again. Now, instead of dreaming up scandals or inventing things for him to say, they were more interested in applauding him. 'This guy is no one-season wonder,' said the *Spark*. 'He came from nowhere, but he's certainly showing no signs of going back,' agreed the *Morning News*. For now, they were more interested in the miracles he was performing on the pitch than investigating any possible indiscretions he was involved in off it. His number one fan, in his *Daily Reporter* column, noted that Christie's form had made for 'the most exciting start to the season in recent memory . . . Mile End aren't good enough to be on top of the pile, but no one is able to stop their star striker. When teams score two or three goals at home, they expect to win; they don't account for players like Christie. If they score one, he scores two. If they score two, he scores three. At the moment, it seems that the man doesn't actually know how to miss.'

According to the *Football Stats Centre* on TV channel Sport One, Foster's last comment was almost entirely accurate. In his five games this season, of which Mile End had won all five, he'd had 38 shots. Incredibly, 36 of them had at least been on target, either forcing the goalkeeper into a save or else – in one of every three instances – finding the back of the net. For the record, he'd also been responsible for 148 successful passes out of 162, and 42 clean tackles out of 48 attempts. He'd not received a yellow or red card – in that month or in his career to date – and he'd never been accused of diving, time-wasting, play-acting or even so much as a stray word. As Rick Palmer, host of Channel One's *The Big Match* said to close the show one night, 'he isn't just playing the beautiful game – he is the beautiful game.'

Which led, in early September, to the first mention of a slogan, which across the course of the month avalanched into a full-scale media campaign: 'Christie for England'. Harry Foster, surprisingly, wasn't the man to coin it – that honour belonged to Troy Wilson in the *Mouthpiece*, who got the graphics department at his newspaper to create a cut-out-and-wear badge for the bottom of his weekly column. 'Regan and McLean are top class attackers, who rank up there with some of the best in the world,' he wrote, 'but John Christie is something else. This boy is dynamite – let's give him a chance to explode on the national stage, starting against Portugal. Otherwise, we may not even have the option of seeing him do it at the World Cup. Come on Mr Hardcastle [England's constantly under-fire manager] –

it's got to be Christie for England.' Those words first appeared on 3rd September. Two days later, they'd been repeated in some form or other in at least twenty other media.

During the next month, John, unaffected by the growing interest in his rapidly rising stock, kept focusing on the pitch and picked up exactly where he had left off. Four goals in his next two games cemented Mile End's place at the top of the league – a full three points ahead of the almost-unbeatable London City. His team-mates were beginning to pass to him at every opportunity; the club shop was running out of '9' transfers; the crowd had already developed a whole album-worth of chants and songs about him.

And then things got really big.

One Sunday afternoon in mid-September, John was relaxing at home with his family. The telephone, which was often unplugged to provide respite from an onslaught of journalists and well-wishing fans, rang loudly, disturbing the board-game that they had all been immersed in. Becky, who'd left her chemist job to become her brother's PA, answered it efficiently. It was Greg Hardcastle, the England manager, for John.

As Becky relayed this fact across the living room, John's stomach flipped over inside him. England now? Could this roller-coaster climb any faster?

'This is John Christie,' he said, clasping the phone tightly so that it didn't slip as he shuddered.

'Hi John, Greg Hardcastle. How are you?'

'Oh, great, just chilling out after the game yesterday.'

'Ah yes, a very fine performance I thought.'

John began to realise where this might be heading. 'Were you there then?'

'Yes, saw your goals. Very impressive, particularly the second. You're having a great season young man. I do hope you intend to carry on like this?'

'I'll certainly try – of course, it's mostly down to the rest of the team,' he offered magnanimously.

There was a booming laugh on the other end of the phone. 'Come on John, let's be serious. The rest of that squad is barely Premier Division standard, barring maybe Barton and the goalkeeper. You're virtually carrying the team on your own.'

'Well, that's your opinion, sir.'

'Anyhow, the reason I'm calling is this: I'm sure you know we've got two important games coming up at the end of the month – World Cup qualifiers against Portugal and Tajikistan.'

'Yes,' said John his heart racing and his grin broadening.

'I'm just calling round the players now to tell them that they're in the squad.'

'Right.' John's non-phone-holding hand was flapping freely as if trying to swat a fly.

'I wanted to talk to you first though . . . because I've decided not to pick you.'

'Oh thank you sir,' gushed John, 'I can't believe it! I . . . . Oh, right, I see.' His face turned the purple side of red as he realised what Hardcastle had actually said.

Hardcastle was equally embarrassed. 'Look,' he explained, 'you've been in excellent form, and the reason I'm calling is because I truly see you as an England player in the future. But it's all happened so quickly for you, and I think it'll probably be better for you in the long run if you don't take another step up just yet. Concentrate on establishing yourself, maybe for a couple of seasons. Then you'll be able to make the transition to international football. But I wanted to say well done so far, let you know that we're keeping an eye on you, and that we rate you very highly here.'

'Thank you sir,' said John, annoyed that he'd allowed his pride to swell, and hence had fallen over it.

'We've got a training camp in January for the squad. Maybe you could come and join up with us there?'

'Yes sir, that'd be great sir.'

'Good to speak with you John. Goodbye.'

'Goodbye sir.'

John wobbled as he walked back across the room, where his mother and sister were hugging tightly, awaiting the chance to burst into celebration at another milestone passed.

'What did he want John?' asked Becky. 'Are you in the England squad?'

'I'm an idiot,' moped her brother, looking close to tears. 'I've let myself get too confident. I'd even thought to myself, after Harry told me about that stuff in the papers, that I might be in the squad. What right have I got to go thinking that? I've been given so much in the last year, and still I start to want more.'

'So . . . is that a no then?' Marilyn pried.

'He just wanted to tell me that he thought I was playing well – that was all. I'm not in the squad. And why on earth should I be?'

'Because you're the top scorer in the country?' Becky argued firmly. 'Because you've been playing brilliantly?'

'It's human nature, isn't it?' said John, mostly to himself. 'It always gets the better of you. Well I'm not going to let it. I'm not going to forget how much I've been given. I'm not going to lose sight of where I've come from. Please Mum, Becky – don't let me become like the rest of them.'

'I don't think there's much chance of that, son,' said Marilyn, throwing her arms around him and sobbing soft tears of pride. 'I don't think there's much chance of that.'

The following Wednesday, the biggest game of John's career so far had arrived. A repeat of the final fixture of the previous season, it saw his team travel to the massive City Stadium, to face a team that currently held both the league trophy and the European Cup. Once again, their starting line-up would include eleven pure-bred internationals; once again, despite being league leaders, Mile End would go into the match as second favourites to win. Because quite simply, no one ever won here.

John went into the game with something to prove to himself. In spite of all the adulation, which even he could not ignore entirely, he was determined that his ego would not be allowed to spiral out of control. The Lord had given him all this, he thought, and the Lord could take it away again. If he abused it, he was sure that it was likely to disappear as quickly as it had arrived. He resolved to ensure that John Christie the footballer would always behave just as John Christie the electrician had done. It was the only way *to* behave.

With that in mind, he made sure before the game that he shook hands with every player in the opposition's ranks. He even tried to make conversation with some of them – although without an interpreter present, this was tricky in some cases. He already had their hard-earned respect after his performance in the May game; after this, London City's players not only said of him 'good player', but also, if their language skills stretched that far, 'nice bloke'.

But it was the former quality which came to the fore during the ninety minutes. After just eight minutes, Mile

End had silenced the masses, and John's goal tally had progressed to seventeen – an unprecedented average of more than two goals per game. With Frank Crumb having chosen a more adventurous formation this time round, John had attacking company in the shape of Carl Barton, who, despite loathing him off the pitch, maintained a grudging respect for him on it. Carl picked up the ball in the left wing position, beat City's Italian full-back, and swirled in a perfect cross which found John in space. Instead of going for the more obvious header, John leapt up and met the ball in mid-air with what looked like a kung-fu kick, and which thrillingly despatched the ball straight into the corner. It was so good in fact, that Carl even shook John's hand – although he didn't stretch to looking at him while he did it.

It remained 1–0 for over an hour, and then the defining moment of the game, and possibly the season, arrived so unexpectedly that the next morning it made the front pages as well as the back. After breaking up a City attack, Helmut Mahel lashed a long ball in the direction of John, who was standing a little inside his own half, marked only by D'Alex Smith. Feigning to trap it, he instead allowed it to run beyond him, meaning that it was now a straight race to goal between the defender and him. John was one of the paciest attackers in the league, but even so as he advanced, D'Alex met him stride for stride. That was until suddenly, painfully, the defender stopped, shrieked and crumpled to the floor. Something in his left leg had given way, and he was out of the race. Now it was just John on the goalkeeper, and the other twenty players mere interested spectators.

John kept going, but the scream that left D'Alex's lips as he fell was audible even above the desperate cries of the crowd. Realising that he was now alone, John took a second to look back over his shoulder, and saw the player on the ground a little way behind him. Instinctively, he stopped.

The 2,000 travelling supporters screamed for him to continue towards goal. Frank Crumb screamed in terms unsuitable for the family enclosure which his bench was situated beneath. Carl Barton covered his face with his hands. John looked back at the goal, in which the frightened 'keeper had frozen, then at D'Alex, whose face was a picture of agony. Then, very deliberately, he launched the ball high into the stand behind the goal. It was certainly not a shot (the *Football Stats Centre* didn't hold it against him the following day).

Every Mile End heart sank. Their golden boy had just squandered their best chance of ensuring an impossible victory. Had he missed, or forced the goalkeeper into a fantastic save, they could have forgiven him. But this – what was this? Didn't he know that this was *professional* football?

Those hearts, however, only amounted to a tiny percentage of the total in the ground. To salute this incredible, unexpected, unmatched show of good sportsmanship, every London City fan in the ground, and every one of their players, stood and applauded. That morning, John had set out to show the world, and prove to himself, that he was still the good man who he'd always tried to be. By late that afternoon, he'd achieved his aim.

From that point on, John's every touch of the ball was cheered – by the opposition supporters. That show of admiration even extended to the final minute when John, almost unthinkably, scored again, this time with his head. It remained 2–0 until the final whistle, when, despite suffering their first home defeat in recent memory, John was ushered from the pitch by another standing ovation.

The flurry of reporters, TV cameras and radio microphones which overwhelmed him as he entered the players' tunnel kept him from the changing room for over an hour. When he finally made it there, he was immediately met by the solemn figure of Frank Crumb, who prodded him hard in the chest.

'I don't know what on earth you thought you were doing out there today,' he snarled, 'but that little stunt could have cost us a lot.'

John was shocked. 'I . . . I . . . .'

'Fortunately,' Crumb's face melted almost instantaneously into a vivid smile, 'you're also a little genius, and you just scored two goals against London City. Who we beat. At home. So you've very nearly inflicted two heart attacks on me this afternoon.'

'Right. Er, sorry about that.'

Crumb laughed loudly, patted him on the arm and went off to plan his celebrations. Just as he reached the door, he spun briefly on his heels, and looked back at his walking *cause célèbre* with warmth in his eyes.

'You do realise what you did will be everywhere tomorrow?'

'Really? But all I did was kick the ball out for an injury.'

'I think you'd better call your agent, son' said Crumb, before setting off to find his chairman and punching the air.

Just as Crumb had predicted, John's act of sportsmanship became massive news. For a game dominated by constant accusations of greed, corruption and ill behaviour, this was a massive shot in the arm, and the journalists responsible for reporting on its many foibles were more than happy to write about something positive for a change. Some, like the team at the *Spark*, seemed to lack the mental capacity to understand why he'd done it. 'The inexperienced Christie seemed to misunderstand the precedent to carry on in this type of situation' they foolishly claimed. Others, such as Ade Akintola in the highbrow *Business Daily*, found a deeper comprehension of the act. Akintola called Christie 'a throwback to the gentlemen footballers of yesteryear, an all but forgotten breed in the cynical modern game.' The *Reporter* – who had rightly determined Harry Foster's role as makeshift agent to John a conflict of interest – were similarly positive. Alex Knight, writing a rare sports editorial, called it 'a moment to savour, the like of which we're unlikely to see until . . . well, the next time John Christie steps out on a football pitch.'

Not having to write up the match was something of a blessing to Harry, who's hands were well-filled by a plethora of requests from his media colleagues, all of whom craved access to his 'client'. By now John was a lot more media savvy, and gamely worked through the list. That weekend, he was the most interviewed footballer – and possibly individual – in Britain, and was able to share a little of his world-view with men and women who usually made a career out of dark cynicism. A range of nickname phrases began to spring up for him, although it was unclear which would remain permanent. That he was described as an 'angel,' a 'gentleman' and a 'true role model', all on the same day, was some tribute to the power of his simple act of honour.

It took just one more week of incident to see public interest in John Christie reach critical mass. Already he was the mysterious 'Messiah of Mile End' – already he had eighteen goals to his name for a season less than two months old. But true, enduring superstars are not born overnight, and while the sports pages were full of references to John (including an entirely fictional story that Club de Paris were lining up a £10 million bid for him), the wider media remained interested, but not obsessed. On form, he might have been every bit the equal of a Billy Regan, but in the world of celebrity, he was some way behind him. For the moment at least, his shaggy hair and soft tones had not yet caught on.

Exactly a week after the London City versus Mile End game, England played host to Portugal in a game billed as a World Cup qualifying group decider. In a group out of which only the winners escaped automatically, with the second placed team going to a two-leg play off, Portugal were top, just as they had been since the first game. England, after their recent recovery, had managed to claw their way back into second place, and only two points behind the leaders. A win in this match would see England leap-frog their opponents at the last minute, with only a game against the minnows of Tajikistan left between them and automatic qualification.

In Monday's *Foster's Eye*, Harry, who'd been barred from even mentioning John's name in print, predicted a Portugal victory. His rivals were split on the issue – some had allowed their patriotism to overwhelm their football knowledge; others had faced the fact that Portugal, and their superstar striker Hugo Veiga (also of Moss Side), were by far the better team. All acknowledged, however, throughout three days of heavy hype and build up, that this was the biggest test of an England side for years, and that everyone would be watching.

As expected, Portugal were awesome. Hugo Veiga, free from the expected shackles of the injured D'Alex Smith, ran the game as if everyone else was moving in slow motion. The patched-up England defence did their very best to repel his repeated and varied attacks, but even they knew that it was only a matter of time before

Veiga found a way through them. What they did not expect – and neither did an incredulous Veiga – was that their team would score first, but that's exactly what happened. Paul Kerridge burst up the right-hand side of the pitch, spotted Billy Regan (his eyes now refocused), and picked him out with a cross. Regan leapt as if leaving a trampoline, and his head met the ball a millisecond before the flailing punch of the desperate goalkeeper could reach it. Goal – 1–0 to England.

Portugal bit back like an angry tiger. As half-time hovered into view, they looked likely to score at any moment. But somehow, through a combination of whole-team defending and the marvellous form of Lloyd McGrath in goal, England made it to the whistle unscathed.

The final forty-five minutes followed a similar pattern to the first – relentless Portuguese attacking; an abundance of continental skill, but little penetration. When the referee blew his whistle to end the match, the visiting players, and their tiny band of supporters, could not quite believe what had happened. When a team has 75 per cent of the possession and 90 per cent of the shots, it's unus- ual to see them lose. And yet that was exactly what had happened here – Portugal had suffered from a smash and grab that seemed so unfair that it should have been against the rules. England *were* going to the World Cup. 'Christie for England' would go back on ice for a while.

That was Wednesday. The next morning's papers eulogised over what little they could – praising England's 'fighting spirit' and 'sterling defensive work', but no one was under any illusions. There was simply no way that victory had been deserved. Opinion on whether that mattered or not was divided (except back in Portugal) but, England were going to the World Cup (barring a slip against the part-timers from Eastern Europe). Once victory was confirmed on Saturday night, in the little-visited city of Dushanbe, the celebrations could truly begin.

Harry and John watched the game in Tajikistan together, in the comfort of the former's front room. They, like the England players and the rest of the country, were looking forward to a straightforward performance. In the home leg, only the incompetence of the England forwards had kept the result at a respectable 3–0 – had they been firing on even half of their cylinders it could easily have scored ten. On that evening, Tajikistan's own attack had been as blunt as infant-school scissors, and nowhere near as colourful. Tonight, exactly the same was true. The two forwards looked like they'd have trouble getting in the Ariel Hill side, let alone passing for internationals. If Lloyd McGrath had dropped the ball on his own penalty spot, then walked off the pitch with the rest of his defence and sat down for a cigarette, it was still unlikely that either of these two could have scored.

Of course, keeping the opposition out was only half of England's problem. Portugal, who were playing at home to Poland, were winning 2–0 within three minutes. A draw would not be good enough and, simple as it sounded, England did need to ensure that they came away with the win.

'I've got twenty quid on Regan for the first goal,' lied Harry (actually it was £200), just as that player squandered a tremendous chance to score. 'You know, I felt quite dirty inside when I put the bet on.'

John chuckled. 'I think you might feel even dirtier if he carries on like this. The strikers look overconfident – I reckon our first goal will come from midfield.'

'Hmm,' Harry bit his lip and looked slyly at his betting slip. 'I'm hoping you're wrong there.'

'Well, just as long as the goals come from somewhere, eh?'

An hour later, the goals still hadn't come from anywhere. Portugal were now four goals ahead of Poland, and back on top of the virtual group. McLean had laboured long and fruitlessly, and had been replaced, and Billy Regan looked no closer to making Harry any richer.

John and Harry sat in silence for most of the second half – the energy slowly draining out of both of them – as each had been too scared to verbalise what they and half the country were beginning to think. When the clock in the corner of the television coverage ticked into the 80s, John could bear it no longer.

'I don't think we're going to score,' he spluttered.

'No, no, don't worry,' Harry reassured him, while not believing his own words, 'they'll nick one. The other team are tiring now. They'll get at least one. England always do this. I'm sure–'

He stopped as, on the screen, Billy Regan finally broke free of the normally well-marshalled defence to go one-on-one with the goalkeeper.

'This is it,' shouted Harry. 'Come on you hateful little girlfriend-beater, I want my money!'

John gave a stunned glance in Harry's direction, disturbed by the outburst, and turned back to the screen just in time to see another woeful England miss.

Harry screamed in agony. 'No! You monkey. What are you doing?'

'It's not the end Harry,' offered John, 'there's still almost nine minutes left.'

Harry was not consoled. 'The point is, I want *him* to score. He's the one I've got the money on.'

'But surely the most important thing is that England win?'

'Yes but . . . well, no . . . I mean, it's complicat–'

Again Harry was stopped by another incident in Dushanbe. 'Handball!' he bellowed, as a Tajikistan midfielder haplessly caught a Simon Brazier shot with his left arm. The referee blew: a free kick just outside the enemy box, and the man on Harry's stub of paper was getting ready to take it.

In his nervous excitement, Harry left the slip on the floor in front of him, and John was able to discover the real amount of the stake. He just managed to prevent himself from expressing his surprise and dismay – although in his ultra-focused state, it's unlikely Harry would have heard him anyway.

Regan took the free kick, driving it past the right-hand side of the wall and – wide of the goal. Another throw of the dice had not worked out. Harry sank to the floor in disbelief.

For the last five minutes, wave after wave of England attack surged over the minnows, but like real surf, each wave faded and died. Almost at the same time as Portugal's 5–0 stuffing of Poland was confirmed, so was the horror result in Tajikistan. England had failed to score against a team ranked 103 in the world. For the moment at least, England was not going to the World Cup after all.

The panel in the television studio were wearing the same shell-shocked expressions as John and Harry. Almost the first comment made was not even a reflection on the match. Jesper Klein – who, not being English, seemed to have far greater access to a vocabulary at this point than his fellow pundits – verbalised the nagging thought that in Harry's living room, John had been trying desperately to suppress. 'You've got to ask yourself, would John Christie have missed all those chances?'

Less than a minute later, the phones in Harry's house and the one next door began to ring and ring, clogged up by people wanting to ask the same question.

Harry sat still and ignored them. 'I should have gone for nil–nil,' he said, completely vacant, 'it was on at 16–1.'

Eighteen

For consolation after defeat, both Harry and John instinctively sought comfort in the same place – the arms of a woman. For Harry, that meant yet another lunchtime drink with his 'friend' Jessica, whom he'd been seeing in that capacity now for several months. They were not 'going out' in school-yard terms – the only kisses they'd shared had been quick cheek-pecks whenever they said hello or goodbye – but they were meeting regularly, talking deeply, and missing one another when apart.

At the same time, and in the same Ariel Hill street, John and Elaine were holding hands across a restaurant table. They'd now been going out – in very much the school-yard sense – for two and a half months, ever since the day after their first meeting in Paul Kerridge's mansion. Back then, they'd met for dinner and shared a lingering kiss afterwards; ever since then the pattern had been pretty much identical on a twice a week basis. Once again here they were, staring into each other's eyes, imitating lovesick teenagers.

Their tender moment was interrupted by the arrival of a well-dressed skinhead – he looked like an Alsatian in a frock – who arrived at their table and tapped John on the shoulder. As he did so, Elaine covered her mouth to prevent a frightened cry from escaping.

'Excuse me mate,' said the man, who had the twangs of a Midlands accent and several missing teeth. 'You're John Christie, aren't you?'

John committed to neither a smile nor a frown. He simply answered: 'Yes'.

'Just wanted to shake your hand. I'm a London City fan, me, but I've got a lot of respect for you – especially what you did against us the other week. We were well impressed.'

Elaine beamed with pride.

'Well, thanks very much,' said John, offering the requested hand. 'Very nice to meet you.'

'Yeah. Hey John – did you see the game last night? Awful weren't it? How come you weren't out there – you've scored about a hundred goals already this season. Are you gonna be in the squad for the play offs?'

'Er, no,' replied John, a little embarrassed. 'I'm pretty sure not.'

'Well more fool old Hardcastle – I reckon he'll get the sack if we don't qualify. You'd be in my team every time – and most of the fans I know feel the same.'

'Well that's very kind er . . . .'

'Vince.'

'That's very kind of you Vince. You have a nice lunch.'

'You, too, John – see you again sometime.'

'Sure.'

Elaine leant across the table as soon as Vince had retreated out of earshot, and grabbed John's hand back. 'I'm so proud of you,' she said. 'How on earth did I ever get to go out with a Premier Division footballer?'

'Hey,' said John, with so much humility that it came out defensively, 'I'm just a normal bloke. There's nothing special about me. Please Elaine – I love spending time with you, but you've got to drop this inferiority complex. The fact that I'm a footballer is not that amazing.'

She recoiled – this being the first raised word of their relationship, but then nodded in acknowledgement. 'I'm sorry,' she said. 'It's John Christie the man I'm lucky to be with, not John Christie the footballer.'

He smiled reassuringly at her. 'Well,' he replied, 'I feel just as lucky to be with you.'

'OK,' she chuckled, 'and maybe I'll get to waitress for England someday.'

'Don't get carried away. Concentrate on your club form first.'

'Like you? Bet you'll be in the England squad soon, just like that man said.'

'I don't think so Elaine. I happen to have it from a good source that it won't be happening for a while. So please, don't go on about it.'

At which point a red-faced 50-something man appeared at the restaurant window, with a particularly unimpressed 50-something woman in tow. Harry waved and banged hard on the glass, frightening several nearby diners. Before security could get to him, John was already outside.

'What is it?' asked John.

Harry stopped to cough. Jessica was not finding him terribly attractive right now. He pointed to John, and tried to speak in staccato statements.

'It's you. You. You're in the squad.'

'What?' John's heart went from 0 to 60 in half a nanosecond.

'For the play offs. It's against Sweden. They announced the squad. Straight after the draw. Hardcastle tried to get you. You haven't got a mobile. You're in the squad John. Your mum saw it on TV. She rang me. Told me you were at this restaurant.'

John's face was pale – his gaze was somewhere distant but his smile was unstoppable. Suddenly Harry's condition brought his focus back to the now.

'Where have you come from?' he asked, seeing the unnatural colour in his face and the sweat on his brow, and hearing the rattle in his chest.

'Just down there,' answered Jessica. 'The restaurant about ten doors down. We were out for lunch.' She didn't attempt to hide her annoyance.

John looked concerned, especially when his friend chose to slump to a seated position on the pavement. 'You got like this from running ten doors down?'

'No,' wheezed Harry, 'thought this place was at the bottom of the hill. Stupid mistake really.'

John couldn't stop himself from giggling. He helped Harry back to his feet, thanked him, and apologised to Jessica, before sending them back to their lunch. Then he returned to his own table, where Elaine had waited patiently. He managed to keep a straight face.

'That was interesting,' he said, sitting down calmly.

'What was it?'

'Oh, just Harry needing to tell me something.'

'What?'

'Well, you know just a minute ago, I told you off for saying that I'd be in the England squad soon?'

'Yes?'

'Well, I guess now I'd better apologise.'

She took a moment to process that, then launched herself full-length across the table and hugged him tightly. She burst into tears, and then, from nowhere, so did he.

Arriving at his first England training session, two days prior to the flight to Stockholm, was for John a little like arriving at Paul Kerridge's party. Many of the same faces were there, along with a host of other superstars who he'd seen on television but only ever met as opponents. Among them was Simon Brazier, the captain, who took him to one side almost immediately upon his arrival.

'New boy,' he said, emotionlessly, 'so, you reckon you've got what it takes.'

John chose to say nothing, unsure of what was meant.

'Seems like everyone else thinks so,' Simon continued. Then, unable to hold his stony expression any longer, he melted into 'I happen to agree.'

'Thank you.'

'I've played against you mate. Most of us have – and most of us have been on the wrong end of one of your displays. Carl says you're the best striker he's ever trained with – Lloyd rates you; so does D'Alex. A word of warning though. Just be a bit careful around Billy Regan. He gets a bit sensitive when new strikers come in; he feels threatened – thinks you're after his place in the team. Which, I guess, you are.'

'Oh, no,' protested John. 'I don't want to upset anyone.'

Simon laughed. His long, jet-black hair swished across his shoulders. 'Carl told me about that, too. I think you're going to have to learn a bit of arrogance and selfishness if you're going to be an international striker John.'

'I hope not,' replied John, very seriously. 'Otherwise I'd rather not be an international striker.'

Simon looked straight at him, his thick eyebrows furrowing like crawling insects. 'Are you for real?' he asked.

Greg Hardcastle called the squad together. D'Alex Smith, who was still on crutches after his abortive race with John, caught the new recruit's eye and gave him a reassuring smile.

'Gentlemen,' Hardcastle boomed authoritatively to the assembled circle of players, 'the next seven days will determine my future as manager of this team. It could also determine some of your futures, too. If we lose this play off, not only will we rightly incur the wrath of a nation starved of success, but you will see a new man come in to take my place, with new ideas on how to play and who to pick. You, as you can tell from your presence here today, are *my* best twenty-two. But another man may not see it that way. So as you approach these games, remember that you are playing for three reasons – for your country, for the fans and for your own futures.'

There was a general consensus of nods. Shivers passed up several spines.

'To the older players I say this,' he continued, 'this World Cup could well be your last chance of true glory. Play well in these games and I shall not consider you too old next summer. To those of you midway through your international career, remember that the end could come quicker than you imagined. And to the new boys–'

John was acutely aware that Hardcastle was staring directly at him. He gave half an awkward smile, then realised he probably shouldn't have.

'–you need to realise that this may not be your first chance, but your only chance. Fail us in these games, and you may never be considered for international duty again. And I say all this not to scare you, but to force any of you who hasn't realised the severity of our situation, to wake up now. Your clubs may be fighting for points in the league, or facing a big European game in the next round of matches, but you need to put club football out of your minds. Same goes for marital problems, tabloid exposés and new dogs. For the next seven days, your bodies, your minds, everything, belong to this cause. This week, nothing else matters. This week, we beat Sweden.'

There was a loud cheer of approval after those last three words. Again they broke apart, while the training staff set up some training equipment, and John took the opportunity to act on Simon's warning. He strolled up to Billy Regan, who had immediately taken a ball to the nearest goal and begun practising his for-the-camera long shots, and tapped him gently on the shoulder.

'Hi there Billy,' he said affably.

'Oh. It's you. The new striker. Wish I could say I was pleased to meet you.' Regan replied, with his tongue in his cheek.

'Actually, we have met once before. At a party.'

'I don't think so,' said Regan, 'I don't remember that.'

'Yes – at Paul Kerridge's mansion.'

'We've never met.' Regan was suddenly stern. John decided against arguing.

'I just came over to . . . I just wanted to say, I'm not after your place and–'

Regan sneered and squared up to him. 'After my place? I'm England's number 9 mate, everyone knows that. That number is sewn on to my skin. I ain't worried about you or anybody else coming after my place. I'm the greatest English striker in history, undisputed. After my place? Don't make me laugh.'

John completely forgot himself for a moment. 'I just thought after all those misses in Tajikistan, you might be a bit nervous . . . .'

Regan exploded. 'YOU WHAT?' He pushed John hard, sending him flying backwards. 'Think you're clever do you? You want to make something of it?'

'No, no,' pleaded John. 'I'm sorry! That came out wrong.'

Three nearby players dived in to separate them. On the first morning of his first England training session, John was issued with an official conduct warning. It was not a good start.

The stadium in Stockholm was small but impressive – like a scaled-down replica of the City Stadium in London. The one other major difference was that the crowd, although smaller, was much closer to the pitch than in London. In fact, there were only a few yards of grass between the touch-line and the front row. That meant the 32,000 Swedish fans, huddled together and painted yellow, actually sounded louder from the pitch than they would have done in a bigger stadium.

This acoustic effect was not immediately comprehensible for John, as his starting berth for the match was in the middle of a plastic-sheltered bench. He'd been named as a substitute, which was quite impressive for his first squad, but might even have made the starting eleven if it hadn't been for his spat with Regan on the first morning of training. That incident – although not really John's fault – had placed a black mark on his card as far as the manager was concerned. In his personal notebook Hardcastle had written next to his name: 'great skill, questionable temperament – not sure how he'll handle big game pressure.' Some of that, of course, was fair comment; accusations of bad temper were hardly deserved. John took it on the chin though – for him, and for his family and friends back home, it was an honour just to be sitting on the bench.

Sweden came into the game as slight favourites. Although they didn't boast any outstanding individual talents, they were a well-drilled, experienced unit which played as a team. In the previous World Cup, that kind of approach had seen them through to the quarter-finals. All but one of the players who'd taken part in that defeat were lining up to play now – a testament to the stability of the team.

The national anthems rang out around the ground. Both were observed respectfully by a crowd too nervous to boo. World Cup qualification is too big a prize to be decided by knock-out ties like this, and most of those watching had been unable to eat that day. The atmosphere was loud, but every individual's cheer was punctuated with a shiver of nerves.

England, seemingly inspired by Hardcastle's relentless rallying team talks, started brightly, producing fluid passing movements which raised the spirits and expectations of the 3,000 officially-ticketed travellers (as well as those hiding among the sea of yellow). The clever passing though – however aesthetically pleasing it happened to be – did not result in a shot, and the halfway point was reached without a single meaningful attack from either side.

It was boring, but that was exactly Hardcastle's point, just as he underlined at half-time. A 0–0 draw here would be a great result for England, and a 0–1 win would be practically dreamsville. But the important thing was not conceding, and that was exactly why he would persist with his tactical system – which he referred to as 'the lockdown' – for the rest of the game. Five defenders, three defensively-minded midfielders, one striker and one man just behind him. It was a little more constructive than a ten-man wall, but not much.

His services still not required, John made his way back to the bench for the second half, praying for a little more action this time to keep him awake. His prayers were answered ten minutes later, although not quite in the way that he had hoped.

A brilliant shot from the edge of the box was produced – but not by England. It was from the Swedish Striker Jonas Lamberg, and it stung Lloyd McGrath's fingers on its way into the net. Hardcastle swore and cursed. 'The Lockdown' had failed.

Almost immediately, Hardcastle became twitchy, fiddling with his pencil and notebook and whispering to his coaching staff. He glanced at Carl Barton, who was sitting next to John, and then to John himself. There was more discussion, more fiddling, and then a broken pencil. Suddenly the manager jumped to his feet, and turned to the substitutes.

'You two – Barton and Christie. Warm up. You're on in two minutes.'

John felt as if he'd been struck by a lightning bolt. His moment – his final step up the ladder – had arrived. A wave of excitement and determination to serve the cause washed over him. As the camera picked him up, stretching on the touch-line and removing his track suit to reveal the red England away kit, a roomful of people at the top end of Ariel Hill went high-pitched and squeaky.

Clinton McLean and Wayne Webster were the men being replaced. Neither looked too upset to be making an early exit from proceedings. Carl was sent into midfield, John was told to support Regan in attack. Both were warned again as they went – despite conceding the goal, 'the Lockdown' was still in force.

Ultra-defensive formations were not a problem to John, as Carl pointed out when they ran on together. The greedy child in front of him might be, however. Regan would expect John to pass, not shoot, and send forth his wrath if he tried anything else. Gamely, John determined to play as selflessly as possible. He had no grudge against Regan; the way he saw it, the training ground incident had been mainly his fault. No, as a way of making amends in fact, he would try to set up his striker for a match-changing leveller, and shy away from attempting to grab it himself.

Just five minutes after John had come on, the ball, which took some time to bagatelle around the heavy skeleton of 'the Lockdown', reached his feet in a promising position. A little way outside the box, and a few yards from the nearest defender, John had a clear shooting chance. He also – as denoted by a screaming, flailing, tantruming red blur ahead of him – had the option of swinging a deep cross in the direction of Regan. He remembered his promise, and chose the latter.

A perfect cross bisected the defenders and the goalkeeper, and beelined towards Regan's head. The ball connected with it – and sailed high and wide of the goal.

As they ran back from the attack, Regan caught John's eye. 'Better ball in next time please,' he snarled. 'What am I supposed to do with that?'

John did not reply. Instead he swallowed any fragment of pride, and nodded. He'd try to do better next time.

The next time did not arrive until the final minute. This time, John found himself isolated on the right wing. The left back had clearly tired, and was not even attempting a tackle. Out of the corner of his eye, John spotted Regan – and only Regan – ambling up towards the penalty area. To assist his aging team-mate, another Swedish defender stepped across to try to win the ball from John, who was practically standing still as he waited for Regan to catch up. But John saw him coming – as he dived in, studs showing, John flicked the ball away with the instep of his trailing foot, leaving the bemused Swede to tackle only his shadow. Next, John attacked the stand-offish full-back, using his pace to glide past him and into the back corner of the penalty area. He looked up, and saw Regan shouting hungrily on the penalty spot. John calmly laid the ball back – perfectly – for the easy tap-in. Regan swung and missed. It was still 1–0. Again John took a barrage of blame from the real culprit.

There was no injury time. The final whistle blew, and England's place at the World Cup was fading like the evening sun.

There was no time, in the four short days that followed, for idle conversation, family visits or sitting down. There was barely provision for sleep. All was focused on steering the ship on a sharp about-turn; on putting the awful results of the past month far behind; on beating Sweden in the return leg, by the two clear goals now required. All else was forgotten. Nothing mattered besides a now improbable victory. Greg Hardcastle, but more importantly the nation of England, demanded it.

The media were very clear on what was expected. After expressing their disappointment, every columnist and reporter reiterated that for this country, failure to appear at a major tournament was not an option. On the morning of the match, the *Morning News* went into six pages of detail, explaining how the match could be won, and by whom. By contrast, the front page of the *Mouthpiece* displayed only a few chilling words – 'Lose, and be disowned'.

City Stadium was packed to the rafters for the second game – a sea of white and red with a brave but tiny yellow-and-blue stream in one corner. The nerves of the previous game had now been replaced by angry determination, and England's supporters were more riotously loud than ever. John's performance in the first leg, coupled with the general prerogative for attack and the abandonment of 'the Lockdown', had earned him a starting place, alongside both Billy Regan and Clinton McLean. This time though, Hardcastle had begged him, if he had a chance to shoot, he should take it.

For the first time, he stood in line for the national anthem. A forty-piece band was drowned out by the wailings of the fans who attempted to join in. It was an impressive choir – at least in terms of sound – and their combined impact lifted John's heart. It sank again straight afterwards, however, as the Swedish anthem began, and a sizeable hissing contingent of the crowd decided that it hadn't. As the players shook hands moments later, he made a point of apologising to every member of the Swedish side for the fans' ignoble conduct.

From the start, England looked hungry and Sweden looked scared. The three-pronged English attack appeared dangerous from the very first minute, when McLean hit a Regan knock-down narrowly wide of the Swedish post. John sent a fine cross into the box four minutes later, and Paul Kerridge forced a smart save from the goalkeeper. The pressure mounted – England gained confidence as Sweden lost theirs – and with ten minutes to go in the half, the ball was in the net, after defender Carlo Sweet had headed in from a corner. The players wheeled away in celebration, but the sudden muteness of the crowd told them something was up. The referee had, he claimed, seen pushing in the box and called a foul. No goal – England no closer to the tournament.

The referee soon began to stand out as the pivotal figure in the match. It may have been a coincidence, but the majority of his decisions seemed to go against the men in white. Regan was called offside when the linesman's flag had stayed down; Wayne Webster got booked for a tremendous and fair tackle. Temperatures around this little bald man, who was clearly unaware that his chances of leaving the stadium with his head still attached were decreasing rapidly, rose almost as quickly as the looming chances of a Swedish win.

The interval came; Hardcastle vented his frustration; the interval ended. The second half continued in the same vein. McLean's claims for a penalty were waved away; John's excellent chest-down to set up a shooting chance for the same player was somehow deemed a handball. The referee seemed to be attempting to establish himself as a great villain of English history, on a par with William the Conqueror and the Viking hordes.

And then came what was to prove the central moment in the tie. On eighty minutes, with the game still goalless, Billy Regan burst through on the Swedish goal. As he did so, John noticed a slightly different look in his eye – more determined, more angry, more sure. This time, somehow, John knew that despite all those misses, Regan was going to score. About 10 yards from his target, he set himself to strike – and received a clear punch in the kidneys from a defender who was desperately trying to catch him. He fell down in the centre of the box, clutching his back and with his face screwed up in pain. All 75,000 pairs of eyes looked straight at the little bald man in black, who pointed . . . for a Swedish free kick. He made a diving motion towards Regan, still prostrate on the floor, and ran away. Regan staggered to his feet and ran after him with his fist clenched – Simon Brazier only just got to him in time to prevent a punch being thrown – screaming and raging in terms which forced the television camera to refrain from close-ups. Seconds later, a red card was produced. Amidst desperate screams and the sound of 20 million English hearts breaking, Regan was dragged from the pitch in shame.

Hardcastle, although an experienced manager, did not know what to do or say as his players looked to him for a last-ditch plan. All his ideas were spent; his dreams and his job were slipping through his fingers like ashes. With only a few minutes left to salvage the tie, against a team which for over 170 minutes had successfully prevented them from scoring even once, and against a referee who appeared insistent that such form continued, his hope was all but gone. It was bad enough when it had been twelve men against eleven – now the balance was just far too uneven. His only instruction was to the two remaining front-men – 'close it up at the front.' Clinton McLean and John would now both play in Regan's central position, and hope that someone else could provide a decent cross for them to get on the end of.

The clock, seemingly blown round quicker by a suitably chill wind, soon found its way to ninety minutes. An official on the touch-line signalled that there would be two additional minutes to compensate for injuries. It was now or never. Carlo Sweet launched a massive long ball towards McLean, who trapped it and laid off to Brazier. He thought about shooting, but dipped his shoulder instead and found his way into the box. Suddenly, eighteen other desperate men swarmed in to join him – all jostling for prime position as he prepared to cross. Brazier lobbed the ball into the midst of them, and those at the front gasped as it travelled, almost in slow motion, over their heads. Those at the back post tensed as the ball slowed and failed to reach them. And right in the middle, just the correct side of two Swedish markers, was John Christie. The ball connected perfectly with the middle of his forehead, and flew past the 'keeper like a bullet. There was a split-second of utter silence as everyone in the whole world looked at the referee, and then, as he began running back to the centre for a restart, scenes of utter, unbridled jubilation. The eruption of noise nearly blew up the Channel One microphones. John was mobbed by nine besotted team-mates. In pubs and clubs and living rooms around the country, grown men cried and kissed one another. And they hadn't even qualified yet.

Sweden were in total shock. At the point of Regan's dismissal, they had all reached a point of utter self-belief that they were unbeatable. They had assumed, when the referee had awarded a straight tenth disputable decision their way, that victory in the tie was their destiny. Now, with the game suddenly levelled, their legs turned collectively to jelly. The crowd, which had become less and less noisy as time had elapsed, was suddenly back at maximum volume. How Sweden needed the final whistle, so that they could recompose themselves for extra-time.

But there was still a minute left. While Sweden were reeling, England were suddenly swamped by a spirit of belief. Straight from the Swedish kick-off, the ball was given away and passed to the advancing Brazier. John and his forward partner began hurtling forward, striking fear into shattered Swedish hearts as they went. As the ball came to his feet, via a great headed flick from McLean, a sudden flashback of his first competitive start, for Ariel Hill against Kingston Town, passed in front of John's eyes. Losing the ball clumsily to a brittle-looking defensive midfielder, he remembered the perseverance he'd learned from his initial failings at Mile End, and won it back again. All the experiences; all the incredible, high-rising moments of the last year were coming together as one. He sensed, as the last defender missed both him and the ball, that in some unearthly sense, his time had now come. And suddenly, as he stood one-on-one with the goalkeeper, and everyone looked on spewing indeterminable half-words, he knew what he had to do. Very deliberately, he drove the ball straight and true against the left-hand post. The crowd gasped in distress. Unlike them though, John knew what he was doing. Just like the overweight tramp in Ariel Fields, the goalkeeper threw himself to his right, to cover the shot, which bounced back off the metal post and came spinning back toward John. Then, just as he had on that cold December day, he flicked the ball up, spun around and flipped himself upside down. The ball came back towards earth, John's foot swung out, and the match-winner flew directly into the middle of the 'keeper-less goal. There should have been scenes of wild celebration. Instead, there was three seconds of stunned disbelief. Then – ten times more powerful and glorious than before – the celebration came. It continued long into the night. England were going to the World Cup finals.

On the telephone later, after he'd managed to dodge a hundred bloodthirsty news-hounds, John cried on the phone to Marilyn and Becky, and calmed himself slightly to talk to his girlfriend. But when Harry came on, neither man could remain composed for long. Although it was lost on everyone else, Harry understood the more subtle significance of that wonder-goal.

The morning's newspapers were both the victims and the chief proponents of Christie-mania. The *Spark*, which boasted 'Twelve pages of pictures and analysis' (although in truth it was mainly pictures and advertisements), called it 'the greatest moment in recent English sporting history'. The *Morning News*, for once abandoning its commitment to highbrow comment and common sense, claimed 'England now have a player capable of winning them a World Cup'. And the *Mouthpiece*, the most widely-read newspaper in the land, went even further, crowning John with unimaginable praise. 'A year ago,' wrote the original Christie-for-England campaigner, Troy Wilson, 'no one had even heard of John Christie. Then he emerged, as if from nowhere, as one of the top strikers in the Premier Division. After the thrilling finale to last season, this newspaper referred to him as "The Messiah of Mile End". But we stopped too short, for in sweeping aside

Sweden in a match we had no right to win, he has confirmed that he deserves to be identified by an even more glorious title. This man is not just the hero of his club – he is heaven-sent, the chosen one, brought to save this nation in our hour of need. And I believe that he *will* lead us all to our promised land. Because, as I see it readers, John Christie is *England's Messiah*.'

Nineteen

And with that, John Christie was a superstar. In one instant of sublime skill, the park-kick-about-nobody of one year ago had barged past stars of stage and screen to the front of the A-list, and absolutely without trying. Overnight, the majority of the non-stop phone-calls that Harry and Becky fielded were no longer journalists in search of a quote, but marketing men looking to put John's face on an advert, or a cereal packet, or the bonnet of a special edition car. The interview requests from the sports writers continued to flow in, but they were pushed out by a flood from every other kind of media. Women's magazines wanted his life story, music magazines wanted to know what he listened to in his spare time. Even *Pets Are Great Monthly* got in on the act, calling to find out if he had a hamster.

John walked between Harry's study and his own front room in disbelief as the offers and requests rained in. Though he'd seen many examples before, it was only now that he truly understood what Harry had meant all those months ago when he'd described football as a national obsession. When he tried to go out to buy a newspaper that morning, he'd been accosted three times; he'd not even managed to get to the end of the street. It was not that he couldn't understand it – he was not so naïve as to believe that 'he'd just scored a couple of goals' – but even so it was difficult to stand at the epicentre of all this excitement and activity and comprehend it. Right now, too many things kept happening for it all to make sense.

At 11 o'clock on Thursday, just thirteen hours after the event that changed everything, he heard a shriek from the corner of his living room. There, Becky was shaking, a still-wet fax in her hand. 'You'd better take a look at this,' she said.

John read, then nearly fell to the ground, and asked his sister to read it back to him in case he'd gone mad. But he had not. *Hey!* magazine – the weekly of choice for the discerning celebrity obsessive – were offering him £500,000 for an exclusive photo shoot. At that point, John needed some air and headed for the garden. This most certainly did not make sense to him.

Outside, the flash of camera bulbs from paparazzi hanging over his back fence prevented him from calming down – instead having quite the opposite effect. Knocked off balance by the offer from *Hey!*, he was now sent into hyperventilation by reporters from their chief rival, *First!*. Chased back inside by the relentless flickering, he was met by his sister, who was receiving another offer, this time by phone.

'It's the Crumble Chocolate Company,' she announced excitedly, with her hand clasped over the receiver. 'They want to name their new special edition chocolate bar after you.'

John said nothing, retreated to the darkness of his bedroom, and locked the door.

After careful thought, and agreeing – on the understanding that it would not be publicised – to give his staggering fee in its entirety to an AIDS charity, John accepted the offer from *Hey!*. He also made two further stipulations: first, that contrary to their initial request, Elaine would not be involved in the shoot (the thought terrified her even more than rats and spiders), and second, that the word 'Messiah', with which he was growing increasingly uncomfortable, would not be used anywhere in the text. These were both hastily agreed to, and so the following Monday – having received a hero's reception in Mile End's weekend victory over Teesside (in which he scored, again) – John was taken by limousine to the West End of London, where he breakfasted with the magazine's editor and creative director. The latter, a full-framed flouncing woman with all too-obvious facial enhancements, gushed sickeningly at him over croissants:

'John – darling! This is our most exciting shoot in years. I mean, we did Princess Augusta's wedding a couple of months back, but this is sooo much bigger. The public is desperate for you right now John – and we don't want to disappoint them.'

She stopped to draw breath, and expected some level of enthusiasm in response. John forced a smile, and buttered his brioche.

The editor, a freakishly young-looking man with dyed blonde hair and enormous earrings, interjected on his behalf. 'I'm sure he's well up for it Sandra,' he said, in voice of purest 'geezer', 'you just got to give 'im a chance to wake up.'

'Anyway,' Sandra continued at pace, 'I'm thinking that we could really define your look in this shoot. I'm thinking that hair of yours is a feature. It's messy – let's not make it neat, because then that wouldn't be you would it? I think we should go messier – more defined – more you.'

John looked for confirmation from the editor, who seemed slightly more level-headed, and received a fervent nod. Sandra looked pleased.

'So what do you say John? Our stylist on Sylvia Street can do the hair; for jewellery we'll send someone out to Ben Stone, and the clothes we've already organised. Are you excited?'

John forced his lips up to reveal his teeth. 'Mmm. Can't wait,' he lied.

The doors of the studio swung open, and John exited feeling the dual torture of embarrassment and awkwardness. His hair, which had been pumped full of three kinds of expensive gluey gunk, was sticking up at every conceivable different angle. His clothes, which graciously the folks from *Hey!* had let him keep, were so torn and tattered that, had he not known they were ultra-hip designer items, he wouldn't even have thought them fit for a jumble sale. He caught his reflection in a mirror as he left the building. *Hey!* apparently, had 'fixed' his image for the shoot. But now he'd been 'fixed', he didn't feel like himself anymore.

Three showers, followed by a trip in sensible jeans and jumper to the hairdresser in Ariel Hill High Street, rectified matters. After his experience with the gunk, he decided that it was high time he dispensed with the messy look and pull himself together. This was just the photo opportunity that the paparazzi had been waiting for. He left the hairdresser to a blaze of flashbulbs, and the front pages of the next morning's tabloids were full of 'Christie's new look'. Real news never had a chance on a news day like that.

Elaine woke John early on Saturday morning, rattling his bedroom window with a print-fresh copy of *Hey!*. They sat and read it – as much as it could be read – together, their mouths agape. Then John got angry, and not just because they'd plastered the word 'Messiah' across both the cover and the first spread.

'It says here I'm single,' he shouted. 'I never told them that. I told them I was in a relationship with a girl who preferred to stay out of the limelight.'

Elaine grabbed his arm. 'It's OK,' she assured him.

'No it isn't. They've lied. They've made up things I'm supposed to have said. Look at this: "I'm currently playing the field, but at the moment I haven't met anyone worth teaming up with." Is that supposed to be a joke?'

'I don't mind John. I know you wouldn't have said that.'

'That's nice Elaine, but I do mind.'

'They paid you £500,000 to do these photos.'

'And I look ridiculous. Look at my hair. It's like I've just had 40,000 volts sent through my body.'

'But it was so much money. And it'll do so much good.'

'I know that Elaine. And if it was just about me looking stupid then I really wouldn't care. But they've made up words and put them in my mouth – not just about you – about my family, my team-mates, my ambition. I never told anyone that "I want to become the best player in the world". That's just not a thing that I'd say. They made it up – and because they paid all that money they think they've got the right. So is that the price of truth? Half a million?'

'John, you're upsetting me. I've never seen you like this.'

'Tell me Elaine,' said John, pulsing with anger. 'If half a million buys you the right to lie, what does a million buy you? Or ten million? This stinks.'

'John?' Elaine did not know this John Christie. Neither, until now, did John.

'I've got to get some fresh air. Please, stay here for a while.'

He stepped through the hall and out of the back door, hoping that he hadn't woken his mother upstairs but presumed that, in the adjoining bedroom, his notoriously heavy-sleeping sister had almost certainly missed his outburst. Outside, he caught a cool breeze in the face, and began to regress from his anger. Then he heard a noise in one of his trees, like a bird's pecking. He glanced up to try to catch sight of it, and instead saw a badly camouflaged photographer clicking at his every move. Very calmly, he walked inside, and then let out an almighty roar. Now even Becky would be awake.

'I know it's a lot easier to say than do,' said the Reverend Paul Miller, 'but you've got to be prepared to turn the other cheek.'

John sat in the front pew of St Peter's with his head in his hands. He had nothing to say; he had come here in the hope of hearing some wisdom.

'The world is far from perfect John,' continued the vicar, 'but it's the world we've been called to live in. And all these people who live in it with us, they're not so bad. They're all just the same as you in the end, all born with that gap in their soul where God should fit. Some of us, John, like you and me, we put God there, and try to live by his rules, and it works out OK for us. But the others, they find different things to put there first. Football, money, celebrity worship – they're all just an attempt to fill that hole.'

John looked up. 'I'm not sure I know what you're talking about,' he said quietly.

'I'm just saying, that these people who you don't understand – the celebrity-hunters always after your photograph, or the obsessive fans who stop you in the street – they're all just the same as you. They're just following their religion – demonstrating their faithfulness. Except that their church is a football stadium, or their Bible is a copy of *Hey!*.'

John suddenly looked very anxious. 'Well then, where does that leave me?'

Paul shook his head. 'What do you mean?'

'Reverend, they're calling me their Messiah.'

The next day, for the first time, John had to abandon his own religion for the benefit of another. For television scheduling purposes, Mile End's home tie against Billy Regan's Docklands had been switched to a midday Sunday kick-off, meaning that John was unable to attend his own church or any other. He expressed his disapproval at the idea when it was first mentioned, but even he, with his new-found mega-star status, didn't have the sort of kudos required to influence a TV company into changing its mind.

Although the media knew nothing of their less-than-fragrant relationship, the game was billed as a battle between the two England striking stars, and few were in any doubt over who would come out on top. As the players prepared to exit the tunnel, John sought out Regan and offered him the hand of friendship. It was duly declined, even eye contact was avoided. As Allan Strong quietly pointed out to his team-mate as they entered the pitch together, Regan looked terrified.

As predicted, the game *was* all about Regan and Christie. As early as the first minute, the former signalled his intent by hitting a hopeful shot from all of 40 yards. It didn't trouble the Mile End goal, but it demonstrated that he wouldn't require an excuse to shoot. He tried again five minutes later, this time from a little closer in, but reaped the same reward.

Then it was John's turn. He received the ball in his own half, exchanged passes with Carl Barton, and dribbled into space. The defenders, whose minds were possibly still on what they had got up to on Saturday night, back-pedalled instead of making a challenge. It was all the assistance John required. Seeing the defence open up like the Red Sea, he let fly from just outside the box. As the ball travelled inevitably goalwards, one voice could be heard over any other screaming 'No!' It was Billy Regan.

The goal spurred Mile End, and John, on to dominance. For the final twenty minutes of the half, only the brilliance of the Dockland's goalkeeper prevented them from taking a commanding lead. As the whistle blew for the break, the visiting defence collapsed in unison with near-exhaustion. Their star striker, by comparison – a lonely figure who'd barely had a meaningful touch for the final half an hour – was left scratching his head and cursing his rival. He walked back to the tunnel pursued by a loud chorus of 'You wish you were John Christie,' and spat in disgust.

The early exchanges of the second half only angered him further. First, John found himself in space on the right wing. Instead of merely attempting to outpace the full-back, however, he decided to flick the ball over his head using the outside of his wrong foot. It worked perfectly, left the defender in a daze, and resulted in a chance that François Rieux only narrowly failed to convert. The crowd was lavish in its appreciation, cheering and chanting at their hero's display of skill. So then, Regan decided to demonstrate that anything John could do, he could do better. In a similar position, he attempted an even more complicated trick, back-heeling a bouncing ball between two onrushing defenders, and running around the outside of them to collect it again. But, almost inevitably, it didn't work. The ball simply looped straight up in the air, travelling no distance forward, and came down onto the grateful chest of one of the defenders. Regan, meanwhile, had already set off in pursuit of a ball that would never reach him. This he realised, midway through his stride, and desperately turned toward the ball's actual position. For a moment, he was running in two directions at once, before simple physics caught up with him and he went twisting and tumbling to the ground. The crowd enjoyed this even more than John's clever trick, and showed their appreciation with a gigantic collective wolf-whistle. For their pleasure, the giant screen in the corner of the ground replayed the moment three times. Regan's face burned with anger and shame. At exactly the wrong moment, an entirely sincere John arrived to help him to his feet – and felt a blast of acidic language scorch him full in the face.

The wound in Regan's pride was gaping, and John's very next act was, quite unintentionally, the footballing equivalent of pouring an enormous salt-cellar directly into it. Taking advantage of some tired defending, he intercepted the ball just outside the box. A suddenly flustered centre-back took a swing for the ball, and John tapped it past him. Another quicker defender tried to shoulder-barge him into losing control, but John's newly-impressive upper body allowed him to keep his balance. A third player attempted to stop him and missed. Then a fourth – and all the time he was inching closer and closer to the goal. The goalkeeper, panicked that his defence had suddenly lost the ability to stop as much as an ice cream van, dived towards John's feet, spreading his body like a parachute. John had seen him coming though, and flicked the ball over him just as his body hit the ground. Somehow, John had walked a goal in despite the attentions of five other players. As the persistent replays and the subsequently granted 'Channel One Goal of the Month' award proved, it was truly a wonder-goal. Beyond that though, it provided a dangerous spark to Billy Regan's suddenly-exposed blue touch-paper.

At the resulting kick-off, Regan deliberately belted the ball directly at John. Although it was hit hard, John seemed to see it in slow motion, and brought it under control when it would have simply bounced off of most players. Pleased to receive the gift, John advanced, at his usual breakneck pace, toward the other end of the field. Unopposed by a midfield that was now resigned to losing, he continued at speed, and slowed only slightly to check for a team-mate in need of a cross. As he looked up, he did not see a team-mate. Instead, he saw Billy Regan, diving towards him at full stretch, his studs extended like the prongs of a vengeful porcupine. Instinctively, he knocked the ball out of the way, but as those studs tore into his flesh, he realised that Regan had never even been aiming for the ball. He fell to the ground, cushioned slightly by the cries of a stadium-full of angry supporters, and hit his head on the turf. His scratched forehead began to bleed. He tended to it with his hand, and saw Regan encircled by his team-mates, then presented with a red card by the hollering referee.

'No, no,' he called, from the ground, 'I'm sure it was just an accident. . . .'

The nearest player, Allan Strong, was wearing an expression which he could not read. He looked across and noticed that François Rieux was wearing it, too. So were most of the crowd. Then he realised that the crowd had suddenly hushed. The numbing initial effects of shock began to wear off, and utter agony rushed through his body, as if he'd been tossed into boiling water. He looked down at the source of the pain – his bloodied right leg – and saw a large piece of bone poking out of his skin. Instantly, through a combination of utter terror and unending pain, he lost consciousness, and a clutter of medical staff, friends and supporters swarmed over him.

A few moments later, John's limp, broken body was lifted from the pitch on a stretcher. Then, there was only silence.

Twenty

Harry, Elaine, Becky and Marilyn squashed onto one long bench in the waiting room. There were other seats nearby, but they each found comfort in the closeness of one another, as they watched a flurry of doctors and nurses racing in and out of the treatment room. Through the curtained window in front of them, John's injury was receiving an initial assessment, as a constant stream of anaesthetics was pumped into his body and he drifted around, just the right side of consciousness. Meanwhile, through the shuttered window just behind them, a contingent of reporters and cameramen was growing in size by the minute. Upon the arrival of their high-profile guest, the management of this small private hospital had already begun to divert other patients to another three miles away. Now, two hours after John's admission, the decision was made to close the doors even to emergencies.

Slowly, over the course of a third hour, activity within the walls of the hospital became less frenetic than that occurring outside. A statement from the doctors was requested by the restless reporters, and then subsequently demanded. Sport One started broadcasting a constant shot simply of the locked hospital doors. The beginnings of a media frenzy had already been unleashed – even before a proper diagnosis had been given.

In the waiting room, where John's four closest allies had maintained a silent vigil, a tall, bearded doctor cleared his throat.

'Excuse me,' he said to Harry, his hands trembling so dramatically that his voice wavered with them. 'Are you John's father?'

'I'm his mum,' Marilyn cut in. 'How is he doctor?'

The doctor looked down, and wiped some sweat off of his glasses. 'He's . . . OK. He's suffered a very serious injury, and he lost a fair amount of blood, but he's doing all right.'

'What is it?' asked Becky, glancing at her own wheelchair. 'Is it bad?'

'It's a very serious double break. But you have to know, he's in no pain. He's receiving the very best medical care possible. We'll keep him heavily anaesthetised while we restructure the leg.'

'Will he play again?' asked Harry solemnly, believing that he already knew the answer.

'I can't say. We've got to get him walking again first. I'm afraid that sometimes, with breaks like this, the body just doesn't heal up again like you might want it to. Really, it's too early to say.'

'Are you saying he might not be able to walk again?' asked Becky, her voice heavy with the strains of bubbling emotion.

'No, I'm not saying that. It's just a matter of whether he'll need some kind of walking aid for support.'

'Like a stick?' cried Elaine with horror.

That was when it truly hit Harry. Almost as instantly as it had begun, the adventure had now, tragically come to an end. He had thought, with more than twenty John Christie goals on the board by November, that the records were lining up to be smashed. He had believed, after the glorious win against Sweden, that John would go on to establish himself as a world great, and then a World Cup winner. He had assumed, that after suffering such undeserved misfortune for so many years, the

Christie family's luck had changed. But he had been wrong on all three counts.

As the doctor braced himself, then headed gravely for the door where he would address the media, another realisation hit Harry so hard – like a jackhammer in the chest – that he was forced to sit down again. Through a small gap in the curtains he caught sight of John's sedated body, hooked up to various machines and fluids. And for a split second, it was not his friend's face which he saw there, but his own, nearly forty years previously. Because just like the rise from the lower divisions, the signing of a Mile End contract and the taking of an all-or-nothing penalty kick, this career-ending injury was now yet another fate they shared. Though it made no sense, their lives, decades apart, seemed to be inextricably linked; one following the other like a carbon copy. He glanced across at Elaine, looking pale, terrified and all cried-out. Was this John's Jessica? He felt sick.

His hopes dashed and his dreams slaughtered, Harry heaved himself to his feet without speaking and dragged himself towards the door. On the steps, he passed the doctor, being bombarded from every angle by desperate newsmen. Even despite his well-known attachment to John, in this scene of utter pandemonium he was able to slip past them all without being recognised. Then he left the grounds of the hospital, wiped a steady stream of tears from his eyes, and sought out the nearest public house, where he remained until the night.

'Is this the end?' asked Harry soullessly, staring into his coffee cup.

Across the table Jessica gave an encouraging semi-smile, but said nothing.

'Can I do this any more?' he continued. 'Can I give any more? This game . . . it's taken everything I have. And what do I get in return? This. Not just the once – all over again.'

Jessica reached across and took his hand. She narrowed her eyes sweetly, and gazed up at him. 'I know this must be very hard for you,' she said softly, 'seeing what happened to you happen to John. But you've got to find something positive to pull out of it. You've been getting angrier and angrier with this sport for years, and yet somehow it's remained your obsession all this time. Well now it's hurt you too badly to expect forgiveness – so consider this your clean break. Put football behind you. Live another life instead. Maybe with me.'

Harry gave a slow, resigned nod. He tried to smile, but the slightest gesture of emotion only tipped him into raw depression again.

Jessica stood and moved around the table to him, and cradled his head in her arms. As he closed his eyes and prayed again that this was all a nightmare, she couldn't resist half a smile of long-awaited satisfaction.

The following Saturday, *Foster's Eye* did not appear.

The little light that appeared came from the most unlikely lantern. Two days on from the disaster, the front page of the *Mouthpiece* was devoted to a huge picture of John in full striking flow, underneath which was placed the caption 'Six months, three weeks and four days until the plane leaves. Get well soon, John.' Inside, the newspaper's editorial read as an ode to the British fighting spirit. 'We do not give up, even against impossible odds,' it said. 'This is the nation that produced Churchill, and which bred his bulldog spirit. The experts say that it would take a miracle to get John Christie to the World Cup, but that should not strip us of our hope. We have already seen one miracle performed by this remarkable young man; why is it so ridiculous to hope for another?'

The next day, the *Mouthpiece*'s editorial meeting was abuzz. They'd received an unparalleled number of calls to their switchboard, and seven heaving post-bags of letters when on most days they were forced to make up most of their feedback page. The front page, and the daring, unusually bright editorial, had captured the imagination of half a country. Every word was of praise – and every comment asked for more of the same. 'With positive thinking like this for a change,' wrote one correspondent in a letter read proudly at the meeting, 'we might even create the miracle ourselves.' The editor, understandably, was thrilled with the response. He had always seen his newspaper as the voice of the people, and for once he had been proved resoundingly right. The question, therefore, was how to fully exploit the gold reserve that they had struck upon.

One of the paper's lesser lights, a humble sub-editor, suggested they focus their attentions on John's forthcoming operation, due to take place at the end of the week. They could rally people, he explained, to send their positive thoughts in unison to John at the time of his surgery – creating one giant wave of positive mental energy. The editor saw the brilliance of the idea in an instant, and in the same moment took ownership of it as if it had always been his. 'Yes,' he said, grinning maniacally. 'We'll print a picture of the X-ray, and get everyone to touch it and think positively.'

'Don't you think that's a bit flat,' interjected a deputy. 'Positive thinking? It sounds a bit wishy-washy doesn't it?' There were a few uncommitted murmurs which indicated some agreement.

'What do you suggest instead?'

'How about prayer? How about we get everyone to hold the X-ray during the operation, and say a prayer for John's leg?'

The editor wasn't sure whether he loved or hated the idea. He just looked blank. Finally, he asked: 'Do you think that'll sell more papers?'

There were a few nods. Others, who had been less committed, joined in to form a consensus.

'Good – prayer it is then,' said the editor coolly. 'We'll print up special different ones inside for all the major faiths – that should steer us clear of any press complaints. Hey, maybe we could do a mocked-up prayer mat for the centre pages.'

'I reckon we could get an advertiser interested in that,' added the deputy.

The first month was by far the hardest for John. For a start he was in a wheelchair, just like his sister, which brought her to tears virtually every time they met. Beyond that, though, he also had to watch as his football team ran out of ideas and steam without him, losing four consecutive matches and being firmly deposed from the top of the Premier Division. Likewise, he could do nothing as his good friend and neighbour launched himself into his first steps away from football. Harry's heart was broken; he'd lost his faith, and John couldn't help but think that it was his fault.

Jessica, by comparison, was delighted by the change in her former fiancé's outlook. Partly on the recommendation of the steady drip of advice which she offered, Harry had decided to take a sabbatical from his newspaper column (Alex Knight almost had a heart attack as a result), and backed away from offers of punditry and reporting. Although it felt unnatural, with Jessica standing by for support, he even managed to wean himself off of watching Channel One's *The Big Match*. Although he blamed no one in particular (barring Billy Regan, on whom he already blamed most of the problems in British society) he couldn't cope with what had happened to John, and with the sudden stark reminder of what had also once happened to him.

Taking the long view, the game had not been a good friend to Harry, and now, he had been helped to realise, it was time to let that friendship die.

The second and third months, which took John into a new – and World Cup – year, were more hopeful. The wheelchair was exchanged for a shiny pair of first edition crutches (which several newspapers offered considerable amounts of money to adorn with their logo), and the messages of goodwill, which during the first month supporters had been too mortified to send, began to stack up in one of John's spare bedrooms. Elaine, faithfully arriving each and every evening in the runabout which John had helped her to buy, was also a great source of help and encouragement, full of common sense but never patronising him as he agonised over his predicament. 'When I'm back on my feet again properly,' he told Becky one night, 'I think I might propose to her.'

The media, which had allowed him a little time to recover – 'too many wheelchair pictures will freak the public out', one sports editor told his staff – began to show renewed interest in John after Christmas, and the quick-fading anti-Billy Regan hate campaign passed. The *Mouthpiece*, whose initial paper prayer mat had gone down a storm, sent a large editorial delegation to his home in what they termed 'a gesture of goodwill'. They were fronted by the editor, a small, round working-class northern lad made-good, and the paper's Chief Sports Writer, Troy Wilson. Marilyn did admirably well with the catering, as the hastily arranged meeting took place in John's front room. Harry had been invited, but even though he had offered constant support and friendship to John ever since his injury, declined to attend. Becky, who'd quickly pulled on a suit in an attempt to look official, took Harry's place by John's side.

Wilson did most of the talking. 'John,' he said, talking almost unbearably fast. 'We're obviously still gutted about your injury, but we've not given up hope. Have you?' The sentence ended so quickly that John was unprepared to give an answer.

'Er . . . hope of what?' he asked.

'Of making the World Cup.'

John laughed. Becky smiled and gripped his hand. Wilson's face fell slightly.

'There's no reason why you can't recover in time,' he said, defensively. 'I understand that they've got the very best physio team working with you.'

'They have,' replied John, 'but their focus is on getting me walking, not playing football.'

'But once you walk, surely then you can start thinking about running, and then after that . . .'

'I haven't even thought about it. The club are waiting for another few weeks but they're already preparing to pay up my contract and make an insurance claim.'

The editor broke in at this point. 'That's not what we'd been led to believe John,' he said. 'Your club told us that anything was still possible, depending on how successful the surgery was. Even Greg Hardcastle has publicly announced that he'll pick you for the World Cup if you're fit. A lot of people still believe that you can make it.'

'It's a nice thought,' answered John calmly, 'but I'm afraid you're wrong to get your hopes up. As far as I'm concerned, my footballing career is over. But you don't have to worry about me; I've come to terms with it long ago.'

'No,' said Wilson suddenly. 'No way. This story is not over.'

'Which is why we're here,' interjected the editor.

'Yes, that's right,' Wilson agreed, 'we came here with a proposal. We'd like to launch a campaign in the

Mouthpiece – along the lines of "We're supporting John's World Cup dream". We'd print a countdown in the paper each day, of the time remaining until the first game of the World Cup, maybe with a new photo showing how you're improving. The important bit would be a short update from yourself on your progress on the previous day. We'd pay you for it of course–'

'We'd pay you *well*,' added the editor.

'–and the only thing we'd ask is that you don't speak to any other media' Wilson concluded.

John looked at Becky, who returned a shrug. He thought for a few moments, causing the delegation to tap their feet and chew their pens nervously. Finally, he announced his decision.

'I don't believe I've got a chance of making it; you obviously do. I respect that – I mean, more than that, I'm encouraged by you. But I wouldn't feel right leading all your readers on, if I actually knew that a full recovery was impossible. So I'll tell you what: if when this plaster cast comes off, and they do all their tests, any doctor tells me that I've a chance of recovering sufficiently to play football this summer, then I'll agree to what you've asked. But that's my final decision – please don't try to persuade me otherwise, because you'll be wasting your time.'

The semicircle of *Mouthpiece* staff turned inwards for a few moments, murmured a lot, and then turned back to face John and Becky.

'Very well,' said the editor, producing a business card. 'Call me the moment you know.'

They filed out rapidly, paying respectful thanks to Marilyn as they went. John sighed, and for the first time began to wonder whether his initial pessimism about the injury had been too hasty. Within hours, that doubt had festered into a catalyst that re-launched his previously-subdued World Cup dream. And suddenly, from a standing start of general acceptance, he was in a dangerous place – hoping desperately that a near-impossible wish might come true.

The fourth month was difficult – Mile End's sequence of losses and draws equalled the worst in the club's history – and a bad illness kept Elaine away from John for the best part of two weeks. But the fifth, March, brought unexpected developments. Scans on the injured leg revealed that the bone had healed fully, and the plaster was able to come off a few weeks earlier than expected. Checks were made for a full day, but almost miraculously, it seemed that John was virtually able to walk unaided as soon as his plaster was removed – even if only for a few steps at a time.

At haste, a meeting and video conference was arranged. Soon, John found himself seated in the majestic chairman's office at Mile End's stadium, around the same giant table as Frank Crumb, several surgeons and physio staff, and video screens bearing the visages of Greg Hardcastle and a famous American specialist. Dr Cole, the club's Chief Medical Officer overseeing John's recuperation, chaired the conversation.

'Well gentlemen,' he began, with a hint of a grin, 'it seems we have some good news. We've removed John's cast, and it appears he *will* be able to walk unaided. We'll need a good week or two of physiotherapy to be sure, but the signs are very encouraging.'

'Do you think he'll play again?' asked Frank, straight out.

'It's too early to say. We don't know how the bone will react to stress, or how his general posture, flexibility and so on will be affected.'

'So?' pushed Frank.

'So we can't say for sure that he definitely *won't* play again.'

On his screen, Greg Hardcastle's eyes widened. 'Well that looks like a mighty big improvement from where I'm sitting.'

'I must stress,' said Dr Cole, 'that the chance of getting him fit and ready for any sort of football match, ever in the future, is still well below the 50 per cent mark. The chance that he might make a recovery in time for this summer's World Cup, which I suspect is what you're wondering about, is still rather minuscule I'm afraid.'

The American doctor chose this moment to join in. 'It's not impossible though,' he said, with a nasal, Brooklyn twang. 'If the boy wants to play, and he really puts his mind to it, there's a chance he could recover. We've already seen that his body heals unusually quickly – we didn't expect to have that cast off yet. So let's not be undeservedly pessimistic here Dr Cole; there's still a chance.'

Reluctantly, Cole conceded that the more experienced man had a point. 'Perhaps. I suppose I hadn't factored in the psychosomatic element.'

The best course of action was then discussed between the medical staff, but the football men weren't listening. Crumb and Hardcastle wore smiles of content, and John just thought about how he was going to tell his family.

But first, he asked to use the phone. He had a promise to keep.

The *Mouthpiece*'s daily progress updates caught the imagination of its readers instantly. Within days of its launch, backed by a heavyweight advertising campaign, 'Christie-watch' was becoming a must read for every football fan and patriot in the nation. When, in early April, John expressed that he was feeling frustrated, nineteen sacks of cheering-up post was delivered to the newspaper's offices. Later in the month, after he'd managed a light jog for the first time, nationwide pub-takings saw a massive one day spike. His journey toward recovery was still a long and painful one, but now there were several million people going through it with him every step of the way, willing him on toward a highly unlikely goal.

Their obsession came from the media-propagated myth that an England side without John might as well not bother flying out to the championships. After his late double strike against Sweden had somehow snatched qualification from the jaws of utter devastation, John had become the talisman for an England that could win – even though he'd only played for the national team twice. When the fans had seen the leg-breaking tackle – over and over again on two weeks' worth of news bulletins – their hope of success at the World Cup finals had all but died. Now, mainly thanks to the positive propaganda, those hopes had been resurrected.

Harry Foster, meanwhile, was not allowing himself even an inch of hope. In his mind, there was not a chance that John would recover. It was simpler that way, now that his self-imposed removal from football had taken full effect, and although he still paid daily visits to his neighbour, he refused even to notice any progress, convincing himself that a great setback would surely lie around the next corner.

In particularly unromantic fashion, he had re-established his long-abandoned engagement to Jessica. Her presence over the last six months had been rock-like to him, and the compassionate companionship which she embodied had melted his heart and soothed his stress. He loved her – he was pretty sure that he had always loved her – and with his long love affair with football finally buried, she felt that things had changed sufficiently for their relationship to work. They set a date for the middle of the summer, and set about filling their time with wedding preparations – which also assisted Harry in his attempts to ignore 'Christie-watch' and the like.

John was increasingly beginning to believe that he could do it. By early May, his leg was feeling solid, and, as documented in newspapers and celebrity magazines in the UK and beyond, he even managed to kick a ball with his injured leg. The publication of the photographs sent the nation over the edge of fingers-crossed belief and headlong into total hysteria. 'Christie-watch' was extended from an eighth to a third of a page. Many churches, on the demands of parishioners they'd never met, put on special 'Pray for Christie' services – one of which was even broadcast on Sport One. The hope, the prayers, the belief was working – John was winning the race.

Twenty-One

John ran – yes, ran – into Harry's front room to tell him the news. Moments earlier, he'd been interrupted from his rigorous stretching programme by a phone call from Greg Hardcastle. The resulting conversation had been brief – lasting less than 30 seconds – and Hardcastle had done almost all the talking. It had gone like this:

'John, it's Greg Hardcastle.'

'Hello there, sir.'

'John, I've just submitted the final World Cup squad to the WFF.'

'Yes, sir?'

'You're in it John. I'm taking a chance on you.'

'You are, sir . . .? Th– thank you, sir.'

'See you in a couple of days. That's all for now. Goodbye.'

As he relayed the story to his friend, he was bouncing on his injured leg. And although he was still experiencing several problems, most notably an inability to kick the ball hard with the injured leg, the hardest part of the impossible had already been achieved. His broken body had healed in half the time he might have expected, and twice as well as anyone had hoped. John Christie was going to the World Cup finals, and what's more, there was every chance that it could be the same John Christie who scored against Sweden.

Harry did not take the news as John expected him to. Instead of breaking into tears of joy and engulfing him in a bear hug, he slid down on to his couch, turned pale and looked away. Inside his every sinew was bursting with happiness and excitement; simultaneously, his heart throbbed painfully with devastation. Having just spent six months on a strict cold-turkey programme, the hopes and dreams of the previous fifty years had appeared unexpectedly once more. He felt like the jilted lover who has just rebuilt his shattered life, only to find his true love at the door once more. The emotional cocktail was too much – he didn't know how to cope or respond. So he said nothing, and thrust his head heavily into his hands.

From the middle of a crumpled heap therefore, came the words: 'I'm so proud of you son.'

John did not understand Harry's reaction. He had known that the injury that he had suffered had hit Harry badly; he had known also that *Foster's Eye* had ceased for the moment, but he had gathered that the cure for the former had been the reason for the latter, and that with Jessica in tow, Harry had now found a greater degree of happiness than ever before. But the crumpled heap did not look happy, to any degree. Neither did he look interested in conversation.

'I'll let myself out,' said John as he retreated towards home. 'Come by later if you want to talk about anything.' And he was gone.

Harry waited for the sound of a closing door, then released the tears that had been clawing away behind his eyes. He poured himself a large drink, then another, and tried once again to reassess his life, as not for the first time, the goalposts shifted significantly.

The England squad, complete with Messiah, left Heathrow early one morning at the end of May. The airport had been brought to a virtual standstill by surging crowds, all desperate to catch a glimpse of their hero as John-Christie-fever reached a supremely positive conclusion. The *Mouthpiece* ensured that as 'the official John Christie paper', they made their presence felt there, handing out cardboard cut-outs of 'the leg' to wave as well as the usual 'Come on England' flags and plastic hats.

The players, themselves decked out in designer suits decorated with both the English Football Federation logo and the three roaring lions, were shocked by the scene. It buoyed them, however, as they prepared themselves for the seven-hour flight to New York, where they would be based for the first part of the competition. It instilled in them, if such a thing was needed, a realisation that the whole country was behind them. None of the players cared that so much of the nation's attention was being focused upon just one of their number, and a man who hadn't played football since early in the previous November. Almost to a man, they shared the sense of pride that the nation felt for John Christie, and drew inspiration from his courage. They had also bought into the hype – they, too, believed that his presence on that plane to the USA considerably multiplied their chances of bringing the trophy back on the return flight.

There was one notable exception to all this flag-waving, soul-baring, wide-smiling patriotism, however, and not just because of the time of day. At the back of the party, the one player who had refused to wear the national tie was seething through narrowed green eyes. He was the one man in England who had rooted for John to fail; he was the person who had hoped that the odds would prevail. Now his destiny – as England's greatest ever striker and their World Cup hero – was under threat. As another camera flash went off in John's face ahead of him, the anger uncurled in Billy Regan's throat, and he could not stop himself from snarling.

A few days of US acclimatisation, during which John was introduced to cultural wonders like 'Buffalo Burgers' and three-course breakfasts, were followed by an intensive period of training and practice games. Despite his presence in the squad, John was still unable to take part in the vast majority of this, and was often left to run or practise on his own while the rest of the party trained together. He was a spectator for both of the 'friendly' matches to take place in the run up to the tournament's opening, against New York Dynamos and the Pennsylvania Titans, and watched as Billy Regan and Clinton McLean – both of them under real pressure for their places for the first time in years – hit a rich vein of striking form. Finally, with only five days remaining before the opening match against Norway, the medical staff allowed John to take part in the regular daily training session, followed by a five-a-side game.

He had expected to feel rusty, but not quite that out of touch. Drills and exercises were not a problem for him – the leg seemed now to have healed completely – but match-play was more tricky. His first touch of the game, which was at first played at walking pace for his benefit, sent the ball spinning out of control and straight to an opponent. His second, executed with the pressure of the initial mishap still weighing heavy on his shoulders, was even worse: attempting to trap the ball with his instep, he instead only managed to get a knee on it, and then after recovering, he sent the pass a full 10 yards wide of it's intended recipient. He looked puzzled because his feet weren't doing what his brain was telling them to; his team-mates looked terrified that the real John Christie might still be in London.

Although his skills seemed to be suffering from jet-lag, the leg itself was holding up well. He hadn't yet suffered a heavy challenge from anyone, but he felt strong and confident when he ran. And the next day, in a repeat of the same session, John's skill began to catch up with his body in terms of recovery. He began to regain his excellent close control; his speed when running with the ball was back up to 95 per cent of what it had been before; and he even started to find the back of the tiny five-a-side nets. By the time the practice schedule switched over to 'light training', two days later, the physios had labelled John 'almost match fit'. 'Almost' was quite good enough for Greg Hardcastle, who quickly informed the British media and the player – in that order – that John would start against Norway. And with that, the miracle was complete.

Harry, still at home and fully immersed in wedding plans, heard the news from Marilyn, twice in quick succession. First, he felt his own home shaken by the joyful shrieking emanating from next-door. Then, he heard banging at his front door, through which tumbled a breathless, ecstatic middle-aged woman with tears running down her cheeks.

'He's in! He's playing! He's starting!' she screamed, without pausing for breath and bouncing up and down like a 10-year-old.

Harry's face didn't move. 'He's starting? John's starting against Norway?'

'Yes! John just phoned to tell me! They've told him that he's match fit! Isn't it wonderful?'

'Yes,' replied Harry, his body language saying anything but. 'It is wonderful.'

England's first two group games would take place in New York, with the third in Dallas. Norway, first up, presented potentially the least threat, and so, with a highly improved Australia and second-favourite France lying in wait, an opening victory was imperative. Hardcastle's plan was to go all out for victory in the first two matches, since a team which earned 6 of the possible 9 points in the group stages seldom failed to qualify for the second round. A good result against France would then be a bonus, rather than the only way to avoid an early flight home. John would, he was told early on the morning of the match, be playing as part of a front two with Clinton McLean. Billy Regan – who a year ago had fully expected to be leading the line in this match – was one of five on the bench.

After breakfast, and prior to light training, John retired to the hotel room which he was sharing with D'Alex Smith to call Harry, whom he had not spoken to since leaving the UK. It was already the middle of the day in England, and so John did not expect the gruff response he received.

'Harry?' said John upon getting through. 'It's John – I just wanted to call to say hello before the game.'

'Oh, yeah, of course. Thanks John,' said Harry coldly. There was an awkward pause.

'Er . . . how are things going? Wedding plans and all that?'

'Good, yeah. Everything's fine.' Clearly everything was not fine.

'Well, OK then – I just thought I'd give you a quick call. Are you going to watch the match tonight?'

There was a quiet, undefined murmur on the other end of the line.

'Harry?'

'Mmm?'

'Are you OK?'

'Fine. I'm fine. Hope it goes well tonight.'

The change in Harry was so drastic, that it both upset John, and left him with nothing to say. The conversation was dry now – and he knew that it was time to go. 'Alright then Harry,' he said. 'It's a shame you can't be out here. I'll try and score one for you.'

'Mmm.'

A few minutes after John's call, Jessica returned from the supermarket, where she had bought fresh bread and cheese for lunch. She found Harry slumped once more on the couch, as he had been on and off for the last few days. Deep down, she knew what was wrong, but continued to feign ignorance.

'You OK darling?' she asked innocently.

'Yeah,' he lied, dragging himself to his feet. He was acutely aware, of course, that he could not reveal the truth. That truth was that ever since John's unlikely recovery from injury had materialised into reality, the previously extinguished flames of his primary passion had become partially rekindled. Half of him was rejoicing that his dysfunctional relationship with football had at last been replaced by something more tangible; half of him still hankered for his long-term mistress. With John in a wheelchair, on crutches or even limping around a park, Harry had been able to put that mistress out of sight and out of mind. He had felt that she'd betrayed him beyond any forgiveness. But then, thanks to a combination of miracle and modern science, the situation had dramatically changed. Now, there was nothing that half of him would not give to be in the New York City Soccerdrome that evening. The other half was happy here, though, and now, just as for much of the past few days, what he couldn't quite compute was which half was bigger.

He played around with his food in silence, as Jessica attempted to throw a few interested questions in to break up the grating grey awkwardness. He barely responded, even with grunts, until out of sheer frustration, she threw in a dart-like question which he could not ignore.

'Harry,' she said, very calmly, 'are you thinking about John?'

Harry looked up guiltily, like a boy caught with his hand in the cookie jar. He said nothing, so she tried again, even more explicitly.

'Harry, is your heart in America right now?'

Again, Harry said nothing, but now the guilt on his face increased tenfold. Jessica stared at him for what seemed like an age, her own mind whirring through the situation. After some time had passed, she spoke again:

'If you want to go out there, to support him, then you can. If you drove to the airport now, I expect you could even get a flight that would take you out there in time for the game. If that's where your heart is Harry, I can't hold you back.'

Pieces of bread fell out of Harry's mouth as his jaw hung open. 'Jess – do you really mean that? You'd let me fly out there – even in the middle of all this planning, and for football?'

Jessica was not smiling. 'That's what I said. Of course, you wouldn't need to worry about the planning. There'd be nothing to plan for if you left me now.'

Harry's face plummeted again. Now he realised what she was getting at. 'But Jess–' he started.

'But Jess what?' she snapped. 'Half a lifetime ago, I fell in love with this ridiculous boy who was more interested in a sport than he was in me. Then I find him again, half a lifetime later, and I find he's finally grown up, and at last he's ready to have a mature relationship. And now suddenly, you're telling me he's regressed again?'

'I didn't bring it up,' he protested. 'You asked me if I wanted to fly out!'

'As if you needed to bring it up,' she shouted, getting to her feet. 'You've had a face like a dying man for most of the last week. It didn't need a brilliant psychologist to work out what was going on in your head.'

'Jess,' pleaded Harry, 'this isn't just about football – it's about John. Isn't that a bit different? He's almost been like a son to me over the last year and a half – I can't deny that there's a part of me that feels like I should be by his side right now.'

'Maybe you should listen to that side of you then. Fly out there. Join your adopted son. Leave me here. But if you do, then this time it really is over – and you will never see me again.'

'Jessica, please don't do this to me – not again.'

'Choose.'

'Losing you the first time is the biggest regret of my life.'

'Choose.'

Moments later, Harry realised which half was bigger, and followed the appropriate course of action.

The New York City Soccerdrome was a magnificent beast of a building, constructed specifically for the tournament and with an awesome retractable roof, which on this evening stood gaping open, as the sun slowly descended and a cool breeze rushed through and soothed the pitch. Though the United States had only warmed to 'soccer' in the relatively recent past, this stadium, like most of the others that were due to host games in the next five weeks, was all but sold out. A handful of tickets were still available, mainly through the small army of touts outside the ground, but the vast majority had been snapped up on their release several months ago, and mainly in this instance from the city's wealth of Italian and Irish descendants who had football – not soccer – in the blood.

John and his comrades stepped out onto the pitch around an hour before kick-off, just to get a feel for the ball and the playing surface. As they did so, they were greeted by an eager and almost packed house of nearly 60,000, the majority of which seemed to be clad in England white. On John's first touch of the ball during the warm-up, there came a mighty roar from three corners of the stadium. That told them all that their supporters were here in force.

Even so, John felt lonely. Despite his gentle insistence, Becky, Marilyn and Elaine had all declined the opportunity to join him at the tournament. Each of them was burningly proud, but also uncontrollably nervous and immensely terrified of any sort of limelight. In view of the media machine which was bound to follow John around the tournament, they had all come to the decision that they would stay in England together and support him from afar – remaining on the end of a telephone line if ever he was in need of comfort or a chat. This he had come to terms with – he certainly never wanted to force anyone into something they didn't want to do – but Harry was a different matter. It felt strange that the man who had been with him through every step of his football career, without whose intervention he would certainly not now be warming up at a World Cup, was not here for the biggest leap of all. It felt wrong. His heart sank again as he thought about it.

Greg Hardcastle's assistant shouted from the tunnel for the team to return to the changing rooms for the pre-match pep talk. With his heart still a little heavy, John followed the others and left the pitch to rapturous applause and chanting. As he reached the tunnel's edge, however, he was sure he picked out one voice among all the rest, screaming his name with a greater intent than simple adoration. He stopped, looked up, and tried to find its source. Then he did – a stubby, wrinkled man directly in front of him, one side of a huge crowd-control barrier. And though they couldn't embrace due to the huge chunk of metal, both of them welled up with tears and beamed with joy.

'Harry! You made it!' cried John.

'Of course I did,' Harry replied. 'I wouldn't miss this for the world.'

Twenty-Two

England were magnificent. From the first minute to the last, they crushed the Norwegians with a steamroller of attacking genius, and repelled their futile offensive blows with a rock-solid defence. True to the hype, John Christie was the centrepiece, privately buoyed by the surprise appearance of his friend just before kick-off, and relishing the chance to play in a match that seven months ago, none but the clinically insane would have possibly envisaged he would be fit for.

After just twenty minutes his World Cup scoring account was open. A 40-yard ball from D'Alex Smith set Simon Brazier free on the left hand side, and his over-hit cross reached all the way to Paul Kerridge on the opposite flank. Kerridge's cross was better measured, and found John unmarked almost directly on the penalty spot. His well-directed header hit the inside of the post on its way in, and the goalkeeper could get nowhere near it. It was 1–0 to England, and Hardcastle's master-plan was underway.

It was 2–0 before half-time. This time, John got the assist, expertly shielding the ball from the desperate Norwegian defenders, before threading a cute reverse pass into the path of the on-running Brazier. During the break, when no substitutions were thought necessary, the manager's instructions were cheerfully simple: more of the same please.

Those orders, although undemanding, were strictly adhered to. England were 3–0 up on the half-hour mark, and again, John was involved. His flick-on from Lloyd McGrath's goal kick put Clinton McLean clean through on the overworked Norway 'keeper, and, eager not to sacrifice his place in the next game to an increasingly red-faced Billy Regan, made no mistake with his finish. After that, England slowed their pace, containing any half-hearted opposition attacks with consummate ease, and by the end, were practically running the game at walking pace. It stayed 3–0; a final score that sent a clear message to those who'd doubted England's potential before the tournament. John took the man-of-the-match award – his second in three appearances for his country – and all was very well indeed.

Back home, Christie-mania was back with a bang. A special, delayed edition of the *Mouthpiece* (the time difference meant that the game had been played during the British night) appeared with the cover splash '*Our John Sinks the Vikings*', while normal television programming was regularly interrupted by repeat showings of England's emphatic win. The *Morning News*, which was generally more conservative than most in its sports predictions, noted that 'Christie played like he was very deliberately making up for lost time – in his first competitive match for half a year, he scored one and set up two more. If this was his comeback match, and a chance for him to blow away some match-practice cobwebs, how Australia must fear facing him at full strength.'

Bookmakers across the country had responded quickly to the game, just in time to protect themselves against the patriotic flurry of betting that followed it. Odds on England winning the title, which had been as long as 25–1, were now reduced to 10–1 and below. A handful of punters, who'd had the courage to back England before the game, and at the

longer odds, were now licking their lips in anticipation.
'You're going to make me rich if you keep playing like that,' enthused Harry, with his first words to John as they finally hugged after the game. He unfolded a piece of paper tucked deep into his wallet. '25–1! Look at that!'

'You put £2,000 on us to win?' John recoiled in shock. 'Are you mad?'

'I got nervous at the airport while I was waiting for my flight. The odds took my fancy. Anyway – I'm told they're not even offering half that on you now.'

John smiled. He was too delighted by his friend's arrival to worry too much about his flaws. 'Come on,' he said. 'Let's go and get something to eat. We've got two weeks to catch up on.'

'No John,' said Harry, placing an arm around him. 'We've got seven months to catch up on.'

Australia, five days later in the very same stadium, presented a very different proposition to the men from Scandinavia. While Norway were a team in the depths of a footballing slide, the Australians were the very opposite – a side on-the-up, packed with flair, pace and invention. In their first game, they'd narrowly lost to the highly-rated French, but only by three goals to two. That they'd scored twice against a defence held in such regard was a concern to the England coaching staff, who chose less attacking tactics for this encounter. Also, this game – for the sake of British television – would be played in the midday sun, and a climate far more recognisable to the boys from down under. That meant a 5–3–2 formation (five defenders, three midfielders, two attackers), with the emphasis on plod and battle.

Hardcastle, much to Billy Regan's chagrin, named a carbon copy side of that which dispatched so effectively with its first opponents. That meant another chance for

John to impress, and he duly took it. With Harry – now enjoying a better view from a special box reserved for players' families – roaring him on, his confidence and ability seemed to reach another level as the opponents put before him improved.

In the first ten minutes, both he and Clinton McLean struggled to see much of the ball. Between themselves, they decided that John would drop into more of an attacking midfield position, in order to provide a link between the attack and the midfield, which seemed to have its work cut out coping with Australia's tricky young side. In this deeper position, John immediately gained a greater share of possession, and was soon setting McLean off in pursuit of the first of many clever through-balls.

England had several good chances in the opening third of the game but failed to convert any of them, and were caught by surprise when their fearless opponents scored first. Lloyd McGrath fumbled a deeply hit corner, and managed to drop the ball directly onto the outstretched foot of their Scottish-based forward Ewan McGee. Again, the crowd was heavily biased towards England, and there was a chilling quiet directly after the goal which made it seem unreal. Despite the silence, it *was* still a goal, and at half-time, England trailed.

This time, Hardcastle found more to say in his team talk. England's chances of qualifying for the next phase were hanging in the balance, he told them. News had already filtered through from the other game in the group that Norway had unexpectedly held France to a dour 0–0 draw. That meant that if England could turn this match around and win – a job not to be underestimated – then they would have guaranteed their place in the last sixteen with a game to spare: the original Hardcastle master-plan. Of course, the flip side of that coin was that the mighty France would now need to win their final game – against England – in order to be sure of their own qualification. All in all, the message was obvious – they needed to win this one, and quick.

In pubs across the UK, many fans were demonstrating how brittle their dream really was. At 1–0 down against the nation's old sporting enemy, few were even speaking coherently. Many armchair pundits were already writing off the first game as a fluke, and with it England's overall chances in the competition. They had such little faith.

Around eight minutes after the game had restarted, England levelled. D'Alex Smith, the centre-back, surprised the Australians by embarking on a marauding run from one end of the pitch to the other. The attackers didn't bother to try to tackle him, leaving him for the midfielders, who in turn were too busy marking other players to consider that his rampage might continue. Thus he was unopposed until he reached the very edge of the Australian box, when eventually a frantic defender arrived to block his progress. This forced Smith, who did not possess a subtle through-pass in his armoury of skills, into giving the ball a good, honest thwack in the direction of the goal, with the end of his toe. It was as straight as an arrow – straight at the 'keeper in fact, who was anticipating it – until it hit the leg of the defender, and bent off in the opposite direction. The goalkeeper was completely wrong-footed and simply watched the ball fly into the back of the net. In no sense was it a wonder-goal – Smith's trundle up the spine of the pitch had been well short in the grace and poise departments – but it was effective, and it brought England back to 1–1 at exactly the right time. Back home, the bars were alive with chatter and activity once more – their faith had been instantly restored.

There was still the small matter of a winning goal to seek, however. England had to wait for it – until the

78th minute when Ewan McGee, who'd earlier been Australia's hero, now turned villain as he hopelessly missed a clearing header and caught the ball full with his hand instead. The referee, who'd had a superb game, saw the incident clearly and awarded a fair penalty. The decision was not a difficult one to make, but the Australians, sensing that they were slipping out of the tournament, surrounded the referee in protest anyway. As they did so, Greg Hardcastle took the opportunity to send on fresh legs for the tiring McLean – in the shape of Billy Regan, whose absence from 168 minutes of the World Cup had nearly deflated him entirely. He appeared a subdued figure as he emerged from his track suit, far from the raging ball of jealousy that had occupied those clothes previously. At last, grudgingly accepting his place in the pecking order, he did not even consider asking to take the waiting penalty. But John, seeing his sullen demeanour, called to him as he entered the pitch. 'Billy – do you want this?' Regan's reaction was one of shock, but after less than a second of thought, was followed by an unmistakable gesture of acceptance. Several players on either team scratched their heads in disbelief as John strode away from the penalty spot, and Regan assumed the striking position. Seconds later, after Regan had successfully slotted the penalty into the very corner of the net, those thoughts were all forgotten and replaced with equal measures of joy for the English and despair for the Australians. And as he wheeled away, celebrating what turned out to be a winning goal with more passion than he had ever celebrated in his life, he was not slow to acknowledge John's sacrifice. For the first time in their lives, they actually shook hands.

Two games, two wins, and England were already through to the knockout stages of the tournament with a game to spare. So with the first stage of the plan successfully complete, Greg Hardcastle allowed his troops a reward: some well-earned R and R in central Manhattan.

D'Alex Smith knew the area well and suggested that they spend their evening at an exclusive jazz club – Tiny's – with a reputation that stretched far beyond Greenwich Village. According to D'Alex, there were only two types who had a hope of getting into Tiny's: obscenely rich famous people like themselves, and the criminally poor jazz musicians who would provide entertainment way into the small hours.

Inside, Tiny's was anything but. A sprawling, underground lair filled with smoke and mirrors, it seemed to go on for miles in every direction. As they entered – a huge group of mainly-white men in sharp suits – the music and the conversation momentarily paused in disbelief. Nervously excited, John immediately dragged Harry to the nearest couch, where a make-up-splattered waitress instantly appeared, genie-like, to offer them drinks.

'This place is cool,' said John, bobbing his head unrhythmically to the beat.

'Yes John, but it appears you're not,' Harry laughed.

John giggled, and exaggerated the bobbing. Harry scanned the vast room for a toilet.

'Do you mind waiting here for the drinks?' he asked, having finally spotted a neon sign. 'I won't be a minute.'

John nodded, in out-of-time bobs, and Harry walked away shaking his head.

The 'rest room' was also massive. There were eight cubicles, seven of which were empty, and a row of ten sinks each decorated with a proliferation of hand lotions, face creams and after shaves. Overwhelmed by the choice, Harry chose a cubicle. On departing from it, moments later, he bumped into the man leaving the next one along. It was Billy Regan, stumbling a little, with the wide unfocused eyes that John had encountered back at Paul Kerridge's party a year earlier. Each man looked at the other, and did not speak. Then Regan found something hysterically funny, and sprinted back into the main bar area.

On his way back to John, a concerned Harry took Clinton McLean, who was bobbing his head in a far more credible manner, to one side.

'Clinton,' Harry began, 'I've just seen Billy Regan in the toilet – he looked absolutely hammered. He wasn't drinking on the way down here was he?'

'I don't think so mate,' came the reply.

'It's funny, because . . . his eyes . . . I swear he looked drunk.'

McLean looked serious. 'No Harry. He ain't been drinking.' He looked both ways to make sure no one was listening. 'You're not a journo any more, are you mate?'

Harry shook his head, wondering what he was about to hear.

'What Regan does, none of us is happy with. But the fact is, it can't be detected, and if he wants to mess his own mind up, that's his business.'

'I'm sorry, I don't understand.'

'Billy takes Zanthone – it's a designer drug that the testers don't seem to know about and the screening process can't pick up. He tells us he's not addicted, but I'm not so sure, the amount he seems to take it.'

Harry shook his head in disbelief. 'Who knows about this?'

'Most of the older lads know. Obviously the boss doesn't. Look, Harry, I hate it too, but he's Billy Regan for goodness' sake. He does what he wants. Take comfort from the fact that he'll destroy himself in the end.'

'You know Clinton, a year ago I might have agreed with you. But now that doesn't comfort me at all.'

John was really getting into the music now, and had barely touched his non-alcoholic cocktail. When Harry returned, a little pale and shaky, from his excursion, John just wanted to extol the virtues of the genius saxophonist who'd transfixed him.

'Hey Harry, this guy is fan . . . what's wrong?'

'Regan. Regan's a junkie.'

'WHAT?' John nearly jumped out of his seat, and the saxophonist was jerked into hitting a bum note. 'What? As in a drug user?'

'Zanthone apparently, whatever that is. He's on it right now.' They both looked across the bar at Regan, who was dancing foolishly, and alone.

'But . . . but . . . that's wrong. He can't do that. They've got to make him stop.'

'I know,' Harry reassured him, 'but apparently this stuff doesn't show up on drugs tests.'

'He's a role model – there are children all over England who want to be like him. . . .'

'John, I'm as upset as you are about this, but . . . .'

'Really?' John snapped, his eyes raging. 'Was your sister paralysed by a drug addict then?'

Harry said nothing.

Neither of them felt like socialising any longer. They switched the glamour and panache of Tiny's for the less salubrious surroundings of a nearby branch of Zwickburger, and sat in silence for an hour munching junk food. John was stung, and his mind was racing in fifty directions, each fuelled by a different emotion. And then he hit upon an idea. As Harry went to the counter to fetch apple pie for dessert, John reached into his friend's coat pocket and retrieved his diary. In the front, as he suspected, he found a number for the *Daily Reporter*, which he quickly scribbled onto his hand. Then he slipped the diary back into the pocket, just in time to avoid Harry's returning eyes.

Back in his hotel room by 11, and with room-mate D'Alex still deep in the bowels of Tiny's, John went straight to bed. He didn't sleep at all that night.

In the morning, as soon as D'Alex had disappeared for his shower, John took the course of action that he had arrived at over a full night of mulling. Picking up the receiver of his room's phone, nerves meant he dialled, mis-dialled and re-dialled the number on his hand several times over, which was beginning to melt away from the sweat on his palm. Eventually he made a connection.

'*Reporter* Sport,' came the curt answer.

'Hello,' he shuddered, 'this is John Christie.'

'John Christie? Is this a joke?'

'No, I'm serious. It's me – I'm calling you from my room in New York.'

'Wow! It is you, I recognise the voice! Hey – you're doing a great job out there so far. I mean, it was a bit twitchy for a while yesterday but–'

'Thanks,' John cut him off, 'but I've got to be quick. I've got something to tell you. Some information that I think would interest your readers.'

'Hang on,' said Burke. 'I'll get my editor.'

Twenty-Three

One day of relative tranquillity in the England camp passed without incident. Then . . . .

'Are you really so naïve?' screamed Harry. 'What in blazes did you think you were doing?'

John sank into his seat, said nothing and looked away.

The plane journey to Dallas was turbulent and uncomfortable. It was nothing to do with external weather factors, however – the disruption had come from within. At Lite-Cola airport, scores of reporters had accosted John, Hardcastle and others, begging for comments on the report in the British *Daily Reporter*. Struck dumb by the shock of the unexpected and by the ferocity of the questioning, no one said anything, as the airport security was almost overrun by the heaving mass of media.

At the back of the all business-class charter, John received a severe grilling from the management and EFF officials. Displaying a backbone that he had previously kept hidden, John remained defiant, insisting that what he had done was the only right thing to do. Just as Alex Knight at the *Reporter* had done, they pressed him hard for a name. He refused, insisting as he had done to Knight that he was only prepared to reveal that *a member* of the squad was taking narcotics. This, he explained, was a warning – a chance for the player in question to realise his mistake and cease his habit immediately. John did not want to ruin anyone's career – he simply wanted the drug abuse to end.

The EFF did not share his sense of mercy. A few flustered radio-phone calls between London and the middle of the air over America later, the punishment for this unwarranted outburst to the media – the like of which the squad had been seriously warned about pre-tournament – was meted out. John would be banned for the final group game against France – by his own football federation. And ironically, his place in the team would go to the very person his silence was protecting.

In Dallas, no one spoke to John. Even Harry was too angry with him. John did address some of his team-mates briefly, but his words did little to calm their frustration. 'I'd do it again,' he said.

Back in England the next morning, things turned nasty. The *Mouthpiece*, horrified that John had given the 'England squad drugs claim' story to another newspaper, turned on their former favourite son. 'Christie has misunderstood his role, and the value of his own self-righteousness,' spat their venom. 'The boy needs to shut up, and concentrate on his football. Otherwise he'll find his popularity will hit a deeper low than the cold turkey suffered by his imaginary drug addict.' Rival tabloid the *Spark* was similarly offensive: 'John Christie is in danger of going from hero to zero in the space of a few poorly chosen words. He's lucky – had England needed a result in the game for which he's now banned, this outburst could have cost the country very dear. Hopefully he will not be foolish enough to pull a stunt like this again.' Speculation over the identity of the mystery junkie was also rife. Five different newspapers contained five exclusives on the truth, each featuring a different player – none of which were Billy Regan.

Alex Knight's sports editorial in the *Daily Reporter* was a lone voice in protesting John's innocence. 'Here is a man,' he argued, 'who sees wrong, and cannot simply stand by and watch. This, surely, is the role model our young people need? A man who has such a sense of honour and mercy, that he would rather fall on his own sword than see the villain betrayed? Many of you will attack him for what he has done, but I say that he is now twice the hero he was before.'

No one listened to Knight. The wide consensus throughout the media, and subsequently among those who consumed it in the pubs, offices and homes around the land, was that John Christie should keep his mouth shut for the foreseeable future. Wrapped up in the excitement of potential World Cup success, most had insulated themselves from caring if a member of the squad was dabbling in drugs. If he helped England to win a World Cup, most people didn't care if he was a serial killer, too.

There was no justice. As John sat in the stands of the Dallas Zwickburger Stadium, regularly blinded by flashbulbs more interested in him than the on-pitch action, he looked on helplessly as Billy Regan single-handedly demolished France. He scored twice, either side of half-time, with strikes that John himself would have been proud of. At the end of the game, and in the next day's press, the fickle pendulum of support had already swung back towards the previously forgotten man. In the briefest of moments, Regan was king once more. And when questioned after the game, though he ducked all questions about John, Greg Hardcastle confirmed that whoever the opposition, Regan would definitely start the second round match.

John was overcome with disappointment; still though, he regretted nothing.

As promised, John started the second round match, against fourth-favourites Argentina, from the inside of a track suit, on a bench in the Chicago Megastadium – the largest soccer arena in the USA, which would also be the venue for the final two weeks later. As the teams ran out, he was sure Regan, with whom he had not shared a single word about the controversy, aimed a sneering wink in his direction. It hurt him, but he did not react, cheering on the team with the rest of the bench and half of the 80,000 crowd.

The game, the latest in a notorious line of fixtures between these two giants of world football, was edgy and tense, with few chances at either end. Lloyd McGrath, who'd only conceded a single goal so far and had been named the goalkeeper of the first round, was again on fine form, keeping out the best chance of the first half with a cat-like leap to the very corner of his goal. Regan, though fired up for the game, was no match for the classy Argentine defensive pairing – a virtually error free duo who also played together at Club De Paris, hence sharing an enormous understanding – and failed even to get a shot on target.

At the break Hardcastle, still mad at John, decided against the obvious substitution, and left his most talented player to rot next to him. But after twenty further minutes of dullness, during which Argentina still had marginally the better chances, he began to feel the game slipping very subtly from his grasp. At any moment, he realised, a single Argentina goal could potentially send them spinning out of the tournament. Clinton McLean again looked tired, and though he had looked more likely to make an impact than the shackled Regan, it was he that made way for John's belated re-introduction to the side.

McLean did not offer the customary high-five as they switched places. Furthermore, John realised that none of his team were even looking at him as he entered the fray.

Plenty of the opposition players did, however, and talked among themselves in low voices laced with concern.

John could not score, however, if his team-mates did not pass to him. As the ninety minutes petered out to a painful 0–0, that was exactly what happened. In twenty minutes, he only touched the ball three times, and that was only when he was making his own tackles. And when he did finally gain possession, it arrived at a heart-wrenching price – a large contingent of his own crowd was actually booing him.

Extra-time arrived, but now both sides were too terrified of conceding even to leave their own half of the field. The longest half an hour in footballing history ensued, as the teams committed numbers to their defence, failed to launch a meaningful attack and put all their faith in their penalty-taking abilities. Eventually, after what seemed like several days, the whistle blew and the terrifying conclusion inevitably arrived. Five penalty kicks a side, and the losers on a plane home by the morning.

Back in England, millions crowded behind television sets, holding their loved-ones tightly and praying to whoever might be listening. In Ariel Hill, three women – who in recent days had been forced through an emotional mill – did likewise.

Simon Brazier stepped up to take the first English penalty. He struck it low and hard to the 'keeper's right, and though he dived the right way, the ball found the net: 1–0 to England. The Argentine captain did likewise: 1–1. The next pair of penalties were also successfully converted. Fingernails here, and around the world, were already getting short, and no one had yet missed.

Paul Kerridge, who'd had a quiet game, got ready to take England's third. Before he started his run-up, he decided that he would put it to the right. However, as he reached the point of contact, he looked up and noticed the goalkeeper was already starting to move in the direction he was about to place the ball. Readjusting his body at the last second, he toe-poked the ball to the left instead. But he over-compensated, and the ball thudded into the advertising hoardings, wide of the post. It was still 2–2.

Not for long though. The Argentina striker Juan Carlos Pablo, was single-minded in his subsequent strike, and it rocketed past the outstretched glove of Lloyd McGrath to give his side the lead. England were four kicks away from going home.

Next up, the revitalised icon and secret Zanthone addict. Nonchalantly, he placed the ball on the spot, waved to the fans, and ran up to dink the ball cheekily into the centre of the goal, directly over the fooled 'keeper's despairing dive. But this was not the moment for nonchalance. Regan had underestimated the goalkeeper's quality, and though he was initially fooled, he recovered quickly, standing up to catch the ball as it ballooned towards him. Argentina were up 3–2, and only a miracle could stop them now.

Lloyd McGrath was feeling miraculous though. He made up his mind, as the fourth Argentine steamed in towards him, to throw himself full stretch to his right. He guessed correctly – the ball zoomed towards his hand as he flew, and he was able to keep it out easily. England needed to score and then save again – their tournament odds were surely now closer to 1,000–1, but at least they were part of the way there.

And then it was John's turn. The villain of the last ten days had the opportunity to become the villain of the next four years. The noise of the crowd was unbearable. John felt crushed like a bug under the pressure. He did not feel ready for this, but the referee urged him on. He placed the ball on the spot, took ten paces back, said a short prayer, and ran in at full pelt. It was the hardest he'd ever hit a football – all the pent-up emotion, frustration and anger surged into his foot as he let fly – and it was past the 'keeper before he'd even had a chance to move. At last, 3–3, but with one more rabbit left in the hat.

McGrath would have to try his best to pull it out. To the collective screams of several hundred million viewers worldwide, he succeeded. The fifth Argentine penalty was poorly taken, straight at him, and easily saved. Still it was three penalties a piece; still the sides were inseparable, and the agony of sudden death was wheeled into view.

England sent forward Wayne Webster – the only other England player who had volunteered to take a kick. If it went to a seventh round of penalties, they'd be wheeling out the conscientious objectors. Webster's arrival at the penalty spot did not fill his team-mates with excitement, since in training he was regularly mocked for his inaccuracy in front of goal. As he gave them a thumbs up though, he was smiling brightly, and as the team huddled together, they assumed that perhaps he had been practising.

In the middle of that huddle, and back in from the Siberian cold of rejection, stood John. Still no one had spoken to him, yet it was clear, with a white-shirted arm covering each of his shoulders, that some degree of forgiveness had been earned.

Webster scored. His uncultured toe-punt deceived the goalkeeper, who'd been expecting something more classy and had flung himself away from the centre of the goal, where the ball trickled over the line. For the first time in what seemed like millennia, England were ahead. Back at home, the millions who'd been preparing for a wake got ready for a street party instead.

In the end it was an Argentine, and not John or Lloyd McGrath, who sent England into the second round. The pressure was simply too much for young Diego Garruda, who at 19 was not meant for a moment like this. His penalty sailed not only high over the crossbar, but also wide of McGrath's post. One country went into mourning, the other into national celebration. England, somehow, were in the quarter-finals.

John did not celebrate with his fellow victors, despite smiling invitations for him to do so. Instead, as captured on film by much of the world's media, he stepped over to console Garruda, who lay alone on the turf, abandoned by his team-mates, and feeling as if he'd been hit by a train. They did not speak the same language, yet John was all too aware of how grateful this young man was of a comforting hug, even coming from his enemy. The little Argentine's tears soaked the back of his shirt, and for the first time, John realised the crushing relativity of a football victory. In the past, he had only thought of how the fans in England would be cheering, dancing and singing with joy. For them to experience that, however, there needed to be a matching set of people, on the other side of the world, who were now crying, cursing and contemplating acts of mindless violence. Winning was not as clear-cut as he'd thought.

That night, instead of joining in the England celebrations, he opted for an early night. He was beginning to like this game less and less.

Twenty-Four

If England were to make the semi-finals, they would face the favourites and undeniably the finest team in the world. Brazil, who'd put Turkey to the sword with a devastating display of skill and proficiency, already occupied one of the berths in their half of the draw. England had one eye on the other. First, however, they had to overcome the might of history-steeped Italy, again in the lofty Chicago Megastadium.

John, whom the media had left alone in all the post-penalty shoot out elation, was restored to the starting line-up alongside Regan. He would, he had been reassured in training all week, again receive passes from his team-mates following their collective sulk in the previous match, but he'd been instructed to play in the gap behind Regan as a second striker-cum-attacking midfielder.

Italy were a fine side. Although notoriously slow starters in competitions such as this, they had recorded a thumping 5–0 demolition of Denmark in their second-round game, and in Marco Spizzo boasted the top-scorer in the competition so far with six goals. They also named Tyneside's Luigi Spagnoli and London City's Gino Di Ginetti in their starting eleven, so they had plenty of inside knowledge on the England players. With that in mind, John noticed that they had directed Di Ginetti, a defensive midfielder, to shadow him man-for-man for the match's entirety. John had been man-marked before, but never by a player of di Ginetti's quality, and he realised that he would need to raise his game if he was to come out on top.

As early as the second minute, their first confrontation arose. In England's first attack, John received the ball 25-yards from goal. He set his body to launch a long pass, switching the play to the far left of the pitch, but as he did so Di Ginetti was too fast, stealing the ball off his toes and breaking up the attack. It happened again just five minutes later, as a solid tackle removed the ball fairly from beneath John's feet. By the time he lost out for a third time, against the same player, he was beginning to believe that he had met his match, and that he would reside in Di Ginetti's pocket for the remainder of the game.

Football, however, and life in general, had taught John a few things in the last year and a half. Early on in his time at Mile End, he'd been forced to learn perseverance, and that was clearly the order of the day once again. So he tried harder, giving himself less time to control the ball and attempting to run faster than ever before. Still Di Ginetti matched everything he did. So he tried harder again, dropping into unusual positions, making later and harder-to-track runs forward, constantly staying on his toes. At last, after forty minutes of fruitless toil, he got his reward. At a corner, Di Ginetti lost concentration for a split second, and, lifted by his sudden burst of freedom, John leapt up to head the ball. It was the most important goal he'd ever scored, which he realised as his team-mates mobbed him and a crest-fallen Di Ginetti offered him a grudging look of respect.

The second half, the manager implored them, was about defence, not attack. Italian sides, he claimed, were notoriously bad at coming from behind, and 1–0 was very much the final score that England should aim for. Another forty-five minutes of 'versus-Argentina-style' defensive monotony then, should see them through to face Brazil.

John, however, did not understand such tactics. He'd complied with them in the previous game of course, but mainly because at that time none of his team would even acknowledge that he was on the pitch. The way he saw it now, attack was the best means of defence, at least among the attacking players, and Italy's enforced change of tactics, which had seen his marker Di Ginetti switched to a different position, meant that he and Regan would now have far greater scope to do just that. Judging by his advanced position – despite orders from Hardcastle to the contrary – Regan seemed to agree. They were on their own then, but John felt that their combined might – despite their mutual disapproval – could well be enough to put the game beyond reach against a weakened and unprotected defence.

His hunch proved correct. As the Italians pushed forward in search of the equaliser, they fell to a sucker punch as John and Regan exchanged passes just outside the box, and John rifled in his second of the game as Regan screamed for a return pass. There was no high-five between them, just a reluctant nod or two.

Italy poured forward in even greater numbers, but the English fortifications stood firm. Then D'Alex Smith pounced on a loose ball, and belted it up the pitch to where Regan had wriggled free of the only remaining defender. Using immense pace, John managed to join him, and almost resentfully, Regan played him in, one-on-one with the goalkeeper, whom he beat easily for his first international hat trick. The Italians had been defeated, Brazil were next, and though they remained far from friends off the pitch, on it Messrs Regan and Christie were beginning to develop the most potent striking partnership in the competition.

In the stand, Harry Foster unfolded the pink piece of paper in his wallet, and kissed it repeatedly. In two matches time, he could be £50,000 the richer.

Three goals were the price which bought back the affections of the British media. Suddenly, it was *'Our John'* in the *Mouthpiece* again. All the major newspapers – tabloid and broadsheet – printed stick-in-your-window posters of John celebrating the quarter-final win. One part-time television channel, Sport Two, replaced its usual 'Programmes start at midday' logo with a picture of John scoring a goal.

The text was even more emphatic than the images. 'Though he confused us with his outburst,' wrote Troy Wilson, 'that is the way of the true shaman. Perhaps only after he returns the holy grail to its proper spiritual home, in little over a week's time, will we begin to understand his actions.' The editorial in the *Spark*, though, was slightly less mystical: 'Just keep your mouth shut for one more week John, and then you can say what the heck you like.'

England's continuing success – reaching their first semi-final for a significant while – came at the price of a gruelling travel itinerary. From Chicago they would now head back to New York, where, if they were successful against Brazil, they'd be sent boomeranging back west for the final.

Though the squad had been to this city in the very recent past, arrival there spelt surprises for two of its number. In what Greg Hardcastle assumed was a masterstroke of man-management genius, he announced that for the three days leading up to the semi-final, John and Regan would be room-mates. Both men were underwhelmed; each approached the management individually to argue. The decision stood.

Time spent awake in the room together was kept to a silent minimum, and John used every possible excuse not to be there. Most of the time, that meant visiting a coffee shop with Harry, or else going for a long walk. The evening before the game, they combined the two, walking along Broadway with giant paper cups in their hands.

'This is incredible, isn't it?' said Harry rhetorically. 'You and I, being here now, on the eve of a World Cup semi-final in which you're playing. It didn't seem possible a year and a half ago. Or even, half a year ago.'

'Yeah, it is amazing,' agreed John. 'I kind of wish Mum and Becky could be here to see it, and Elaine. Hey – have you spoken to Jessica today?'

'Oh yes,' lied Harry. 'She said the wedding plans are all under control. She doesn't even need me.' He paused awkwardly. 'So . . . how are you feeling about the game tomorrow?'

'Good,' replied John honestly. 'Really good. The team's playing well, me and Billy are working well together . . . .'

'And how is that? The room situation, I mean.'

'Oh, you know . . . could be worse. We don't really see a lot of each other, but he's civil enough when we do. I think kicking the drugs has brightened him up a bit.'

'You're sure he's done that?'

'After what happened? I should hope so.'

'Hmm. Well, junkie or not, I don't know if I could stand rooming with him. I've got a lot of respect for you for managing it.'

'Maybe he's not so bad. After the tournament is over, whatever happens, I think I might try to patch things up with him. I mean, underneath it all, he's probably quite a nice bloke.'

John awoke around 1 a.m., to strange sounds stemming from the bathroom. It sounded like Regan might be in pain. Without turning on the light, John crept to the door, and peered in. In the darkness, he could just make out the figure of Regan, sitting on the edge of the bath, staring at a plastic container in his hand. Then, Regan took a deep breath from the container, and again made the strange noise that had roused John.

'What are you doing?' asked John, half-knowing the answer.

Regan coughed and looked up, shaken at first, but then relaxing with the drug's help. 'Get out of here Christie,' he wheezed. 'Leave me alone.'

'That's Zanthone, isn't it?' John was not about to leave. 'Is it Zanthone?'

'Yeah, whatever.'

'Billy, come on, I gave you a chance. I missed the France game because I wouldn't tell them your name.'

'Did it ever occur to you that if you'd not said anything at all, then that might not have happened?'

'But that wouldn't have been right Billy. This isn't right.'

'What's it to you, you do-gooder? Nobody cares about this, you idiot, it's not doing anyone any harm.'

'It might do. You don't know that.' Pictures, memories, recollections flashed into John's mind. He suppressed them.

'Come on John. Don't patronise me. Only stupid people let themselves get hurt by this stuff.'

'Oh yes?' John's voice raised a notch. 'Really? And what about the people who didn't even have a say in the matter? What about my sister? She was run down by a driver high on stuff just like this. Is *she* stupid?'

'Yeah,' he giggled sickeningly, 'your stupid sister should have looked where she was going.'

The words made John feel sick. Great fiery hatred rose within him, and for a second he wanted to hurt Regan badly for saying that. Somehow, he controlled himself. But he could not stay in the room any longer.

'We can't run that story,' insisted Alex Knight. 'I'm sorry John – I appreciate what you're trying to do here but it's misguided.'

'But he's still taking it,' protested John to the payphone, loading it with a barrowful of quarters as he did so. 'It's so wrong.'

'I know John – I'm with you on this believe it or not. But I'm not prepared to do this – not to England, not to you. And I promise you, there's not a newspaper editor in the land who'll print it either. Maybe, after the tournament is over, we could possibly run it, but not now.'

'But why? Why won't you print the truth?'

'John, this country is in the middle of the biggest natural high in years. People are singing with complete strangers in the street. Shop assistants are actually smiling and enjoying their job. City bankers are even leaving work early to see their friends and watch the games. What you want to tell them – it will puncture all of that. You can't do it John. I won't let you – none of us will.'

'We'll see.' John slammed down the receiver, and headed to breakfast.

Back in London, Knight furrowed his brow and thought for a moment. Then he called to his assistant: 'Burke – you'd better get the EFF on the phone. Christie's trying to announce the name.'

John's breakfast tasted bitter. But something even more unpleasant was just around the corner.

He was joined by a tall, red-faced man with a small designer beard. He was an EFF official, and had been part of the tour party for the last month, but had remained faceless, and blended into the background, until now.

'John, good to see you,' he said, every word laced with threat. 'I understand you've been making some calls this morning?'

John dropped his spoon and gave away his surprise. 'How did you know that?'

'The EFF has many friends, John. And you know, we'd like to consider you one of them.' He produced a folded piece of paper from his wallet, and laid it silently on the table.

'What are you getting at?'

'We know what it is that you think you know John. But I'm afraid you're mistaken. And if you're prepared to acknowledge that, then we'd be very happy to reward you.'

'I know what I know,' John half-smiled, tucking in again to his cereal. 'I saw what I know last night.'

'Well in that case,' said the EFF man, sinisterly switching his line, 'would you be prepared to forget what you know?'

John's spoon clattered into his bowl again as the realisation came. 'Wait a minute. You know about Regan?'

'Please John, I'd prefer it if you didn't raise your voice. I believe this will compensate you quite sufficiently for your trouble.' He unfolded the paper, to reveal a financial document which he passed across the table. John's eyes fell straight to the bottom of the page, where the words 'Pay John Christie, One Million Pounds Only' appeared.

'Are you trying to buy my silence?' asked John, incredulous at first.

'If you want to put it like that. Of course, you won't see that money until after the World Cup, and I'm sure you'll appreciate why. All we need then, is a little show of good faith from yourself in the meantime.'

'Right,' said John, trying to think quickly. 'Well I think I've got the gist.'

'So, we understand each other?'

'Oh, perfectly, sir. I'm crystal clear.'

That afternoon, the New York City Soccerdrome played host to a festival of football. Hours before kick-off, the beating of samba drums at one end of the ground could be heard for miles around. A roaring, swarming mob of England fans responded with thunderous songs and boisterous chants. Whatever happened on the pitch, there was bound to be plenty of excitement off it.

The teams entered to an ear-splitting storm of noise. They left to the same. What went on in the middle, was a small slice of footballing heaven.

In the first minute, Brazil scored. Pretedinhio, London City's young master, won a free kick in his very first attack, from the misplaced leg of his club colleague D'Alex Smith. The same player took the kick, and deposited it expertly into the top right-hand corner of the goal.

After a further nine minutes, England equalised. Billy Regan had one of his trademark pot-shots from distance saved, but the goalkeeper haplessly palmed the rebound directly to the feet of Paul Kerridge, who couldn't miss.

Then Brazil scored again. Their two strikers, the identical Ferreira brothers, exchanged passes no fewer than seven times as they took the ball the entire length of the England half. By the time the seventh exchange had been completed, they were less than 10 yards from goal. The result: 2–1.

The second-half was even better. On forty-nine minutes, Pretedinhio was awarded another free kick in a similar position, although this time he had managed to convince the referee of an offence when none had taken place, purely by falling with grace. He had no conscience though, and proved it by thumping his kick into the same corner as the first. Even though Lloyd McGrath knew where it was going, he still couldn't reach it, such was the power behind Pretedinhio's boot.

In pubs across England, it was felt that time had been called on England's World Cup dream. But it wasn't over yet.

John was angry. He'd been bubbling with anger all day, but now, with the unfairly-gotten third goal, the lid had popped open and the flames were bursting forth. Within him, an awesome power welled up. Suddenly he was like a man possessed.

He collected a pass from Regan in an area of little potential danger. Normally in this position, 35 yards and more from goal, he would have looked to the channels to lay on a pass. But something told him not to. Instead, pushing the ball a few feet ahead of himself and taking a high-powered run-up, he shot at goal. Such was the accuracy, and the pace, and the surprise factor of it, that the 'keeper was beaten. It was 3–2, and it had come from out of absolutely nowhere.

There was more. A few moments after the restart, John picked up the ball in a similar position. Fearing a repeat of the goal, the Brazilian midfielders clustered into a makeshift rolling wall in front of him. That, however, left a massive space to run into. John did so, drawing three frightened defenders with him, and spotted Simon Brazier speeding into the box behind him. Improvising, he conjured up a lobbed pass, which Brazier took in his stride. The captain scored, and the game was level with twenty minutes to play.

A place in the final was again up for grabs, and suddenly England looked the hungrier side. Further chances began to come their way – Regan put a free header wide; Paul Kerridge bent a long-range free kick just over the bar. Then, with four minutes remaining, the Messiah arrived to settle matters.

A Kerridge corner sailed over every head bar one, that of a Brazilian defender who accidentally flicked it back out of play again. Kerridge could be heard cursing as he was forced to run across the pitch to take the second kick, then again as his next attempt was headed away by the man at the front post. With their lines cleared, the Brazilians began to push out of the box, but then, to a man, froze as they saw the clearing header sailing towards an Englishman, just outside the box. The ball seemed to take an age to loop towards John, before he cushioned it on his chest and juggled it on his knee. By comparison, it took no time at all to find the back of the net, as he volleyed it, with the speed and accuracy of a high-tech weapon, back at its target. In any game, it was an incredible goal. In this game, it was sheer genius.

Brazil could not recover, and barely even tried. The final whistle, which arrived in a rush, confirmed that England would appear in the World Cup final. All around the globe, small pockets of people in white and red danced and screamed. Streamers rained down on the pitch. Even the Brazilian supporters stood and applauded their conquerors.

In Ariel Hill, Marilyn, Becky and Elaine had finished three glasses of brandy and a complete box of tissues. They thought that they could suffer no further excitement when the voice-over on the television pictures announced that they were 'going live to pitch-side, where John Christie is with Mike.'

There, with a streamer wrapped around his head, and a shirt saturated with sweat, was John, smiling at the camera. The women hugged each other and squealed with delight.

'John,' said the interviewer, 'an incredible game, a fantastic result for English football. It was hard enough to watch – what was it like to actually play in?'

'Yeah, I'm just trying to get my breath back. Obviously when their third goal went in we thought we'd lost it; and let's be honest, it wouldn't have been the nicest way to lose. But we tried a couple of things, and they came off, and obviously now we've got a great chance in the final.'

'How does it feel to be England's number 9 right now?'

John thought for a moment. Then something clicked inside him. 'Er . . . pretty horrible actually,' he answered.

The interviewer laughed nervously. 'I'm sorry?'

'Well, yesterday, I caught Billy Regan taking Zanthone, and this morning, the EFF tried to give me £1 million not to say anything to anyone about it. Oh – whoops.'

The picture cut instantly back to a shocked looking studio, in which no one could find anything to say. The three girls in Ariel Hill stared at each other in similar shock. An entire nation froze.

Within two hours of the interview, the EFF issued an announcement to the media. Half an hour after that, everybody knew that their worst fears had been confirmed. After consultation with the WFF, it said, the EFF had decided to suspend both John, for 'bringing the game into disrepute' and Regan, 'pending investigation into allegations made', for the remainder of the competition. Or in other words, England's two best players would be missing for the final.

The British press took no prisoners. 'Public Enemy No. 9' screamed the front page of the *Mouthpiece* – Britain's most read newspaper by a margin of millions. 'Raving Christie Slaughters England', claimed the *Spark*. Even *Business Daily*, the highbrow pink-sheet, led with 'Christie Outburst Shatters England's Dream'. It was as if the mighty win against Brazil had never been recorded.

The editorials of every newspaper featured a tirade against John. Most were skewed with hate – at least the *Daily Reporter* made a decent case against him. It said: 'If he truly had a claim to make against Regan, and his sense of ethics would not allow him to stay silent, why did he not have the sense to produce some kind of evidence? Instead he has ranted in front of millions, and brought simple charges that have been simply denied . . . . Such foolishness had a mighty cost – his place, Regan's, and the chance of winning the World Cup, for who else can possibly replace those two? He played a wicked game with us – he brought us so close when we'd never have been able to get there without him, then ripped it all away from us just as we'd begun to believe.'

The public reacted, sometimes violently. Posters were torn from walls; numbers were scratched from replica shirts; an effigy of John was even burned outside a pub in Liverpool. England had qualified for the World Cup final – looking at the country one would have sworn they'd just gone out in the first round.

John felt hatred burning him from every angle. Though he was far from the flames in England, he soon realised that the message had got through to the large numbers of supporters who'd rallied in America in anticipation of their team's finest hour. No longer could he walk the streets, even here, without a volley of abuse being fired in his direction by someone.

Harry, whose head was spinning and had been since the EFF announcement, advised him to weather the storm. He was sure that when they returned to Chicago, things would get better and begin to calm down. But they did not – in fact they got worse still. As the team passed through the arrivals gate at O'Hare Airport, a well-aimed egg burst on John's clean jacket, to jeers from a hundred acrimonious onlookers.

Shunned also by his team-mates, John chose to stay away from the official team hotel, checking in incognito to a small three star in the city centre with Harry instead. There, they decided, they would lay low until the controversy finally lulled, or even better, England did win the World Cup and his supposed indiscretion might be forgotten. On the second afternoon, the day before the final, John called home to his fraught family, reassuring them that he was still OK, and that he would be back soon. His mother cried, and he welled up in response. His sister tried to be strong, and made him cry even harder. But when he spoke to his girlfriend, somehow he felt different. Hearing her voice, gently telling him that everything would be OK, another chemical reaction set off within him, like that which had affected him the first time they'd met. She was talking about the future, and about how she loved him, and suddenly it all dropped into place, and he said:

'We should get married.'

All he heard on the other end of the phone was a squeal.

'I know this isn't the greatest or most romantic way to do it, but that's what I want. I want to spend my life with you. And forget about football. I'm through with it – I hate it. I'm going back to be an electrician; an electrician with a wonderful, beautiful wife – if you'll have me.'

'Of course I will!' she wept.

For the first time in days, John wasn't afraid any more. He wasn't unhappy any more. He didn't feel angry any more.

'I'm going out,' he resolved. 'Right now. I'm going to get you a beautiful ring. A beautiful ring for my beautiful fiancée.'

'OK,' she sniffled. 'I'll speak to you tomorrow. I love you.'

'I love you, too.'

John found a large jeweller's shop just before closing, and, after sifting through every ring in their collection, chose a magnificent platinum band with a jaw-droppingly large diamond. He paid, and slid it into the pocket of his jacket. Then, apologising profusely for keeping the staff so late, set off for the hotel, where he was due to meet Harry for dinner.

He first became aware of a presence behind him a few blocks on from the shop. About 30 paces behind him, there was chattering, in what he was sure were English accents. He presumed that these were some of the thousands of England supporters amassing for the next day's final, and on that assumption, tucked his head into his jacket.

Three blocks on, he realised that they had gained on him considerably. Now their voices were clearly recognisable as English. One of them seemed to have a Midlands twang to an otherwise southern voice, and the others, there were three or four in total he guessed, all sounded like Londoners. Then the chattering stopped.

Another four blocks down the street, and only five more from home, he made a casual check over his shoulder, to see whether they were still behind him. Just as he did so, he received a sharp shove in his side, which sent him tumbling into a wide but poorly lit alleyway.

'So boys, it is him,' sneered one of them, a tall skinhead whose accent confirmed that these were the same men who'd been following him.

John tried to get to his feet, but one of the other men, another skinhead, kicked his hand away and pushed him back down. The four – all clad in the dead giveaway clothes of England football hooligans – encircled him, pulling wicked smiles.

'What are we going to do, Vince?' the second skinhead asked the first. 'I say we give him a good kicking.' The other two men, who had hair but apparently no brain cells beneath it, grunted in appreciation of the suggestion.

'No–' said Vince, thinking carefully. 'We're going to let him apologise.'

John's look shifted from abject fear to terrified confusion. He raised an eyebrow, as if to ask for explanation from his captor.

Vince bent down, and placed a strong, heavy hand on John's shoulder. 'You've made a terrible, terrible mistake my son,' he glowered. 'But we haven't got such short memories. So if you apologise, to each of my boys individually, for what you've done, then I will show you mercy, and you'll walk out of here without a scratch.'

John sat on the ground, puzzled. Vince, laughing at his amusing little game, got his 'boys' to line up in readiness for John's row of apologies. But John was not playing:

'No,' said John, quietly. 'I won't apologise. Not for telling the truth. Not for standing up for what I believe in.'

'You what?'

'I wish it hadn't happened the way it did, but in the end I had no choice. I can't apologise to you – or to any of the rest of the fans. I've done nothing wrong.'

Vince's simmering snarl broke into a roar. From his jacket pocket he drew a weapon – John could not see what it was – and launched himself in John's direction. Taking his lead, the others also followed suit, and John found himself helpless and surrounded by four sets of kicking feet.

They stamped on him; they punched him; one of them even pulled out a clump of his hair. They tore his clothes, then his skin, and soon his blood was strewn across the alley. Vince lashed at John's exposed body with his weapon, spewing out vile curses as he did. Then somebody stopped him, and pointed out that John was no longer moving. At first they assumed that he'd simply been knocked unconscious, but closer inspection revealed that their assumption had been wrong. He was dead.

Flustered – they were not sure they'd quite intended this – they picked up John and looked around desperately for an acceptable hiding place to give them sufficient time to escape. A large cluster of refuse bags offered the best cover. Between them, they carried him to a shadowy, closed-off corner of the alley, and, before hastily running away, dumped him there, concealing him with the bags.

There, amongst the rubbish and the filth, and drenched in his own blood, his lifeless body remained until morning.

Twenty-Five

'I knew John Christie very well,' wrote Harry, in a special, final *Foster's Eye*. 'He was like a son to me. In less than two years he taught me more about the world, and about how to live, than any other person I've ever known. Initially I fell into his world because of a fascination with his footballing ability; indeed, if someone must be blamed for bringing this young man to the attention of the wider public, then that person should probably be me. He was, by my reckoning, the greatest English footballer I ever saw play – had he lived to fulfil his potential I've no doubt he would have gone on to be the greatest player in the world. Indeed, so much could be written about John the player, and yet to do so here, in a last glance at his tragically short life, would be to miss the greater part of the man.

'John's gift with a sphere was well documented; yet to those who knew him well it was the least striking thing about him. For here was a man who had his priorities straight in life – a faithful brother and son, a romantic and protective partner. Here was a man who valued truth, kindness, grace and humility above all else, and lived out those values in his daily existence. Here was a man of principle – so much so that in the end he died for his beliefs. Here was a man who, in a world gone mad for the love of money, thought £500 a week a ridiculous wage for a Premier Division footballer. Here was a man of courage, of honour, of love; the like of which we seldom see, and can only hope to see again.

'His mistake – if it can still be called that – was to believe that the rest of the world operated by such values as his own. When he saw wrong being done, he thought that justice should be sought. Now that the hysteria has calmed down, one is left to ask, why exactly was that thought so desperately incorrect?

'I have nothing to say to those who took John's life. What in fact could I say? They would not understand or else they could not have committed such an act. Instead, I am left to reflect that if one small positive can be drawn from John's death, it is that his spirit will live on in those of us who knew him. It is our responsibility to ensure that some of his values remain in the way we now choose to live our lives. When England won the World Cup without him, the very day after his death, the goal-scorer, Clinton McLean, dedicated the triumph to John with these words: "We didn't understand him, and now we'll never get another chance. But that's as well because, quite frankly, he was too good for this world." I can think of no more fitting epitaph myself.'

Despite calls from a widely repentant media for a public funeral, John was cremated in relative secrecy, with only a handful of people present. Harry, Marilyn, Becky and Elaine all stood together in the front row in solidarity; D'Alex Smith and Clinton McLean, who had begged Harry for the location of the cemetery, stood silent and shameful at the back.

Before the service itself began, John's family asked to see his body again. Though it had been cleaned up for the coffin, it was still an appalling sight – with heavy bruising and lacerations obscuring his silent features. Marilyn, Becky and Elaine twisted away in turn after seeing him. Harry, however, draped himself over the corpse, sobbing and whispering apology and regret.

Before he turned to leave, he produced a small pink piece of paper from his pocket and, without unfolding it, slid it delicately between the fingers of John's hand. Then he stepped away.

The Reverend Paul Miller, who also felt a strong sense of loss, struggled through the service with tears glistening on his cheeks. For his brief address, he stepped from the pulpit, and spoke to the six mourners conversationally.

'Reflecting on John's life,' he began, 'leads me to reflect on the life of Christ himself. For like Christ, John was born into a world hungry for a *chosen one* to appear. The Jews of AD 30 were desperate for a saviour to come; a man who could lead them to victory over the Roman army that had taken over their country. The Englishmen of modern times held out a similar hope – although it might sound a little trivial to compare them – they, too, were praying for a saviour, a hero, as one newspaper put it, a *Messiah*. Of course, England hadn't been overrun by another nation's army, it was simply that the country's football team, for millions of people the greatest remaining symbol of national pride, was without a hope of achieving the dream of World Cup triumph. They were desperate to find a chosen one who could lead them to victory over the Germans, the Argentines and the French.

'Into the world of the desperate, downtrodden Jews, stepped Christ. Into the world of the desperate, downtrodden English, stepped John. Neither man was quite what was expected, yet the appearance of each led to great excitement. And for a while, it was very, very good. Christ healed the sick and taught a better way to live; John performed his own kind of miracles on the football pitch, and led the country to the brink of an unthinkable victory.

'But then in both cases, something went wrong. Christ refused to conform to a religious culture, choosing not to stand and fight the Roman army, and though his message was one of love, he made an enemy of the very people he'd come to help. In the same way, John refused to conform to the poisonous culture of commercial football. Even though he tried to live his life in honesty and love, he, too, saw those who had once chanted his name in adoration beginning to spit forth arrows of hate.

'Incredibly, considering what had gone before, Christ was killed in the most ignoble circumstances – tortured and crucified in agony, like a despicable criminal. And tragically, as we know, John met his death in an alleyway – his murderers were a band of men who'd once worshipped him as their idol. They were the very men who'd hoped and dreamed that a player with his talents might be born English, and yet when he was, they destroyed him.

'It makes little sense. If ever a man did not deserve to die, it was John. He wasn't perfect, but he was as close as people get in these dark days. As such, of course it is difficult to find anything hopeful to say. There is an overwhelming sense of needlessness; a feeling which we all share, that he was gone from us far too soon.

'That was how I felt an hour ago. As I prepared to speak to you today, I stood in total despair. There will be no glorious resurrection here. John is dead, and it seemed to me that his death had been for no good reason.

'And then, half an hour before this service, I spoke to a friend of John's, who is here with us now. He told me how he had been gripped with grief for the past two weeks, about how he had been so angry at the world after learning of John's death that he almost took his own life. I asked him why he had not. He said, "It wouldn't have been John's way." I asked him what he meant. He simply replied, "John's way was a better way."

'It is from that statement that we can draw our hope. It is possible that the world will carry on in the same murky way; it is even likely that English football, basking in the glow of that long-awaited World Cup win, will soon forget about the man who made it possible. But perhaps that won't happen. Perhaps John will leave his mark, not just on the filled-in World Cup wall-charts of excited teenagers, but on our hearts. And even if it is just *our* hearts – those of us in this room today – and we try to learn from what John stood, and eventually died, for, then his death will not have been completely in vain. You see, John's way was a better way. Let's not allow ourselves to forget it.'

He sat, and all were quiet.

Outside the cemetery, Harry switched on his mobile phone. He wanted to call Jessica, just to let her know that John had been given a proper tribute. That was all he was going to say to her though, possibly from now until the day he died.

Before he could finish dialling her number, he received an incoming call. He deliberated over whether to answer, but the girls were still inside, waiting to collect John's urn.

'Hello?' he said, not recognising the number.

'Harry! How are you doing?' said a slightly familiar voice.

'Who is this?'

'It's Eddie Chung – Torpedo Books. Harry, have I got an offer for you!'

Harry bit his tongue. 'Eddie, this really isn't a good time,' he said.

'Any time's a good time with what I'm about to offer you. Harry – you were a good friend of John Christie, yes?'

'I'm just leaving his cremation,' replied Harry, still holding his temper.

'Oh. Right. Look, I'll make it quick. We want you to write a book about John. His rise to fame, his injury, his England games . . . his death. We need the highs and the lows; all of the insider stuff that only you got to see. We want the real story. Of course, you'll be rewarded handsomely. We'll pay you a £100,000.'

'No,' replied Harry calmly.

'Plus a big share of the royalties – 30 per cent. And it'll be a massive seller.'

'No way.'

'All right Harry, you've obviously seen me coming – £150,000.'

'Eddie, stop. I'm not doing it. Not for you anyway. Not for a man who wants to tell John's life like some squalid tabloid tale. Not for a man who calls me on the day of my best friend's funeral–'

'Harry,' implored Chung, 'I had to get in first. I haven't bothered you in the last two weeks. The other publishers will all be calling you before long.'

'And I'll give them the same answer I gave you. I don't want to do it.'

'£200,000!' shrieked Chung. 'And that's my final offer.'

'There's not enough money in the whole of Torpedo Books to buy me Mr Chung. Not anymore.'

'At least let's meet for a drink to discuss it!' pleaded a now-frantic Chung.

'Sorry, Mr Chung, I don't drink,' said Harry, and switched off his phone.

It took them ten minutes to row the tiny boat out to the island with the two trees. To begin with, Becky's suggestion that they take John's ashes there was part joke, part wishful thinking. But Harry took her seriously and, by tugging hard at a few strings, had managed to arrange it.

The island was unusually green and overgrown – it had not been visited, according to the park rangers, for five years or more – and when standing upon it, Harry, Becky, Marilyn and Elaine could hear nothing but a gentle breeze. It was serene: everything Becky had always imagined it to be and more.

'I should like to stay here for the rest of my life,' she said, thoughtfully.

The others were too sad to respond. Instead they held on to one another, gazing out across the clear water on all sides, listening to the sounds of the birds in the trees above.

'You know,' said Harry, fighting back the emotion in his throat. 'When you brought me here, and you called this "John's island", I don't think I truly understood what you meant.'

'Do you now?' asked Becky.

He looked at the water, then at the trees, then felt the long grass against his hand. 'Yes,' he said. 'I do now.'

They spent an hour there, standing on the island between the two giant trees. Eventually, one of them drew up the courage to fetch the urn from the boat, and together, they scattered John's ashes across the grass. And as the setting sun shimmered on the lake, and the evening breeze gently shook the trees, there were no more tears. Only memories of a life well-lived.

DAVID STREET'S CHRISTMAS DIARY

Martin Saunders

David Street hates Christmas.

He hates the food, the music, the parties, and the television. And he especially hates the eight-foot dancing Santa on his neighbour's front lawn. Three painful Christmases have made him dread the big day – with the spectre of another pushing him away from the daughter he loves and towards the depths of depression.

It looks like being another desperate December. But the arrival of a blank diary on his doorstep could just change everything. Will David learn to find some meaning among all the materialism? Or will he suffer another Christmas of bad memories and broken dreams?

ISBN: 1-86024-439-4